Malevolent Fairy

~~~

The Tale of Ania, A Troubled Soul

BB CLIFFORD

A Zero Labels Book
~~~

Disclaimer: This is a work of fiction. Names, characters, places, organizations, and incidents either are products of the author's imagination or are used fictitiously. Any resemblance to actual events, places, organizations, or persons, living or dead, is entirely coincidental.

Should you have any questions about the material set out in this book, contact your clinician or doctor. If you need immediate help and you are in crisis, seek immediate, professional help. Here are your options: Call 911 (if it is available in your area), take yourself to the emergency room of your nearest hospital, call a friend or family member, and ask them to take you to the nearest emergency room, call the National Suicide Helpline at 988 or https://988lifeline.org/

Malevolent Fairy
The Tale of Ania, A Troubled Soul

Print ISBN: 979-8-9851024-8-2 (Paperback)

Printed in the United States of America
First printing edition 2024
Published by Zero Labels LLC
143 E Ridgewood Ave, #1484, Ridgewood, NJ 07450

Images in cover photo used under license from Shutterstock.com

~~~

Malevolent Fairy handles some tough issues, including trauma, assault, and suicide, so it is important to include a content warning.

Should you have questions about the material set out in this book, contact your clinician or doctor. If you are in crisis, seek immediate, professional help. Here are your options: Call 911 (if it is available in your area), take yourself to the emergency room of your nearest hospital, call a friend or family member, and ask them to take you to the nearest emergency room, call the National Suicide Helpline at 988 or https://988lifeline.org/

~~~

As ever, this is for my family: M, L, and W. And, of course, our two cats, D and C.

~~~

He asked for their eyes so they could not witness his misogyny. And then he blamed them for it, calling them troubled and gullible fools.

~~~

"I see all the universe in the light of my blindness."
John Milton

"He was blind to the truth that death was his silent companion, always just behind him."
Fyodor Dostoevsky

"Death is the undiscovered country from whose bourn no traveler returns."
William Shakespeare

"The whale has no imagination, but he sees with a kind of blindness."
Herman Melville

~~~
~~~

Contents

Prologue

Misogyny and its accomplice

It came in the night, as all destructive things do. The first Ania knew of it, she saw something shuffling about the shadows of her childish fears. She expected eight legs to emerge, but the moonlight only revealed two that took long strides towards her.

Her mother had been wrong to try to lock Ania up in an impenetrable fortress. He found her anyway, carving deep inside her the shape of misogyny. He did what all men do; skewered a flag to claim her as his own, taking what he desired just because he could. In his pursuit of relentless progress, he left Ania grey, shriveled and a dusky brown. And for what? To make prideful claims about conquests and invaded territories?

Shortly after it occurred, Ania fell into a deep sleep. Some say this protects the body and mind when there is no hope of escape. But what was there left to preserve?

When she awoke, Ania was changed in every way. No longer a child, and unknowable to herself. As if waking into a surreal dream, she drifted through her daily rituals, unfeeling and detached from thought.

The days slipped by, and she told no one. So it became unreal, and she lost touch with everything she had known. Sometimes she would find herself staring into space, adrift. Other times, her limbs would lock up, frozen in space as she became once again powerless to stop it. Rigid, the air became trapped in her lungs, as hardened as a porcelain doll ready to shatter on impact.

Yet deep inside there is something softer, something movable, and it grows with every day that passes. A horror, a cluster of cells to multiply and conquer her. Another way for misogyny to defeat her.

She knows what it is, this cluster of cells, but she refuses to accept it. If she does, she will be forced back into the dirt where she must lie prostrate before them; passive, obedient, and silent.

Dylan could never suffer this fate. No matter how many times her brother changed his pronouns, Dylan could never end up sentenced to nine months in this liminal state; not fully a child to be protected, nor an adult with free will. Not fully a parent to nurture its unborn child nor a victim that must be cleansed of the contamination. Biologically, Dylan is a man, so he will never suffer this indignity.

As the shape of misogyny grows, she remains trapped by men and their acts and declarations that this growth inside her must be revered and protected. Ania is sixteen, barely a child herself, but she is still expected to protect this life that is growing inside of her. And if that means she must sacrifice her own life, then so be it. This is how a horror story grows.

Chapter One

Hard hitter

It feels like Halloween. In the moments afterwards, ghoulishly unfamiliar faces stare at Ania as they wait for her to make a decision. Instead of *Trick or treat?,* the choice is *collapse or retaliate?* The slap, more like a punch, stings her cheek, but that isn't as important as getting to her feet. Staying crumpled on the splintered floorboards leaves her vulnerable to more violence, so she struggles to her feet so she can back away from this broad-shouldered girl who is positioning herself to hit Ania again.

Snarling, the broad-shouldered girl takes a step forward.

Ania fears a concussion because she can't remember how she got to this strange wooden cabin. She also can't remember who this snarling person is, and why she is so angry at Ania.

"Try that again," the girl growls, "and you're getting more of that." Ania wishes she could remember what she *tried* the first time, but all she can do is stare at a badge that is pinned to the girl's shirt. Beneath a line of green apples, the words *I'm Sophie! Your Avaline Camp Counselor!* are emblazoned in bright red lettering. Ania wishes she could understand why this counselor, who seems at least college age, would want to hit a sixteen-year-old.

"Do something," someone shouts from behind Ania. "Hit her back!"

Ania blinks, trying to see who is saying this, but pain flashes through her face, and in the confusion, she mutters a bewildered, "Sorry?"

"Why are you apologizing?" someone screams. "*She* hit *you.*" This girl, with a hard-carved frown and spiky hair, dives over to stand at Ania's side. Her shoulders sloped and fists clenched, she seems well-versed in jumping into fights that don't concern her.

"Leave her alone," the girl adds as she starts to fiddle with her nose-ring, "or you'll have me to answer to."

Ania has seen this type before; a warrior for all sorts of injustices, and she has learned to steer clear, if given the choice. She never wanted to be dragged into trouble that was of their creation. But trouble has found Ania, and in this tiny space, there is no way to avoid this nose-ringed girl.

Already, the warrior has stepped in between Sophia and Ania, her chest thrust at the counselor, practically begging her to take things further.

"Shut up, Daria," Sophie snarls at the girl. "This isn't any of your business." By now, Ania can see that the counselor has a flattened nose; probably from other attempts to inflict her will.

"Please don't make things worse," someone whispers from beside Ania. She realizes there is another girl, and another, and they hold each other as they stand near a metal-framed bed. One of them is quietly crying, and the other smooths the sobbing girl's back. They appear to be fifteen or sixteen years old, and both seem as disoriented as Ania. Hair disheveled, looking like they've just woken up, they are wearing grey tracksuit trousers and a matching sweater, each with the picture of an apple on the top left-hand side of the chest. Glancing down, Ania realizes she is wearing the same outfit.

Ania tries to offer them a smile, but neither girl will meet her eye. They probably fear guilt by association, viewing her as much trouble as Daria. She watches as one of them, the taller of the two, with a chubby head, brushes her hair into a tight ponytail. The girl flinches when she hears Sophie call "Ellie?".

"Yes?" the chubby-headed girl replies. Her hands tremble as she grips the hairbrush.

"You saw that, didn't you?" the counselor sneers. "I was defending myself, wasn't I, Ellie? You can act as my witness."

Ellie stares at Sophie, then at Ania, and then back to Sophie. Her flat face freezes, large and inert like a cartoon moon.

"Don't drag her into it," Daria snarls as she takes another step towards the counselor. She is bigger than Jill and Ellie, and pretty much as tall as Sophie, so she levels her eyes with the counselor's.

"What about you, Jill?" Sophie growls. "What do you have to say about this?"

Now it is the sobbing girl's turn to flinch, tremble, and then freeze. Her skin reddens, highlighting the pimples clustered across her hairline. She looks ready to pop.

"Leave her alone," Daria snarls.

"Quit interfering in my business," Sophie roars back at Daria. "Unless you want to get hurt."

With her obnoxious chin and meaty limbs, Sophie repulses Ania. She's seen this type before, the kind of bully who would probably delight in trapping Daria, Jill or Ellie in a headlock, and watching as their skin flushes a violent shade of purple.

"If you don't shut up, you'll be kicked out of here," Sophie threatens.

"I don't *want* to be here!" Daria snarls. In the gathering light of dawn, Ania can see that the nose-pierced girl has dark circles under her eyes and sharp edges to her limbs. Malnourished and sleep-deprived?

Sophie is upon Daria now. It happened too quickly for Ania to realize exactly who did what, but the counselor and teenager are struggling to find out who is the strongest, and who will end up on the floor in a bloody mess.

"Run," a voice bellows in Ania's ear. She doesn't flinch at the sound; she's heard this voice for as long as she can remember. These are the words of her grandmother, or *Nana*, as Ania's mother referred to her. Nana died long before Ania was born, when Eris, Ania's mother, was just a little girl. Despite never meeting her, Ania believes she knows her grandmother more than anyone else.

"Or maybe you just assume this because we look alike," Nana continues. "As alive as dead. Same cascade of blood-red hair as your mother's. Only, you and I shared the shock of sea-blue eyes that she never had. Believe me, your mother was green-eyed about the resemblance between you and me. Through those hardened emerald eyes of hers, she would watch you stare at the photographs of me, the ones she spent years gathering, framing, and mounting on her walls. And all for me to take you from her, like an abductor in the night. Hardly seems fair."

Nana was right. Rather than her mother's, it was her grandmother's words that were of comfort when the kids at school would trip Ania and laugh as she fell. "They're idiots," Nana would say as they would jeer at her clothes or her hair or the way she spoke. "You don't need them," Nana would add, "because you'll always have me."

"Run," Nana repeats as Sophie pins Daria to the ground. There is a door, just out of reach, just beyond the violence, but she doesn't know what awaits her outside this cabin. Unsure why, she has a sense that she is far from her home in Rotherwell. Something just feels off, maybe the smells or sounds, but she figures she is somewhere far from New Jersey and the East Coast. An intruder in a foreign land.

Straining her neck to peer through a dirty window, she tries to see what awaits her outside the cabin. A forest darkens her horizon, and she spots a raven landing on the branch of a nearby tree. Faintly, she can hear its mournful caw. Something feels familiar about this, a jolt of recognition, and she turns back to Daria, calling for her to join in her escape.

"Dylan," she yells as Daria struggles under Sophie's weight. "*Daria*, I mean, come on. Come with me, Dylan. *Daria*!"

Someone or something knocks Ania to the ground, and her hands land on the splintered floorboards. Sophie notices, pausing her tussle with the nose-ringed girl, and jeering at Ania as she clambers over.

"I told you I'd give you some more," the counselor laughs as she throws her weight onto Ania.

"Stop," Ania yelps. She doesn't want this. She can't bear to feel the weight of a body on hers, so she flips onto her belly and tries to crawl free. One of her fingernails breaks on the splintered floorboards.

"Trauma repeats," Nana murmurs. "Caught like a ripple in time."

"*No*!" she shrieks, but still she can feel the weight pressing down on her.

"Stop," she cries again, her throat aching. How she wishes that her voice could come with a growl rather than a girlish plea.

As Sophie grunts, working herself up into a frenzy, Ania can smell something strange; vapors that seem to trail from the counselor. It is familiar, reminding her of leather and something metallic.

"Don't!" Ania cries, this time using the deeper part of her throat, so it sounds more like the croak of an old woman.

"A witch," Nana mutters.

From behind, Sophie grabs Ania's wrists. In one foolish moment, the teenager imagines trees sprouting arms and hands to seize her. Her wrists are squeezed so tightly, and just as she fears they will snap, Sophie's hands slide up to Ania's throat. She braces, half-expecting that to be the end. But she doesn't die.

As Sophie keeps pushing down with her weight, Ania turns her head so she can breathe. The coarse wood of the cabin floor scratches against her cheek. In the distance, from somewhere beyond this cabin, Ania can hear the mournful caw of the raven again.

"Leave me alone," Ania gasps. The pressure of the hands around Ania's throat makes her words come out in a tangled mess of phlegm and desperation.

"Aw, poor little Annie. Do you need your mommy?"

"Please!" Ania croaks. "Why are you doing this?"

"Come on, Annie, you're big and strong enough to be without your mommy."

"I want to go home," Ania tries to yell, but all she manages is a muffled wail. "Let me go," she tries to add, but the tightening hands around her throat leave her thinking it over and over again.

"Let me go, let me go, let me go."

To survive this, she tries to think of what her family might be doing right now. Her Mom, Eris, is probably conjuring up some new recipe to impress her dad, while they both strategize how to best handle Dylan, their errant son. She can't understand why they would've let this happen, how they could let their Ania slip free of the latches and bolts and locks of the fortress that is her family home. Unless…

"I want to go home," she howls in her head.

…Unless they sent her here. Did they come in the night, carrying her from her bed and to an awaiting car? And for what reason were they doing this? Was this camp some form of punishment? What had she done that was so wrong to be sent far away from home?

"I want to go home, I want to go home," she wails over and over again.

Something shifts in Sophie, and she relents, allowing Ania to struggle to her feet. Her head swims with something fluid; ice, water. Thoughts trapped in some kind of snow globe.

Taking a step or two away from Sophie, Ania can now see why the counselor stopped fighting. Walking through the open cabin door is a woman in her forties with long, flowing auburn hair. She glowers at Ania with hard green eyes, and in a moment of confusion, Ania cries, "Mom?"

The woman hardens with a plastic smile, and there is something strange about her eyes. They seem fixed or flattened, as if she is thinking about some other time or place. Or maybe she is trying to remember something.

"Either that, or she's overly medicated," Nana mumbles.

"No, my dear, I'm not your mother," the woman says, "but I hope to look after you with as much care and attention. Now, Sophie, tell me; what is going on?"

Ania can see that the woman is wearing a name tag similar to Sophie's, with the same line of green apples, only this one declares in bright red lettering, *I'm Cynthia! Your Avaline Camp Manager.*

Behind Cynthia appears another girl of a similar age to Sophie. Her name tag identifies her as *Carrie*, and this camp counselor is twice the size of Sophie in height and girth. Ania can hear a snuffling wheezing as Carrie paces on the spot; a nervousness, perhaps, or even excitement that a fight has broken out. Either way, sweat oozes from Carrie's meaty brow, and she stares at Ania with the same strange fixed or flattened eyes as Cynthia's.

"Now," the woman continues as she turns to Sophie, "I asked you a question. I would like an answer: What is going on?"

"She asked you a question," Carrie repeats. The counselor appears proud of herself, that she has managed to make herself relevant. Gloating, she uses the palm of her hand to smooth her long, jet-black hair that hangs under the weight of something oily.

"Quit being her parrot," Sophie growls at Carrie. "You're not in charge of me."

"Correct," Cynthia declares, which makes the oily counselor pout a little, "but I am. And I would like an answer. What is going on?"

"Nothing," Sophie grumbles as she shoves her hands into the pockets of her tracksuit trousers.

"That's BS," Daria yells. "That psycho was beating us up."

Cynthia stands in silence.

"So you're not gonna do anything?" Daria bellows. "I thought you were in charge?"

The woman tries to force another lifeless, plastic smile.

"I'm outta here," Daria barks. "If you're not gonna protect us, I'm gonna find a place to look after myself, and, more importantly, some place away from that lunatic," she adds as she points at Sophie.

Daria darts towards the door of the cabin but Cynthia is quick to snatch a hold of the girl's wrist.

"Let's not try that again," Cynthia hisses, her face barely an inch from Daria's. "You know we will find you and bring you back."

"You can't keep us here against our will," Daria shrieks. Ania is shocked how strong Cynthia appears, the way she can stand so still as Daria tries to struggle free.

"No one wants to inflict any kind of harm on you, no one wants to see you distressed," Cynthia insists as she keeps a tight hold of Daria's wrist. "My job is to keep you safe until the time comes for you to move on, and my counselors are here to help me with that task. We really are here for your benefit, and I wish you could believe that. Trust us."

"Trust us," Carrie echoes.

The nose-ringed girl flinches at this. "*Trust*? I don't even know any of you. Who are you, anyway, and what are you doing with us?"

"We've been through this," Cynthia responds. "Countless times."

"No, we haven't. You've danced circles around it, claiming some BS about a mission or something. You have no right to hold us here against our will. Just let me go home, please, I just want to go home."

Cynthia shakes her head.

"For fuck's sake," Daria snarls, "who locks teenage girls up in a cabin? What the fuck are you up to? For all I know, you're…"

"Enough!" Cynthia shouts. "Carrie, why don't you take Daria for a walk? Think of it as a reset. It will be good for you, Daria, to have some fresh air. There is a beautiful forest nearby where you can take in some nature. Carrie can show you where to get some water, if you are thirsty, and then you can join us for breakfast afterwards. Does that sound like a plan?"

Daria tries to make her escape, but Carrie throws her weight onto her, wrapping a meaty arm around the girl's neck.

"Oh, come on," Carrie adds, "why fight it? Didn't you hear Cynthia say that it will be good for you?" Her eyes twinkle as she watches Daria's cheeks turn red.

"You're hurting me," Daria groans, "stop squeezing me so tightly."

With her overbearing weight, Carrie reminds Ania of the big marshmallow man in *Ghostbusters*; the overbearing oaf that kept smiling as it bulldozed its way through the movie. With the same bluster and smile, Carrie maneuvers Daria towards the door of the cabin.

Ania knows she should do something, but she remains frozen. Her brother, Dylan, would be disappointed in her. "Stand up to the bullies, *Midget*," he would tell her when she shared with him stories about the girls in her grade. Many times, she told him about how they would tease her, ridicule her, and whisper about her when she wasn't out of earshot. Or sometimes they would pinch her or slap her when no one was looking, or when the teacher was too indifferent to intervene. "Fight them," Dylan would tell her, without ever explaining how she should do this.

Her mother, Eris, was just as bad. The goddess of discord and strife would speak of wrath and vengeance, vowing to bring all kinds of violence to anyone who harmed her daughter. But how could she do this when she rarely left her home? In the end, the dangers still found Ania, and even then, her mother could only offer more spells to conjure up promises of wrath and vengeance.

"Empty promises," Dylan would sneer, "she's all talk. Fuck her tangled up mind. You don't wanna get caught in that web, you'll only go crazy," he would add, only just loud enough for their mother to hear, and then they would launch into a tirade at each other. Their battle was always the same: Eris, their mother, claimed that the dangers were lurking outside the fortress of their home, whereas Dylan believed the only battleground was inside their mother's mind. "How is she supposed to navigate the world out there when you hide us from it?" he would yell at Eris, and she would curse and swear back at him. Each time, they would escalate, screaming louder and louder at each other, so Ania was left in the shadows of their discord. Each day, she felt like she was fading away, a ghost to them, and the only person who showed her any signs that she might exist was her quiet father, Paris. Amongst the chaos of a warring mother and son, he would sit and watch Ania, reassuring her, now and again, that he could hear and see her.

"It takes time," her father would sometimes say, "to navigate this world. The teenage years are the hardest because you are slowly letting go of our support and trying to trust people outside of this home. You are bound to encounter some kind of conflict." This would only make Ania feel more lost to him, more invisible, because if he had really been listening to her, he would have known that these girls in her grade had been cruel to her long before the teenage years.

"This isn't an adolescent thing," she would try to say, but she wondered if he could even hear her above the battle cries from her mother and brother. "I've never been liked by any of them. Not once."

"Try to buy your time," her father would say, "by killing them with kindness." She tried to tell him she had been doing this for years, and it only made them hate her more, only made them say things like "*She'd suck anyone off if they would be her friend for the day*" and "*Don't touch her in case her desperation is contagious*" and "*Really, she's gross and pathetic.*"

"If you buy your time for long enough," Paris would add, "then you'll learn who the real friends are, and who are the ones who can't be trusted."

He just didn't get it. It was different for her father, because men and boys can punch each other and end the war. She would watch them at school, the day after their fight, they seemed so free of any tension, and they even acted like they had discovered a new layer of respect for each other. But with girls, there was no end to the war. Nothing ever changed because the animosity was always burning beneath the skin of their smiles, the whispering and ridicule always clouding the air between them. There was no escape from the girls in her school, and, it seems, there is no escape now, from these girls and women at this camp.

"You never know, Daria," Cynthia continues, "you might just come back like a new person, all ready to hear what we have to teach you at Avaline Camps."

Daria shakes her head violently as Carrie strong-arms her out of the cabin.

"I want to go home," Daria shrieks, "Let me go, let me go, let me go."

Still in Carrie's headlock, Daria's skin is now a strange shade of purple as she hears the girl croaking something like "*You have to…*" Carrie slaps a hand over Daria's mouth before she can say another word, and then the two of them are out the door and they have disappeared.

"*You have to…*" she keeps hearing as it echoes in her mind.

"*Run from here?*" Nana suggests. "*Fight them?*"

With the door open, daylight pours into the cabin, but it feels too much, as if the light is artificial; like floodlights of a stadium or the spotlights of an operating room. Every object seems to hiss under the intensity of the brightness.

Even after they walk far from the cabin, Ania can still hear Daria's muffled cries. Suddenly, Ania is back in her house where she can hear the muffled yells of her brother and mother as they stay locked in their disgust for one another. The kind of stalemate that could only lead to mutual annihilation. She knew better than to intervene, having watched too many of her father's failed attempts to mediate. He always ended up bruised and weary of it all, and that was the saddest part of it. He, like Ania, abhorred conflict because it drained them, whereas Dylan and Eris seemed to grow stronger with every fight.

"Maybe the same can be said for Daria," Nana whispers in an attempt to reassure her granddaughter. She had seen how worried Ania looked as she stared out the window, searching for the nose-ringed girl. "She'll be okay. It's your own welfare that you need to worry about."

"Shut the door," Cynthia snaps, but Ania isn't sure who she is addressing. "If you're not careful, we are all going to get ill in this chilly November morning. Now, would someone please shut the door?"

Sophie races over and eases the door shut without making a sound.

Cynthia surveys the room as she seems to make silent calculations.

After a moment, she presses her fingers together and declares, "Now it is time for some peace and quiet. I really cannot have that kind of chaos at my camp, I mean, I can barely think when there is so much noise. I hope no one else is going to cause any problems."

The woman surveys the room, waiting for someone to speak up, but none of the teenagers will look her in the eye. Ania once heard that malevolent forces use a person's eyes to wreak havoc; she thought, perhaps, that they had said something about the eyes being a window or something, maybe a window to a person's soul. She can also now remember how someone said (maybe the same person, she can't be sure) that the dead use people's eyes to come back from the underworld. "When they hold your stare, they enter your soul," she can now remember them saying. Or was that her own voice saying this as she read it somewhere? Somewhere online, perhaps.

Her thoughts are so muddled, memories chopped up, that her head feels like it is filling with too much air. She tries to take a few steps forward, but she staggers a little, so she reaches for the metal frame of a nearby bed. The cool surface stills her mind, freezing her in place so she can try to scan the room again. A cluster of people and objects, coming in and out of focus. Why does everything seem so strange and yet familiar at the same time?

Thudding footsteps, and she can see that Sophie is stomping over to Cynthia.

"Why are Sophie's shoulders so broad?" Nana asks Ania. "And

why is her jaw so square?"

Ania notices that same vapor trail again, the strange scent of leather and something metallic. This counselor reminds Ania of someone, some man that she knows, but she isn't sure who.

"Maybe she is a man," Nana mutters. "Stranger things have happened."

For some reason, Ania starts to tremble. Her mind drifts to the nightfall that lies ahead, when Sophie will be tasked with keeping watch over Ania and the other girls. She can imagine how the counselor will take pleasure in this power she will have over them, as she lingers in the shadows of Ania's fears and waits for her to succumb to sleep.

"…just about enough of it. Isn't that right?"

Ania realizes, too late, that Cynthia has been speaking to her.

"What?" Ania croaks.

"Really, Ania, I would like it if you paid a little more attention when I am speaking to you. Very well, then," she continues with a sigh, "I will ask Sophie." She turns to the counselor and spreads her hands out, welcoming her input. "I am sure I can depend on you to keep up with the conversation, so you tell me the truth. Tell me, what was happening when I walked into the cabin this morning? It looks like I was interrupting something."

"They were mucking around," Sophie remarks as she points at Ania. "So, I was just trying to get them into some kind of order."

"By what means?" Cynthia asks.

"What?"

"How were you doing it? This *getting them into order*?"

"By telling them what to do," Sophie retorts.

"There seems to be a missing step in your account. Your *giving them orders* does not involve rolling around on the floor with them," Cynthia explains, her words becoming more like a sneer. "What is the missing step, Sophie? In your account. There seems to be a missing step. I would hate to find out that you have not been entirely truthful with me. What are you leaving out of your account?" As she asks this, Cynthia turns back to face Ania, and she stares at the cheek that Sophie had punched. Ania hadn't thought about any bleeding or bruising, but now she has lifted her hand to her cheek, she flinches at the pain that roars through her veins. Something feels wet, blood, perhaps, so she snatches her hand away, terrified to draw any more attention to herself.

"I asked you a question, Sophie," Cynthia snaps.

Sophie shrugs in reply, which is clearly the wrong response because Ania can see that a rage has tightened throughout Cynthia's body, and now the woman's hands are trembling.

"I despair of you, Sophie, I really do. I can't leave you alone for more than a minute without chaos erupting. This is not how Avaline Camps is to be run. Not under my watch. We are supposed to be helping these girls, not traumatizing them. We have been through this already, and I thought you understood."

Again, Sophie shrugs her shoulders.

"Very well," Cynthia continues, "if you can't handle a group of girls yourself, perhaps you would like to think long and hard about your future here. Now, I am going to check on Carrie. I trust you can help these girls with breakfast?"

Still shaking her head in dismay, Cynthia walks to the door of the cabin.

"Quick, quick" Nana stammers, "she's going to leave you alone with that manlike brute. You need to do something."

"Wait!" Ania cries. "Please, I really need to speak to my mom. Or my dad. I think there's been a mistake, I mean, I don't know why I'm here. What is this place? I don't want to be here. I don't…I don't remember agreeing to be here."

A breeze whistles through the gaps in the wooden walls of the cabin. Ania shudders when she thinks of all the creepy crawlies that could sneak in through those gaps. She can almost feel their spindly legs crawling up her spine. And when she has to sleep here tonight, would they burrow in to make a nest of her hair? And then what would they do? Attract others to join them?

"Maybe they would lay their eggs in your hair," Nana suggests, "and you could scare everyone away as you become some kind of *arachnid girl.* Imagine all those baby spiders swarming down your face and neck and arms; an entire army of them to terrorize, to invade and pillage whatever resources they can discover."

"Where's my Mom?" Ania asks. Ania hates the sound of her tight, wheedling voice. So childish, so girly. She wishes she had some of Dylan's testosterone, even if he hadn't much use for it himself. "I need to speak to her, or my dad, or my brother. Can you let me use my phone, and I can call them? They'll come and collect me, I'm sure they won't mind. Just let me use it once, it won't take long."

Slowly, Cynthia turns back to face Ania.

"I see." She hisses this so quietly that she sounds like a leaking gas cannister. "I expected this to happen. I understand it's an adjustment being here, so far from home. It will take time to adjust, but eventually you'll get used to it here. Perhaps, eventually, you might call it your home."

Ania shakes her head.

"I don't want to," she declares. "I already have a home."

From behind her, she can feel a ripple of restlessness from Jill and Ellie. Maybe even Sophie, too. A flash of fear from all of them, perhaps, because, Ania realizes a little too late, she doesn't know anything about this strange woman with the lifeless eyes, or her potential for violence.

"My Ania, my dear girl," Cynthia sneers, her tone dry as ash. "I hope we are not going to have any problems with you. Can you promise me that?"

Ania shrugs her shoulders in response.

"I can understand that you miss your family. We all do," Cynthia continues, "stuck out here for these long, drawn-out days. It is disorienting and depressing. But the more we focus on each other, and why we are here, the sooner we can move on."

"Why *are* we here?" Ania asks.

Another ripple of restlessness from the other people in the cabin.

"Ania, my dear. This is a place of peace and comfort. Make the most of it."

"I don't know what that means, and I don't understand any of this. I just want to speak to my family and go home."

"Okay, I give in," Cynthia concedes as she holds her hands up in surrender. "Come to my office. I have your phone safely locked away in there."

It was such a sudden switch in attitude that it made Ania's head feel light and airy again. She can feel so much air rushing into her head and filling up her body that she is afraid she might float out of the cabin, into the sky, and just as she can see home, a speck of hope in the distance, she will burst with the sharpness of the acidic sunlight.

"Good," Ania finally says in reply. "Thank you. But...But, wait, why do you have my phone in your office?"

"We keep everyone's phones there. Unfortunately, that's one of the rules," Cynthia remarks, a strained smile stretching the edges of her lips so far that it looks painful. "Now come with me." The woman snatches hold of Ania's elbow, and she guides her to the door and opens it. The light dazzles in Ania's eyes, and then there is a rush of fear as Ania realizes she is being led away from the watchful eye of the others, to a room where she will be alone with a stranger.

"Bad things happen to bad people," someone used to say, and she never understood what it meant.

"Let me see if Carrie can come back to the cabin," Cynthia adds as she pauses at the door. "Sophie probably needs help with breakfast."

"I don't need help," Sophie retorts with a humph.

Cynthia uncouples a walkie talkie from her belt that she has kept hidden beneath her sweater.

"Carrie? Do you read me?" she shouts into the handset.

A fizz and crackle on the line, some kind of wail, perhaps of distortion, and then another fizz and crackle.

"Carrie? Are you there?"

A crackle, and then a muffled voice, distant but slowly getting louder, like it is emerging from the darkness of a deep tunnel.

"…there? ….see me? …cold."

"Carrie, for goodness' sake, do you read me?" Cynthia snarls. "You know, I really need to feel like I can depend on you counselors to help me run this camp, but so far, I haven't seen anything that reassures me."

Fizz, crackle. Then a voice, loud and familiar.

"Ania?" the voice calls.

"What was that?" Ania asks.

"What?"

"That. My name. I heard it."

"Not sure. Probably Carrie. Come on, Carrie. We went through the training. You need to press the button to talk, and you need to hold it close to your mouth."

"But it didn't sound like Carrie," Ania insists.

"Oh?"

"Yes. It sounded like…It might have been…someone…Maybe it was someone I know?" Ania realizes how vague this sounds. "Can I speak to them?"

"Carrie, did you hear me?" Cynthia continues as she chooses to ignore Ania. "Come to the sleeping cabin straight away. Over and out."

Turning to Sophie, she adds, "Looks like you're on your own until Carrie can get her act together. Just make sure these two," she gestures to Ellie and Jill, "get to breakfast. Can you manage that?"

Sophie nods, seemingly relieved that she has regained some of

Cynthia's trust.

"Now let's get to my office," the woman insists as she leads Ania out of the cabin and into the cold courtyard.

Another crackle from the walkie talkie, and then a loud and distinct, "Ania, where are you?" It sounded like her brother.

Ania snatches the walkie talkie from Cynthia and presses the button as she yells into it, "Dylan, I can hear you. Where are you?"

More fizzing and crackling, and then the voice comes through again. Only this time, it is a little different.

"Ania, it's Daria. Help me."

Chapter Two

Avaline Camps LLC
Marketing brochure

Welcome to Avaline Camps LLC, a Wilderness Therapy Program in New York. We offer Christian values and loving care for teenagers between the ages of 13 and 18.

Set in the sweeping landscape of The Hudson Valley, New York, Avaline Camps is a rare opportunity for your teenager to rediscover the joys of a Christian lifestyle. We are a firm believer in the teachings of the Bible; something that has been forgotten by most of the youth of today who would rather sit staring at a cell phone than learn about the wonders of Jesus Christ.

At Avaline Camps, we offer a healthy balance of therapy, faith, and nature. Away from the distractions of everyday life, and basking under the warmth of God's sunlight, your teenager can connect with their true self, the person they were supposed to be until modern challenges got in the way. You can help us to help them by delivering your teenager to us and then trusting us as you step back and let us guide them back to a genuine connection with God.

Christian counseling in a beautiful setting, with the hope of redemption for troubled souls. What better way to lift your teenager's spirits? We incorporate experiential programs focused on treating adolescents with behavioral, mental, and substance use disorders. Each program places your teenager in a natural environment so they can keep far away from the temptations of their former life.

At our all-inclusive premier camp, we offer a 40-day program with over a wide range of activities. Each activity has been tailored to support and challenge your teenager, and we pride ourselves on successful outcomes. Each teenager leaves our camp with a better sense of self, a healthier understanding of relationships, and a more disciplined approach to their daily chores. Come explore 150 acres set in a breathtaking landscape. Places are quickly filling up, so don't delay and book your free visit today.

With the support of our Clinical Director, we will design a program that is tailor-made for your teenager's needs. We work with evidence-based practices, and we continuously learn from the latest advances in psychology and neuroscience. Each program uses the latest therapies and research to effectively treat underlying conditions so your teenager can experience a sustained and significant change. We continuously assess the outcomes, examining both the emotional and behavioral changes, and we never push a teenager too hard, whilst also appreciating that some challenges can be extremely rewarding.

For many years, our Clinical Director has made it her mission to help troubled teens, and she is an extremely positive addition to our team. Working alongside two spiritual counselors, our Clinical Director is happy to answer any questions should you need to reach out to her. Take the next step and book a free visit to our camp. If you trust us with your teenager for 40 days, we guarantee that you will see a remarkable transformation that will restore your faith in God.

We have chosen an apple as our logo because we know how precious the apple of your eye is. We hope this demonstrates the trust and love that we will show your teenager. Don't delay and book today.

Avaline Camps LLC.
Planting the seeds of hope of salvation.

Comments:

u/warwound#07:
This place should never have been opened. Death trap.

Source: https//www.[redacted].com
Accessed November 4, 2020, at 7:30 PM

Chapter Three

Anemoia

"I heard them," Ania insists. "On the walkie talkie. First Dylan, my brother, then Daria."

As she snatches the handset out of Ania's hand, Cynthia shakes her head. "You were mistaken."

"No, no I wasn't. I heard them. You think I don't recognize my brother?"

"You can speak to him as soon as we get to my office," the woman snaps.

"Why not now? That was him, wasn't it? I feel like you're…I don't understand any of this. I mean, what is this place? I just want to go home."

"I'm sorry you feel that way," Cynthia replies with a gentler voice. "I know you miss your brother, and your parents. These early days are bound to feel strange, but you'll settle in soon enough."

"I don't know about that, but…What about that girl, Daria?"

"What about her?"

"Is she okay? I mean, that woman, Carrie, I think, she was pretty rough with her."

"I'm sure Daria is fine."

"But how do you know? Shouldn't we check on them?"

"No."

"Okay, then, maybe Daria wants to call someone too. Maybe she has a brother or a parent she…"

"You really should drop this." Cynthia lets out a long, dramatic sigh. "Please don't you worry yourself because Daria will be fine. After Carrie has taken her for a little walk, I'm sure that they will join us. Now can we drop this?"

Ania obeys, falling into step with her as the silence is stirred only by the distant whir of some hidden generator. Usually, she would find the cold morning to be crisp and refreshing, but it only makes her think about the new school year. She can't understand why she has been sent to this camp in late fall when she is going to miss so many classes. Didn't her dad always tell her that these final years before college are too important to fall behind?

"This way," Cynthia says as she points to a dirt track.

Ania can't understand why she doesn't remember any of this from before. One minute, she is in her home in Rotherwell, and the next, she is here.

"Drugged?" Nana suggests. "Abducted?"

Ania has read stories about camps like this, on Reddit and other forums. When kids get out of control, when the parents have had enough of their defiance, they turn to wilderness camps, these pseudo-psychological, but mainly ultra-religious camps, to get the kids back on track. They never go willingly, so the parents or camp officials use whatever means they can to get that body to the camp. Drugs, honey traps, or even violence. And once they have them as a captive audience, all passive and helpless, what better way to indoctrinate them? What better way to mainline that religion straight into their veins?

Ania doesn't think she has done anything to deserve this. Her brother was always the defiant one, fighting with their mom so much that he ended up punching holes in the walls. He even stole their cash, cars and prescription meds. The drugs would always intensify his rages, making him kick and punch the walls even more. Ania did none of this. She chose to keep her wrath to herself, turning it inwards and quietly imploding, so she ended up carving more and more voids from within.

"What secrets have they discovered about you?" Nana asks.

The skin on the back of Ania's neck flares up in reply. The diary. Despite all the roof voids and loose floorboards, there are only so many hiding places inside her family home. Her mother rarely leaves the house, so, in time, she is bound to discover some of Ania's secrets.

"Your *dark* secret," Nana mumbles.

Don't call it that, Ania wants to yell, *there's no shame in it,* but Cynthia is staring right at her, so Ania just walks on, fuming in silence. She can't stand it when her grandmother uses outdated phrases about sexuality, although she suspects that the old woman isn't harboring any genuine hatred towards her. Nana just grew up at a different time.

"Pick a side," Nana once said to Ania. "You can't find everyone attractive."

Poly, bi, Ania was still trying to figure it out by writing reams and reams in her diary; something her parents might have discovered. Was this really why she had been sent away, to a strange camp that felt more like a prison? Was she sent here to be punished or changed, and if that change isn't possible, what is going to happen to her?

Ania stops walking because they have reached the end of the dirt track. Before them, a thick forest looms like a collection of leather-faced old men.

"It's only a short walk through here," Cynthia explains. She notices Ania's wide eyes, so she adds, "You want to speak to your family, don't you?"

"Isn't there a road around the forest?" Ania asks.

Cynthia lets out a dry laugh. "You kids are so delicate these days. You know what they say, that life is a journey, not a destination. I bet most of you have never been for a walk around a duck pond, let alone some woodland or a reservation. Probably spent your life sat scrolling through social media or gawping at video games." Cynthia gestures towards the forest. "Shall we?"

"You're fine," Nana whispers, "you're tougher than you think and stronger than most men, so you can do this."

Ania knows that these words of comfort aren't really for her. Nana was trying to reassure herself, so she could once again face the darkness of a forest that had once swallowed her whole. When Ania was too young to know any better, she kept asking Eris, her mother, where Nana had gone. "But why did she disappear when you were a child?" Ania would ask her mother. "What happened to her?" When Ania became a teenager, she noticed that her mother's body would stiffen in response to these kinds of questions, so Ania learned that she would have to find the answers herself. She searched her home, looking for the truth about her grandmother's disappearance, but at first, she found no clues. Nothing could be revealed by the posed photographs that were framed and gathering dust on each mantel piece. But Ania knew that if she dug deep inside desk drawers and cabinets, eventually she would find something.

"I don't like to be reminded of this," Nana whimpered when Ania found the pathology reports. At the time, Ania was twelve; four years ago by now, but she still remembers every word.

"What made you want to do that?" Ania asked her grandmother. But she got no reply.

As Ania grew, she realized there was never just one reason to drive to a lonely forest track in rural Pennsylvania. Never just one reason for her to become trapped inside the labyrinth of her mind, to choose the thickest part of the forest, to hide in the darkness. Never just one reason to use that cover of darkness to attach a length of hosepipe to the exhaust of a car. It is an amalgam of circumstances, genetics, and sheer bad luck, Ania believed, and the genetic factor was what transformed this tragedy into a horror story.

Still that horror story lurks at the back of Ania's mind. It is what haunts her most nights, when she can hear someone whispering, so subtly that it made the hairs on the nape of her neck stand to attention. In the darkness, the words form, and she is left with a giant question mark to hang over her as she hears the voice groan with a ghoulish wonder: "*What would make you do the same?*"

"Well, come on, we haven't got all day." Cynthia points again at the forest as she waits for Ania to take the first step. This is the kind of place that Ania's parents forbade her from exploring. There was a similar forest at the end of Mount Pelion Way, the street she had lived her entire life, and her mother and father warned her about the wildlife that would roam there, and the oil cans and trash bags that were stuffed full of sharp edges and toxins. But mostly they feared the kinds of people who would linger there in the undergrowth, just waiting for her to arrive.

Ania takes a step, and she can hear a crunch of twigs and leaves beneath her shoe. She takes another step, and then another, and soon they are plunging deeper into the forest, and birdsong is muted, as if they have slipped beneath the surface of a lake.

"…in place. Not when I was doing it alone. Do you know how hard it is to get those kinds of permits?...And when you are alone, the winters bite just that little bit harder…"

Cynthia is trying to tell her a story about the origins of this camp, but Ania refuses to listen. The last thing she wants is to care about this woman or this place. Ania knows that she has a weakness for caring too much about a person who shares their stories with her. When it happens, she can feel nerve-endings growing so they become tethered to each other, and she fears the pain of having to break free. She did it once with someone she thought was her friend, but she refuses to do it again. To lose someone else, to feel that kind of severance, would be unbearable.

There is a stirring of the branches ahead of them. Ania hopes that her brother has been searching, and he has found her. Already he might have stolen one of their parents' cars and driven through the night to get to the camp. She can just imagine how Dylan would rise up from the undergrowth, and how he would be covered in nettles and swamp weed as he wades through that murky water. He won't care about the oilcans and trash bags that have been dumped there because all he wants is to see his little *Midget* again. How powerful it will be to watch as he emerges, terrifying Cynthia away or waging war on her if she doesn't back down. As their mother always said, he is the *battle-lustful warrior*.

"He was never battle-lustful," Nana says with a sigh, "he just refused to put up with my daughter's bullshit."

Ania's eyes adjust to the morning light, and so she can see that it was just a lonesome deer stirring in the undergrowth. The three boys who lived on her street used to throw stones or sticks at the deer that roamed from the nearby forest. They used to try to trap the deer in the nets of their goal posts, and she remembers how scared they looked as they tried to get away. The cruelest of the three boys, Smithson, once got some gasoline and splashed it into one deer's eyes. Ania can still hear the squeals of pain as it thrashed about in the dirt as it tried to get away. Only Smithson laughed, as the other two boys, Cory and Aedean, watched on in silence.

From somewhere amongst the trees, Ania thinks she can hear someone laughing.

"Is anyone in there?" she asks Cynthia.

"I doubt it. Not in this cold. Why?"

"I thought I heard something," Ania replies.

"Probably the wind rubbing the branches together. That can make strange noises."

"Ania," she thinks she can hear. "Ania," she hears again. It certainly sounds like a voice, more than any branches rubbing together. She thinks of her brother on the walkie talkie. And Daria. She thinks of how violently that poor nose-ringed girl had been forced out of the cabin.

"Ania," she hears again.

"I'm getting cold," Cynthia admits. "Let's quicken the pace."

Now Ania has to jog a little to keep up with the woman, and with the quickened pace she can hear more, as if she has climbed out from that dark lake.

A raven caws from somewhere above them. There was once a time when she believed that the natural world was full of her friends who were there to keep watch over her, or keep her company. She thought that she enjoyed a special relationship with Mother Earth because of the close attention she paid to her offerings. She spent hours in her backyard, climbing the apple trees and talking to the birds and squirrels. Those trees, she believed, were full of hope because they transformed from barren branches to beautiful blossoms and then nourishing fruit all in one year.

And then it all changed. The evenings grew darker, and the frost took hold so nothing more could flourish. The change was so violent; one day she believed in hope, the next everything was hopeless. Even Mother Earth turned against her, and she realized her naivety. The natural world was just as predatory, and she was either a source of food or an obstacle in their way.

"You're quiet. Anything on your mind?" Cynthia leans a little closer to the teenager.

"No, I just…How far is your office?"

"Not far now. I'm sure you'll find the walk worth it when you manage to speak to your family."

"You don't carry a cell?" Ania asks as she peers up at the trees. "Seems strange when you are running a camp out here. Anything might happen." She notices that some of the trees are stooped, and their branches look like the arms of angry men in pursuit. She tries not to think of probing fingers as her eyes drift to the smaller branches.

"That wouldn't be fair, now, would it?" Cynthia replies. "If we require you girls to cut off contact with your family, the least we can do is follow suit. I have my cell phone locked away in my office, along with Sophie's and Carrie's."

For a while, Cynthia walks on in silence as Ania trots behind her. The teenager can hear a soft wheezing, and maybe even the sound of something rattling inside of Cynthia's chest.

"Phlegm? Blood?" Nana whispers. "It could be early warning signs of something worse, an illness that could plague her entire existence."

Ania tries not to let her grandmother's fears get to her, but now a cloud of suspicion hangs over her, especially when Nana adds that the wheezing might be a sign of something contagious.

"No contact might seem harsh right now," Cynthia continues, "but I am sure, when you look back, it will be clear that I was trying to make this easier for all of you girls. That is my job, after all. I am tasked with making sure that you girls are kept safe and comfortable at all times."

Ania imagines that the woman probably recited a similar speech when (*if*) her parents handed her over. How persuasive she must have been to insist that they trust her with Ania's safe keeping. What sort of virtues had she extolled (*fabricated?*) about this place, and did her parents feel as unsettled as Ania feels now?

"All part of her manipulation strategy," Nana mutters. "She wants to disorient you, and she's trying to make you dependent on her. Classic mind game, so careful you don't fall for it, any more than you should let her know if you have any suspicions about her or this place. Otherwise, she'll make you look like the crazy one. The truth-tellers are always the scapegoats."

After a moment, Nana adds, with a quieter voice this time, "Maybe that's what this place is. A place for the scapegoats, the truth-tellers, and the ones who don't play the game. They always end up in the jails and the hospitals and camps like this. And if you tell too many truths about the people who are keeping you against your will, they'll manacle you to a bed frame, forcibly medicate you, electro-shock, and even lobotomize you."

Finally, there is a break in the trees, and Ania can see that they are heading towards a road.

"This runs the circumference of the camp," Cynthia explains. "If you're ever lost, you know to head towards the road. You can't go far wrong from there."

Ania appears less interested in the road than what is looming in the distance.

"What's that?" Ania asks as she points to a building made of grey concrete and dirty glass. It is only two stories high, but it stretches far beyond the horizon, giving the illusion that it is endless.

"That is the main building that we are turning into Avaline Camps," Cynthia replies.

"Is it a business center or a mall or something?" Ania stares at the solid mass of concrete, made all the more imposing because of the lack of windows.

"A coffin to seal you within," Nana whispers.

"It used to be a mall until it was abandoned," Cynthia explains. "Now we are lucky enough to own it. Still much work to do yet, but trust me, when we have added a lick of paint and fixed some of the plumbing, it will be a wonderful space. Now come on, you'll catch a cold if you don't step inside."

Cynthia gestures to a pair of heavy-looking metal and glass doors but Ania pauses, glancing back at the forest again.

"What's the matter now?" Cynthia asks.

"I thought I heard...something? Maybe someone? Maybe we should check it out. It could be Daria. She might've got lost."

"I swear, you are sounding like a cracked record. Not that you'd understand that terminology. You're the generation of downloads, not vinyls. But really, can we just move on from this preoccupation with Daria. I mean, you barely know the girl. I would've thought you'd be more eager to get to my office and make that call to your family."

The thought of hearing her parents on the phone, and even her brother, is all the incentive Ania needs to walk up to the entrance of this strange, abandoned mall. Above her head, she can see a dark outline of what was once letters screwed to the fascia. *Polemis Park Mall,* it says in the shadow of dust, and she feels sad for a moment, as if she should grieve these remnants of a life that has ended. She thinks of all the empty malls when the pandemic hit, and the other places that were once filled with people but were so suddenly abandoned. It did make her sad, and nostalgic for that time to return, but really, she had never experienced those kinds of moments in the first place. She never hung out at malls or cafes or swimming pools with anyone because she never really had any friends.

"Anemoia," Nana whispers. "I think that's the word."

With each step, she can hear the crunch of broken glass and debris beneath her shoes.

"I'm sorry about the mess," Cynthia mutters.

"Sure, whatever. But...But, is this place even safe?" Ania asks as she peers at the shards of whatever she is walking on.

Cynthia lets out another dry laugh. "Safe? There you go again, you *Generation of Video Games*! Spent your life locked inside your bedroom so you are too delicate, too fearful of a world where you expect everything to be sanitized and handed to you on a silver platter. Real life isn't like that, Ania. You have to get your hands a little dirty, even your shoes need to get scuffed on fallen debris, and you must discover your strengths from a bit of adversity. Now, where's your sense of adventure?"

"I never played video games," Ania grumbles. "Found them a waste of time. I preferred the soap operas because the dialogue would keep me company. I kept it playing in the background most days, and I even played it to get to sleep. Made me feel less alone."

"Oh?"

"Yeah. I loved how I would find out a little more about the characters each time I watched the show."

"Like a friendship?" Cynthia suggests.

"Maybe."

"Okay, well, if I can't call you *Generation Video Games*, then I'll call you *Generation Instagram*. You're still, at least, all wrapped up in social media, aren't you? Still posting endless selfies, sunsets, and pictures of your food?"

"Not really," Ania replies. "That was for the popular girls in my grade."

Cynthia's smile falters.

"You didn't consider yourself popular?"

Ania shakes her head.

"Hey, popularity is for losers," Cynthia declares. "The popular kids in my school all turned out to be drunk, divorced, drugged up, or dead by thirty. So, count yourself lucky. Otherwise, you might have wasted your time hanging round a mall like this. At least, until they became uncool because of all that virus nonsense."

"Is that what killed this place?"

"No, not at all. I don't think it had anything to do with the pandemic. From all accounts, the owners disappeared overnight, some kind of a dodgy deal that went wrong with some violent people, some sort of fraud or money laundering. I don't know. There are always rumors. Never easy to get to the truth, and sometimes it's never discovered."

"Why was a camp set up in an abandoned mall? Seems a strange place to choose."

Ania isn't sure what she expected. Some log cabins, certainly, maybe even an abandoned farmhouse, but an abandoned mall? Had her parents seen this when they dropped her off (*if they even consented to her ending up here*)? She wishes she could remember more, but there's a small part of her that is scared she might be rudely awoken to those memories as they return with all their violent colors.

"This late into the fall, an abandoned mall seems like a very sensible place for a camp," Cynthia snaps in reply. "Once we move the sleeping area into here, once it is renovated, you and all the other girls who will come here will thank me. Better than spending a fall in a canvas tent, especially when we get so much snow and rain."

"I've never heard of a camp in the fall," Ania mumbles with a shrug of her shoulders.

"There are all sorts of camps for all times of year, depending on the need. We didn't choose this. We just responded to the need," Cynthia explains, without explaining who she means by *we*. "You needed to be here," Cynthia adds, "so we accommodated you."

It's a fragmented story, and Ania wonders if Cynthia is deliberately omitting crucial details, just so she can leave Ania guessing and dependent on this woman.

"It was a steal," Cynthia continues to explain. "With all the repairs that were needed, barely anyone wanted this place. So, Avaline Camps LLC was only too happy to take possession."

She pauses and catches Ania's eye. Still, the stare is lifeless, but Ania thinks that she can see something flickering deep within. Regret? Longing?

"A flame trapped by ice," Nana murmurs. "If you're not careful, you're going to slip deeper into her trap."

"That's not quite true, actually, " Cynthia admits. "I mean, when I say that barely anyone wanted this place, I don't think that is accurate. There was a small group of people, locals, I believe, that tried to cause problems. I think they wanted the land for some kind of community initiative. But Avaline Camps got there first. I hope they see it the same way that we do, I mean, that everything happens for a reason. Besides, we paid a fair price. You can't really argue with that. You'll learn that about me. I take pride in playing fair. I expect that of myself, and I expect that of others."

Cynthia pauses, and Ania knows that she is supposed to offer some kind of reassurance that she will also behave herself and play fair. But Ania can't find the words.

"After you," Cynthia says after she heaves open one of the heavy metal doors. "Better get inside before we both catch a cold."

Chapter Four

Avaline Camps Incorporated
News article

WZBC News: New York Mall Purchase Breaks Record – An as yet unnamed company has secured the purchase of Polemis Park Mall, located in Greenacre, which sat empty for the last two years after owners disappeared overnight. Although terms of the deal remain confidential, some have estimated the land and buildings to be worth around $23 million.

Controversy struck the small community of Greenacre this morning when it was revealed that the Polemis Park Mall site had been acquired by an unknown investor for an undisclosed sum. Nearby residents have been unable to confirm what plans the new investor has for the site, which is set on 150 acres of prime real estate just an hour or two from New York City.

It is now two years since the Polemis Park Mall closed under mysterious circumstances. At the time of closure, the property was owned by a joint venture of three different companies, and the owners of all three companies have since disappeared. Some Greenacre residents allege that these owners were the subject of a federal investigation, although federal enforcement officials have never offered any comment on these allegations.

Ever since the closure, the mall has remained abandoned, with law enforcement officials being called to the site on numerous occasions due to reports of looting, vandalism, and drug dealing taking place at the site. There have also been unsubstantiated claims that the missing owners of the companies have been seen at the site, and one local resident, who wishes to remain anonymous, claims that there are hidden tunnels where they have seen evidence of people being held there against their will. Local law enforcement issued a statement confirming that they have been called out to the property on a number of occasions, and each time, they found no evidence to substantiate these claims.

When the mall came up for sale more than a year ago, Greenacre residents and local business owners formed an alliance to purchase the land and buildings. Each time they bid for the land, a mysterious counteroffer defeated them, and yet the deals never reached closing. As a result, the mall continued to sit empty.

Residents are infuriated by the news that this recent deal has been finalized without any local consultation. We approached members of the Greenacre council who agreed to the terms of the deal, but they refused to comment, stating that they have since stepped down from their roles. There are claims that these council members acted outside of their powers, and one local resident suggested that they were under pressure to agree to the deal, although no evidence has been offered to substantiate this.

Greenacre residents are outraged because, for two years, they have tried to secure a deal which would allow them to acquire the site and transform it into a bustling community center. Plans were shared by various residents and there would have been a mixture of business units, medical facilities, not-for-profit organizations, and even some residential units. Greenacre residents claim that the plans would have benefited the entire community, and eventually a profit would have materialized from the venture.

One Greenacre resident explained that the area was in dire need of community services, and there were plenty of people who were willing to provide those services, they just could not find the land or buildings to provide it. When the mall fell silent, under mysterious circumstances, residents thought this would be the ideal time. Sally and Henry Archard, representatives of the alliance, explained that they planned to encourage locally owned businesses to occupy the mall, with a preference for worker-owned cooperatives. Although the Archards wouldn't comment on this, another resident, who wished to remain anonymous, claimed that the rival bids were always accompanied by threats made to various Greenacre residents, including the Archards.

On behalf of the alliance, Sally and Henry Archard have submitted a formal complaint to the Greenacre council. Although local officials claim the deal was secured before their tenure, they are currently investigating.

Comments:

u/warwound#07:
Why is there nothing about the military use of this site? Talk about a cover-up.

Source: https//www.[redacted].com
Accessed November 4, 2020, at 7:30 PM

Chapter Five

Reborn

"You should've seen the place when we first set up the camp," Cynthia explains as she walks through the doorway. "The damp," she continues, "and the damage from vandals, looters, and roaming animals. We really had our work cut out for us. The buildings had sat abandoned for more than a year, so vagrants and wildlife were trying to stake a claim over the place. We had to fight hard to reclaim the space, but I think we succeeded."

I think isn't the reassurance Ania is hoping for. Is she going to walk into this place and have to fend off some stranger or feral animal?

When Ania doesn't follow, Cynthia turns back to wave the teenager in. "Come on," she insists, but then she notices the fear widening Ania's eyes and she laughs.

"Oh my, your face! Don't look like that. It really is safe. I have eyes everywhere, so don't you worry about anything. I pride myself on keeping watch over the girls at my camp. Now come."

Even from the doorway, Ania can smell the damp clinging to the air.

"Just think of all those black spores multiplying in your lungs as you take each breath," Nana mutters. "Is this the cause of the rattling wheeze in Cynthia's chest?"

"Come on," Cynthia repeats.

Still Ania won't walk past the threshold.

"Do you want to call your family or not?"

Ania can tell that Cynthia is rapidly losing her patience, so she follows the woman into the dark hallway of the mall. From here, she can see that ceiling panels hang precariously as light fixtures and wires dangle above her head. Some lights flicker, adding to the surreal feel of it all, and she can see a pipe dripping in the far corner. Yet still Cynthia sounds upbeat about the state of Avaline Camps.

"I am so proud of all that Avaline has to offer. And word is getting out, so I'm sure that in no time this place will be a hive of activity. We have grand plans to renovate all of this, and eventually we can move the sleeping area into here. I can't wait to get rid of that silly little cabin, and see the transformations take place. I feel like I am a mother birthing this camp, or rather, rebirthing it into something better than it has ever been. We are going to be expanding our offering, widening the age limit, and eventually opening more camps. But it all takes time. You have to find the right people to do the work, and some don't even return our calls."

She walks Ania on, and the teenager can see evidence of the wildlife that Cynthia has been talking about. There are teeth marks gnawed into the edges of wall panels, and scuff marks of claws on some of the door frames.

"I guess, for a while, Mother Earth won," Cynthia admits, "at least in this small corner of her planet. But we're steadily winning the battle, so at some point she will have to concede defeat." The woman points to some vine that has somehow snaked its way in.

Ania can imagine how it might have spread across the entire hallway, but something has made it shrivel and die.

"It only took a bit of weed killer to tackle that," Cynthia explains. "Next on the list is a whole crate of traps to get rid of the little critters."

The teenager tries not to think of lifeless eyes staring out from cages and noose-like snares. Again, she remembers all the different ways the boys on her street would torture the creatures they would find.

"You're ruminating," Nana whispers. "Stuck in a loop."

Once, when Smithson thought that no one was around, Ania watched as he poked a finger into the gaping wound of a fox. From the position she was crouching, behind a bush in her front yard, she couldn't see if the creature was still alive, and she couldn't tell if he liked the taste of the blood that he dabbed with a finger to his tongue.

"He probably believed that made him more of a man," Nana jeers. "The pathetic little fool."

"What are those?" The teenager stares at strange symbols spray-painted on some of the walls.

"Oh, Ania, you have led a sheltered life," Cynthia mutters with a dry laugh. "It's just some graffiti; the work of the competing gangs in this area. I think the official name for the symbols and squiggles is a *tag*. Boys and men like to mark their territory and possessions in any way they can. Well, they can try all they like with this place, but I won't let them encroach on what is mine. *Ours*, in fact," she adds with a squeeze of Ania's shoulder.

The woman watches Ania as she stares at each wall, the symbols coming alive with every blink of the faulty lights.

"Are those spears and shields?" Ania asks. They seem strangely familiar, but she can't place them.

"Yes. Quite odd, aren't they? I believe they symbolize war; probably a warning to the opposing gang. But don't worry, Ania. I won't let anyone get to you. Remember, that's my job; to keep you safe."

They walk on in silence for a little until more light fills the corridor. Ania realizes they have reached a vast atrium where two escalators sit silently. In between, there is an ornamental tree, long since dead and now buckled against one escalator. Withered leaves are scattered on the floor, resembling some kind of confetti for the dead. It reminds her of a time when her dad took her to visit his aunt, and she sat amongst so many dead or dying things. There were flowers drooping over the side of a cracked vase, its shriveled-up petals scattered about the floor, along with dead flies and moths. There was a dead mouse rotting in a trap behind the living room door, and from the place Ania was sitting, she could see a dead bird outside, on the old woman's lawn.

If Ania had been any younger, she would have run from that place, certain that the old woman was cursed. But by then she was a teenager, so she knew that the woman was just old and helpless, and eventually death was going to catch up with Ania, too.

"Don't let it happen," the old woman croaked. Her chest was collapsing in on itself, so Ania could barely hear the words the woman was trying to heave out. She seemed to sense the teenager's fear and disgust, so she repeated her warning. "Don't let it happen.

Don't get old and rotten like me. It starts slowly, like black spores that you barely notice. But then things start to crumble. Everyone around you, everyone you've ever loved, starts to rot and die. Like a horror film, they crumble before your very eyes. Or you think they are just sleeping, and you try to wake them and they're stone cold."

Ania's father had stepped out to the kitchen, making tea or coffee, who knows what, but Ania longed for him to return, just so the old woman didn't keep staring so intensely at Ania.

"You hear me?" the old woman barked. "You have the choice. You don't need to let it happen. I should've acted sooner, while I still had the strength or body and will. Now I'm just slowly leaking away."

Ania can still smell that house. Dirty feet and urine. She was afraid to sit down at the place in case her clothes became coated in that smell. In case her hair, no matter how many times she washed it, started to smell of it too. Just think of the delight of the mean girls then. Ania can still smell it now, even here, in this abandoned mall. It is the smell of desperation, a sad longing for a home that no longer exists for you. It is a sadness that's infectious, a type of social contagion. And it is the kind of intense sadness that makes you do anything for it to stop.

"My office is just behind the elevator," Cynthia explains as she marches on. Ania stops for a moment, certain that something is glinting from the elevator. She screws her eyes up, trying to see inside the glass and steel capsule that is suspended midway between levels. Did something move about inside there?

"Is that working?" Ania asks.

"What, the elevator? Goodness, no. And I wouldn't want to give it a try, either. Probably a death trap after all this time."

Ania continues to stare up, and then she notices movement coming from the glass paneled ceiling just above the elevator.

"Are those handprints?" she asks. "I swear, on the glass roof, I can see hand prints."

"Oh, come on, Ania, your imagination is running wild. Who could get up there?"

The teenager looks again, and with all the dirt and foliage, she admits that she might be seeing things.

"Almost there," Cynthia calls as she paces onwards.

A scuttling sound from behind her, a scampering, perhaps, and a fleeting shadow. Unwilling to be left on her own with whatever that was, Ania races after the woman.

"Here we are." Cynthia points to a small office that is at the far corner of the corridor. Above the doorway, she can make out the dusty shadows of what was once a sign that read *Security*.

The woman reaches the door as she fumbles about in her pocket. She tuts and sighs, the keys getting caught on the fabric of her trousers, before she manages to pull them out.

"She's stalling," Nana hisses. "Maybe she's waiting for someone else to join her. Are you sure you want to go in there and allow yourself to be cornered? Maybe there is already someone in there, and this is your last chance to run for it."

The glass on the door is frosted, with a rippled surface, so Ania can't see into the office, but she can make out a dark outline of something that is inside. A chair, perhaps, maybe a filing cabinet.

"But a chair or filing cabinet doesn't move," Nana mutters as Ania thinks that she sees the dark shape shifting behind the glass.

"Who's in there?" Ania asks.

"There? No one," Cynthia mutters in reply as she struggles to unlock the door. "Just my piles of paperwork that I really need to get on with, if I could just work out this damned door. It's probably the damp, warping the wooden frame, or maybe I'm using the wrong key."

"I thought I saw…" Ania begins, and then she stops when she thinks she hears voices from inside the office.

. . .decision . . . sensible . . . finality. . .

. . . stupid . . . .

. . . reckless. . .

. . . own protection . . .

Finally, Cynthia turns the lock with a slide and thud, and the door swings open as Ania's mind floods with images of men in surgical gowns. They are ready to jump on her and force a needle into her arm, and they are ready to make her succumb to sleep, so Sophie or anyone else can finish what they started.

But the office is empty. The dark object turns out to be a large leather chair that is positioned behind a broad wooden desk.

"So why did it move?" Nana mumbles to her granddaughter, but Ania doesn't have a chance to think about this more because Cynthia has a hold of her elbow as she guides her inside.

"You'll have to excuse the mess," the woman says as she points to a desk littered with paperwork. "Here," she adds as she flicks on a desk lamp, "this might help to alleviate some of the gloom. That's one downside with an office in the heart of a mall. No natural light."

Ania can see that each document on the desk relates to a different camper; she can't quite see the names, perhaps they have been removed because of confidentiality, but she can see other details including their date of birth, eye color, dietary requirements and medical history.

"Recruits from past, present, and future," Cynthia explains. "Apples of my eye, if you like." She offers a dry cackled laugh and points to the apple logo that is fixed to the top-left-hand side of each form. Beneath the apple, *Planting the seeds of hope and salvation* is printed in florid italics.

"Cheesy as a pizza," Cynthia laughs as a few of the forms slide onto the floor. She makes no attempt to pick them up. "Not sure who came up with that one."

A clock is ticking somewhere out of sight, and the sound scrapes at Ania's ears. She could never stand clocks, always conscious that it was like a ticking time bomb, counting down the seconds until her end. Her dad had shaken his head when she tried to explain this to him. He never liked to see her frown and shrink beneath her bedclothes in fear of things so serious. "Why can't you just think of tooth fairies and Santa Claus?" he would ask her. "Mortality is way too heavy a subject for someone as young as you." She wishes that he could have placed aside his own fears and looked into her eyes. Only then could he have realized who his daughter really was.

"Where is that ticking coming from?" she asks the woman.

"What?"

"That. The clock," Ania adds.

"There isn't any clock," Cynthia says with a smile that is crooked with confusion.

"She's lying," Nana snarls, "she wants to mess with your mind. They're all the same, with their long-painted nails, trying to stir up the grey matter inside your skull. Don't let them in."

"I admit," Cynthia adds as she slumps into the leather chair, "that I could make more of an effort to tidy up in here. But you girls keep me very busy. So many newcomers, often staying for such a short time. And yet for each, I have to know every last detail. So much work for so few rewards."

Ania hears a soft click from behind her, and she turns to find that the door has shut. She was always told not to go into a private space with an adult she barely knew, and here she is, sealed into a tiny office with an unpredictable woman in the middle of an abandoned mall.

"Perhaps you could help me with these papers," Cynthia suggests with a flourish of her hand. "There's a filing cabinet over by the door. Would you like to sort them into alphabetical order?"

The walkie talkie crackles with interference. Cynthia unclips it from her belt and presses the button.

"Are you reading me?" Cynthia asks. As she waits, Ania can hear more crackling, only this time it seems to be coming from the depths of the woman's chest.

"Hello?" Cynthia snaps, "I said, are you reading me?"

Interference on the line.

"Is that Carrie? Or Sophie?"

Ania wants to ask if it is Daria, or maybe even her brother, but she sits quietly for a moment. She wants to see how this will turn out.

"The crackling fades out, and then the radio is silent again.

Cynthia shrugs and clips it back onto her belt.

"More hassle than these things are worth," she admits with a sigh. "Did I tell you we found the walkie talkies when we took possession of the mall? Strange thing to leave here, but their loss is our gain. Listen, Ania, I'm sorry if everything feels a little confusing at the moment. It is bound to in these early days. And I'm also sorry if I haven't been patient about your fears and confusion. I've been irritable with you, I admit, and I shouldn't have been. This is a tiring job, emotionally draining, even, so I may not have been in the best headspace to respond to you in a kinder way. I just wanted you to know that...Well, with all these new recruits in the pipeline, and this vast place to renovate, I fear I might have let my tiredness get the better of me."

It sounded reasonable enough to Ania.

"On the other hand," Nana mutters, "her ever-changing moods, this emotional rollercoaster that she seems to be on, could make her prone to overreaction. Dare I say *trigger-happy*? Let's hope she doesn't have a gun."

Ania tries to see if Cynthia's belt area is bulging with a holstered weapon. Nothing visible from this position, but this doesn't reassure her. In fact, Nana's mention of a gun reignites Ania's sense of urgency about getting out of here.

"I need to go home, and I need to go home now," Ania insists.

"Yes, I know," Cynthia grumbles. "You've said that a number of times, and we all want that. Don't think you're the only one with a family you miss. But we are here, so we have to make the best of it.

For now, at least."

Ania shakes her head, refusing to listen to any more.

"No, I'm telling you, I…"

"You won't be here forever," Cynthia adds. "Believe me, it will fly by. Every troubled soul that has passed through here has done so in such a brief space of time." Something makes her stop and glance at a form on her desk. Leaning forward, she traces a finger over the apple logo. "So many troubled souls."

"What I'm saying is…" Ania begins, but Cynthia interrupts her again.

"I try to help each one, but sometimes, you know, they are beyond help."

The woman appears to be doing this deliberately, blocking Ania out so she is forced to sit in silence, and it makes Ania's head throb with a rage that throttles her.

"I'm sure you're wondering what I mean by *troubled*," Cynthia continues. "Well, these girls have been in…"

"Stop!" Ania yells, "you have to stop. Clearly, you've got the wrong person, or someone else has made this mistake. There might be another Ania, there's certainly plenty of Browns. There must have been a mix-up because I am far from troubled. If you mean trouble with the law, then you could take your pick of any girl in my grade. Cocaine, prostitution, theft, you name it, they've done it. But me? I'm boring as hell."

She's talking too much, and breathlessly, so she's starting to feel dizzy. She might not be taking in enough air to think straight, and she's vaguely aware that she shouldn't tell this stranger so much about her life, but she can't seem to stop herself. And Cynthia doesn't appear to mind. She sits in her leather chair, eyes wide with wonder as she listens to Ania's every word.

"The only troubled thing about me is my name, I mean, Ania, *trouble*, they're linked, aren't they? At least, that's what my parents told me. They said they only found out that the name Ania is associated with trouble after I was born. But by then, they had already chosen my name. So, my name was a mistake, and that really sums up what my family is, I mean, not trouble but a bunch of mistakes, or misfits. Nothing ever goes our way, but believe me, I am far from trouble. As I said, I am pretty boring; in fact, my parents would say that I am *quiet, tidy, and well-mannered.* Always the compliant one, the fawning appeaser."

"And yet somehow they still saw fit to put you in this camp,"

Cynthia declares.

"What?" Ania feels sick. "No. You're lying."

"I'm not. It is because of them that you are here."

Ania used to dream of cutting her long hair and dyeing the auburn a thick darkness. Her mother never let her. She wanted to become a malevolent fairy so she could try something new, and now someone was implying that she was, somehow, this bad kid who had done something wrong, and she desperately wanted to go back to how things used to be.

"You're wrong," she insists. "Someone has made a mistake, made up lies about me, I don't know. I'm not meant to be in a place like this."

"Oh, yes, you are. This is absolutely the right place for you. At least for now. I know you miss your family, we all do, but eventually you'll understand how this place is helping you."

"The phone," Ania demands. "I want to make that call."

"Of course," Cynthia says, and she reaches for a drawer underneath the desk. Her sleeve rides up her arm and Ania can see something glistening on her wrists. The lines of scars, perhaps, or even the tracks of an addict after she has spent years injecting herself.

Cynthia catches Ania's eye, and for a moment, the teenager wonders if the woman is going to unleash some kind of violence. Shame can do that to someone because it feels easier to experience outer pain than inner pain. But Cynthia doesn't do anything more than adjust her sleeve, so her wrists disappear from view.

"The phone?" Ania repeats.

"You remind me of my daughter." Cynthia mutters this very quietly, almost silently. "She would never let things drop."

Ania doesn't like the way this sudden intimacy has thickened the air like curdling cheese.

"It became a bit of a problem," Cynthia adds, "the way she held on so tightly to things."

"That's if she even had a daughter in the first place," Nana murmurs. "Could be another mind game."

"In the end, it choked out the life of everything. Do you know what I mean?"

Ania doesn't, but she isn't going to ask for clarification. Instead, she averts her eyes and stares at a point over Cynthia's shoulder. If she can keep doing this, she will have a better chance at avoiding this woman's whirlpool. She cannot afford to believe anything the woman says, let alone start to care. If she can keep her out of her mind, pretend, even, that this woman does not exist, then maybe she will find a way back home.

"And if you allow yourself to fall into that whirlpool?" Nana whispers.

Ania refuses to respond, so her grandmother fills in the blanks for her.

"Then you might really start to unravel," Nana continues, "when you allow yourself to fall into the depths of depravity. Careful, now, to do that might lead you to a dark corner of this mall, where you find yourself bound and gagged…"

"…pondweed grows rampant, choking out the life of it," Cynthia continues to say, confusing Ania, because she stopped listening.

"What then, Ania?" Nana asks. "You've seen the documentaries about these kinds of camps, and you've seen the law firms trying to drum up business by representing the survivors. Those are the lucky ones who, at least, made it out alive. Traumatized, but alive."

Still, Ania will not listen to her grandmother.

"Don't think I am some hysterical old woman. I never grew old, I'll have you know, I never lost my faculties, so you should hear me when I tell you about the kids who have gone missing from camps like this one. Surely your parents heard those stories too, and surely they know the risks of a place like this? How could they willingly sign you up if they had known? Unless they didn't know, unless they didn't sign you up and you've been taken here against your will. Snatched off the street, perhaps, or even from your bed…"

"You look like her," Cynthia explains. "Especially when you frown."

The ticking of the clock is louder now, as if someone has moved it closer to Ania's ear.

"She certainly had a mind of her own. Always finding a point to pick apart, just because she could. Not quite the devil, but the devil's advocate," Cynthia adds.

If the woman was looking for a likeness to her daughter, then Ania thought that she should look to her brother, who was the defiant one, the devil's advocate and, in their mother's eyes, the devil himself. Dylan went by many labels; gender queer at one time, another time it was non-binary, and then there was the time he was gender fluid. But the prevailing view was that he was the picky pedant who could be a pain in the ass.

"So, he left no room for any of your own discontent," Nana adds.

"He ranted so much that your only option was to sit in silence. Dead silence."

"My daughter was troubled," Cynthia explains. "That's why I ended up in this line of work. I knew I had to help others before it went too far."

"Can I go home now?" Ania asks. She tries to steady her breathing, just so that Cynthia cannot see that she is shaking from a combination of fear and frustration.

"You *are* home! Can't you see? I mean, for now, at least, can't you view it as that?"

"No."

"Okay. Then maybe we should call it what it is. Neither home, not that kind of comfort, but also not away, not the desolation of isolation. Instead, this is somewhere in between."

"I don't know what you mean, and I am tired, so just let me go."

Cynthia laughs. "There you go again; just like her. So stubborn and single-minded. So strong. I wondered if I would meet someone like her. It feels like I've been waiting here for an eternity."

Dust motes dance around Cynthia's head, and the dim light from her desk lamp casts shadows to distort her face. One minute she looks kind and the next malevolent. In time, Ania wonders if she would watch Cynthia as she transforms some more; will she see the woman shed her skin, letting it crumble like flakes of ash all over the floor? Ania can almost feel it falling onto her lips, and even the thought of it tickles her nose and catches at the back of her throat.

"Are you okay?" Cynthia asks as Ania starts to cough.

"Yes, I'm fine. I just want to go home. Why won't you let me go home?"

"I get it. You are bound to feel a pull back to your old life. Just relax and let things take their natural course. I mean, just look at me. I thought I couldn't stand another moment longer in this place, and then here you are, to remind me of why I am here, why I am doing this work. We are lucky to have found each other."

A knock at the door, and then a voice from the other side.

"Cynthia?"

It's Carrie.

"Come on in," Cynthia calls.

Ania hears the door open behind her and in wafts a stench of meat or vegetables that has collapsed under the weight of time.

"Can I talk to you?" Carrie asks.

"Can it wait?" Cynthia says with a sigh.

"Not really. Sorry."

The woman lets out a long, dramatic sigh.

"Very well. I hope it's important enough to be interrupted like this." Jumping up, she marches out of the office with Carrie, and she slams the door shut.

From the corridor outside, Ania can hear their distant murmurs and hisses; conspiratorial and urgent, the words come in and out of range like ghostly murmurs from a nightmare.

"…unacceptable to be…"

"…urgent…didn't know…"

"…placating…only thing we can…"

"…fault…know if you…"

Something on the desk catches Ania's eye. A shiny surface glints, reflecting the light from the desk lamp. It's a snow globe, currently in use as a paperweight for the pile of forms on Cynthia's desk. Ania isn't sure why she didn't notice it before but now she cannot turn her attention away from it. She feels like a child again, when she was left alone with a huge slab of chocolate, and her parents returned to find an empty wrapper and brown smudges all over her face. She never knew whether or not it was a test, and she never could rid herself of the guilt of succumbing to temptation. Worst still, she suspected that few other kids her age would even feel guilty for such a thing, especially when it was ten years after they had done it.

"Your guilt may be your weakness, but it could also be a strength," Nana mutters.

Ania picks up the snow globe, gives it a shake, and she watches glitter flurry in a silent explosion. Like ice-white ash falling.

"Or like tiny shards of glass," Nana adds.

Inside the water of the snow globe, tiny figures reach out to one another. Their eyes bulge and their faces are swollen, as it looks like they might be drowning. Ania can't imagine why people would want this as a souvenir; it seems like such a horrific image, this watery tomb where people remain frozen in a liminal state; neither dead nor alive but perpetually drowning.

"Some kind of souvenir?" Nana whispers as Ania slips the item into the pocket of her tracksuit trousers. "If it's a memento of a daughter who has disappeared, she'll kill you if she catches you taking it."

"Not if I don't kill her first," Ania snarls. She doesn't know why she says this, but it makes her feel stronger than the *Midget* that Dylan has always portrayed her as.

The muffled voices of Cynthia and Carrie continue from outside the office.

"…told you not to…"

"…gone…just gone…"

Using every muscle in her body, Ania leans backwards so she can hear more of their conversation. Some of it doesn't make sense, and other words are lost altogether. But she is pretty sure that at some point she hears the words "Daria has gone."

Chapter Six

The profitable troubled teen industry
News article

Wealthwire Today: Troubled Teen Industry Thriving as Billion-Dollar Enterprises.

The troubled teen industry, a sector that focuses on rehabilitating adolescents with behavioral issues, is rapidly transforming into a multi-billion-dollar industry, with estimates suggesting that 45,000 teenagers are currently being held in various facilities operated by private companies. These facilities, often marketed as therapeutic boarding schools or wilderness camps, have become a booming business, attracting significant attention from investors and stakeholders.

A single facility in this niche can charge an eye-watering $18,000 per month per teen, with some services even costing more. One notable player in the industry, Xavine, a privately owned wilderness camp, reported a staggering $700 million in revenue last year. What stands out, however, is that 82 percent of Xavine's income came from public sources, such as Medicaid, school districts, and state and county funding. This high dependency on public money raises questions about the accessibility and accountability of these programs.

For years, private equity investors have found the troubled teen industry to be an attractive investment opportunity. One reason for this is the lack of regulatory oversight and the relatively low barriers to entry for private companies. These factors have led to the rapid growth of the industry, but also raised concerns about the quality of care and treatment offered at some facilities.

One insider, who asked to remain anonymous, claimed that some camps did not even exist, and yet public money continues to be funneled into these phantom facilities. "When I attended the meetings, and I raised questions, questions that suggested impropriety as serious as extortion," the insider explained that "I was quickly dismissed, and then, when I pressed further, they tried to intimidate me into silence. In the end, I would just sit and nod along to their lies, like a ghost, they wanted me there but to see right through me." The insider also explained that the only people who were in charge of these facilities were unqualified family members and friends of the executives from the investing companies. "Many in charge of these facilities have never worked with kids before," the insider added. "Some shouldn't work with kids, but they got the job simply because of who they know."

We spoke to parents of some teenagers who were sent to these facilities, and one explained that "this is a tragedy just waiting to happen. The people in charge are not stable and they certainly shouldn't be working with kids. I've heard of some managers showing signs that they are mentally unwell, or they have lost countless other jobs because of violence or substance misuse, and this is a last attempt to remain in employment."

"The worst of this industry are the camps, the wilderness programs," explained another parent. "Yes, there are adjustment schools and facilities for behavioral modification, but out in the wilderness, there is no one to keep an eye on the kids and those counselors, not when they are so far from the nearest town. Late at night, it can get so cold in those wooden cabins, and I've heard that they make little effort to keep the wildlife away from the kids. It truly is a lawsuit just waiting to happen."

When parents and guardians enroll their teenagers, little information is given about the program. "I'm not sure who is checking these places," another parent added, "but once I handed her over, I never heard from my child. No phone calls, no text messages. Not even an email. It was as if she ceased to exist. I was expected to just get on with my life and pretend someone hadn't just taken my kid."

Many teenagers are enrolled in these programs because of behavioral and emotional challenges, and some parents claim that their teenagers were taken in the middle of the night by transportation companies hired by the camp in question. When we asked camps to verify this, they refused to comment, directing us to their attorneys who never returned our calls.

Critics of the troubled teen industry have claimed that many businesses take advantage of a lack of regulation and loopholes created when teens are sent across state lines. There are reports of physical and verbal abuse, malnutrition, isolation, sleep deprival, and other forms of manipulation.

"We never ate," claimed one survivor. "Rarely, barely, I don't even know. The hunger made us confused, so we lost track of when we had last eaten, when we had last slept, what was night and day. I didn't know where I was, and sometimes I got confused, I wasn't sure who I was. Day one, they took my phone, and they wouldn't let me call anyone. They kept promising that my parents would visit, but they never did. I felt so alone."

Many critics state that there is little evidence to support any claims that these programs make any positive changes to a teen's behavior or emotions. Some go much further, suggesting that these programs make things worse. One insider, who asked to remain anonymous, stated that the strategies some camps use can exacerbate any existing mental health challenges. "If you're already depressed or anxious, if you're already a little paranoid, or delusional, or having psychosis, all these measures can really play with those symptoms. And if you ask questions, you're only made to feel you are the problem. They'll twist it so you believe that you are seeing things or hearing things, so you feel more paranoid, more delusional, more anxious, and ultimately more depressed."

"And these camps have been set up everywhere. It's been spreading like wildfire," one critic added. "Once they found out how lucrative it was for one provider, entire armies of providers started following suit. The idea spread like some kind of social contagion. Everyone wanted a piece of the action."

We reached out to the U.S. Department of Justice, the U.S. Department of Health and Human Services, and the U.S. Department of Education, and no one was available for comment. "And there's the biggest issue," one parent explained, "there is no official oversight. No licensing, no regulation whatsoever. Some of these departments might have some kind of involvement with one or two aspects of what these places do, but, the truth is, there isn't any regulation for the for-profit troubled teen industry."

"It's insane," one parent said. "How can they get away with charging us a small fortune for locking up our kids? And then they claim that they should not be held accountable. Someone really should do something about this."

"They never mention all the lawsuits that are stacking up against them," one parent explained. "There are loads out there, but many have been advised by their lawyers to keep quiet in case it jeopardizes their claim. If parents hadn't been so secretive, we might not be in this mess." This parent, who wished to remain anonymous, refused to elaborate on their own teenager's experiences, but they urged other parents to come forward.

As private companies profit from the vulnerable youth population, critics argue that the lack of regulation and oversight could lead to potential exploitation. Calls for more stringent monitoring and accountability are growing louder, with parents and advocacy groups demanding transparency and a more ethical approach to these enterprises. Yet despite the controversies surrounding the troubled teen industry, it remains an undeniably lucrative market, one that attracts significant investment as it grows into a multi-billion-dollar enterprise. Whether this industry will see increased scrutiny or continue to thrive with minimal regulation remains to be seen.

Comments:

u/healedhelper#20:

None of us are in this line of work for the money. Money? Are you kidding me? What money? Us workers don't see any of those profits. I'm not sure if those figures are even correct, that would be way above my pay grade, but even if it were, none of us clinicians saw a dime of that. If we really wanted money, we would've become a surgeon or a dentist. We chose this line of work because we care deeply about helping others to heal. I find this article re-traumatizing at the least.

u/diegodog#82:

We do this out of love. Not a day of my working life goes by without me shedding a tear for these kids. I work so hard, and for little income. I am certainly not seeing the billion-dollar profits, let alone the $18,000 per month income. I work for minimum wage, and I don't mind until articles like this are published.

u/warwound#07:

I know who you are, diegodog#82. You terrorized me for years, and you still won't shut up. How many times did you wake me up in the night under some BS excuse about folding my clothes or cleaning up the bathroom? You made me stand in the middle of the yard in the chilly night, and left me all alone. There was a forest nearby. Anything could've come to get me, a bear, a wolf, a fox. Who do you think you are, power tripping off trapped kids, and then posting online some sob story about the amount you get paid for the teen camp equivalent of shooting fish in a barrel?

u/rizlasykes#09:

And I know who you are, u/warwound#07. You stole my Pokémon cards and my iPhone. You should be locked up. You were always crazy, making up these stories about people coming after you. Talk about paranoia. You made it hell for everyone, harassing all of us at the camp, and now you're harassing people online. You're pathetic.

u/warwound#07:

Loser, I never took your cards and phone. Probably lost them cuz you're a loser. You know, you lose things. Butt outta things that don't concern you. This is between me and diegodog#82. So, diegodog#82, what do you have to say for yourself?

u/rizlasykes#09:

Stop harassing her.

u/warwound#07:

I told you already. Butt out of this, otherwise I'll come find you and harass you some more. You'll wish you stayed quiet when you hear the creaking floorboards at night, and you see that shadow at the foot of your bed. And what about you, diegodog#82, what do you want to add to this?

u/diegodog#82:

They're coming for you.

u/warwound#07:

What???

u/diegodog#82:

Pitiful. You're caught in a prism, where perpetrator becomes survivor who perpetrates some more.

u/warwound#07:

You're nuts.

u/diegodog#82:

You think you're the malevolent spirit, you think you're the big and mighty aggressor who no one can touch. But really, they're coming for you and soon they'll be crawling all over you. Imagine what it will be like to feel them on your skin, and then inside your skin. Imagine that, for them to writhe about, just beneath the surface.

u/warwound#07:

What are you going on about? Have you been drinking again?

u/diegodog#82:

Just wait, you'll see.

u/warwound#07:

I don't know what you're playing at, but you're not scaring me.

u/diegodog#82:

They're already there. Can you see them? They've found you.

u/warwound#07:

^(#)@#|}{

u/diegodog#82:

Go quietly. It's the only option for you now.

u/rizlasykes#09:

What is this?

u/rizlasykes#09:

Hey, has anyone heard from u/warwound#07? It's been weeks since their last comment.

u/rizlasykes#09:

Anyone?

u/rizlasykes#09:

Hello?

Source: https//www.[redacted].com
Accessed November 4, 2020, at 7:30 PM

Chapter Seven

Sonder

Cynthia returns to the office and quietly closes the door.

"So that's that," she says as she slides into the leather seat. "No more interruptions, at least not for the rest of the morning."

"Everything okay?" Ania asks.

"Yes, of course. Why?"

"You and Carrie sounded animated about something."

"We did? I didn't think so. No, everything is fine."

"Right. And Daria? What's happening with her?"

"Nothing. She's fine."

The woman's replies seem a little too guarded to satisfy the teenager.

"It's just that…I heard something," Ania begins.

"Careful, now," Nana murmurs. "You don't want to reveal her as the liar."

"You heard *what*?" Cynthia leans her elbows on the desk, and it creaks under her weight. She places the tip of each finger on her left hand against the tip of each finger on the right. Ania notices that they do not form identical parallels; one hand appears to be larger than the other, and this adds to the skewed feeling Ania is getting about this woman as much as this camp.

"I heard Carrie. She sounded a bit upset," Ania lies.

Cynthia shakes her head. "You're mistaken. Carrie's fine." She levels a stare at Ania, insisting that the teenager drop it.

Violent images flash through Ania's mind: Sophie's aggression, and Carrie's, and the way Daria was bundled out of that cabin before she could finish saying something. "*You have to…*" the nose-ringed girl had said. Have to *what*? Have to *escape*? Have to *be careful what she eats or drinks, in case of drugs*?

"How do you know they're not doing that already?" Nana murmurs. "Lick your lips. Is there a salty, metallic bite of chemicals? Is there a pin-prick mark on your arm? They could have done anything while you were asleep. Anything they wanted."

Ania licks her lips, and they are dry, but they don't taste of anything in particular. She also pulls up her sleeves to examine her arms. Nothing unusual. So why does she feel so strange? The edges of everything are softer, blurrier, as if she is insulated by something.

"A protective layer?" Nana suggests. "Ignorance can sometimes be bliss, especially if you're not ready to take the full force of reality."

"You seem distracted by something."

"No," Ania lies. "I'm fine. Actually, I'm not. Daria…"

Cynthia cocks her head to one side.

"Daria *what*?" the woman snaps.

"Is she okay?"

"Why are you asking that again?" Exasperated, she lifts her hands up to gesticulate, and her sleeves fall back again.

"There are the scars again," Nana whispers. "Not the tracks of a druggie, but the pain of a self-harmer."

Ania can see the gleaming whiteness of newly grown scar tissue crawling like veins across her wrists.

"She seemed upset," Ania adds, trying not to look at the woman's wrists. "Earlier, I mean, in the cabin. She was really getting herself worked up about something."

"You don't need to be her protector, you know. Is that what your role was at home? Keeping watch over your family members like some shepherd, forever vigilant for your flock?"

Ania shakes her head, disoriented by the woman's choice of words. It sounded slightly biblical, and familiar, but she couldn't place it.

"Daria is fine," Cynthia declares with a sigh. "She's the kind who will always be fine. Doesn't she strike you as pretty strong? The type of kid who will always look after herself?" Cynthia waits for a reply, but Ania just shrugs her shoulders. "Well, I think her defiance will keep her pretty safe without anyone else stepping up to become her protector. Besides, I don't know why you are even worrying yourself about all this. You barely know her."

Again, Ania shrugs. She can't explain it, this gravitational pull towards a girl she has only just met. It feels like she has known her for her entire life.

"She's a friend?" Ania offers.

"A friend?" Nana grumbles, "you're not experienced enough to identify one of those."

"She is? I'm not sure you're quite ready to call her that, at least, not so soon after meeting her," Cynthia remarks. She leans in, making Ania do the same, and she can smell something familiar on the woman. A scent that she can't quite identify, even though she feels like she has known it her entire life. "There's a danger whenever you give too much too soon. Why don't you settle into this place and get to know everyone before you make your decisions and start to label people? Besides, all this preoccupation with this girl you have only just met, and you're forgetting the reason you came to my office. Don't you want to call your family?"

Ania nods.

"Let's see now..." she mutters as she pulls open a drawer underneath her desk.

"Careful what she might have in that drawer," Nana mumbles, making Ania's limbs lock up in fear.

"Of course. You must speak to your family," Cynthia declares, "you *should* speak to them. I would love that too, as would every person in this camp. We usually encourage a clean break, at least during the first period, just so you can acclimatize to your new surroundings. But every rule does not have to be followed to the letter. I am a fair person, and I hope that no one can ever accuse me otherwise."

"Yes. You've said this already."

Cynthia takes her time rummaging about in the drawer, making Ania wonder if the woman ever had a phone here in the first place.

"A ploy to get you alone," Nana mutters. "It isn't paranoia if it is the truth."

"I can't seem to find your phone," she admits, "but in the meantime, you are welcome to use mine." She pulls out a clear Ziplock bag, and inside there is a cell phone.

"We keep everyone's personal effects like this," she explains as she shakes the bag. Along with the phone, there is a small packet of tissues, a set of keys, and some lip balm. It looks like the kind of bag that a hospital or police station hands to the relatives as they sob over the personal effects of their loved ones.

Cynthia unzips the bag, and a strange metallic aroma lingers in the air.

"Here, use it," she says as she places it on the desk between them. Ania stares at it for a moment, suspicious that it might not even work, and this is all just an act by Cynthia to placate her. Yet she can see that the phone has power, at least, and the dull white glow of the display shows that it has a signal.

She longs to hear her mom's voice, and she tells herself that Eris would annihilate Cynthia if she knew that she was holding her daughter against her will. Ania didn't want to believe her brother that Eris was all talk, that the wrath and vengeance were just an illusion as ethereal as the reassurances from her whispering grandmother.

"Even if Eris proves herself to be the goddess of discord and strife, beyond any myths and legends," Nana mutters, "this Cynthia woman seems just as strong. You have to be careful because you might end up caught in mutual annihilation rather than a glorious victory."

"I am sure they are longing to speak to you again," Cynthia admits. Her voice is soft, and she stares into the distance, as if she is trying to remember something. "The absence can be so much harder when we can't hear their voice. They say that eventually you forget the sound of them altogether. I don't know who said that, but I can't possibly believe it. I mean, those kinds of things are burned into our psyche, aren't they? Their voice, the sound of their laughter, and the shape of their smile."

Ania picks up the phone, but she pauses and looks at Cynthia.

"Go ahead," the woman replies, "be my guest."

Ania dials her mom's number, but it gives a call failed tone straight away. She tries again, and she still gets the same response.

"Maybe I'll get a better signal if I go out into the lobby, or even out of the mall altogether?"

Cynthia's body hardens in response to Ania's suggestion. Her fingers curl and tighten around the arms of the chair, and her widening eyes make her look like a wild predator that is ready to pounce.

"I don't think that's necessary," the woman is quick to reply.

Ania dials again, and still the same response.

"Fuck," she hisses under her breath, hoping that Cynthia doesn't hear.

One last time, she tries her mother's number, and again, she gets the same response, so she switches tactics and tries her dad's number. Surely he must be searching for her, distraught that one of his pack has gone missing.

"That's if he didn't put you in here himself," Nana mutters.

Eris would always call him her *shepherd*, the watchful one keeping a close eye on his familial flock.

"Well, he failed this time," Nana adds. "Never thought he was good enough for my daughter. He was calm, yes, but so calm that he took too many rests. He was probably napping when you slipped through his fingers."

Ania presses the phone into her ear, but all she hears is the flattened, dull tone of a failed call.

"That woman was never going to let you call anyone," Nana whispers. "Cynthia wants you trapped here so she can do whatever she likes."

"Having trouble?" Cynthia asks.

"Yeah, kind of."

"It's always been a problem out here," Cynthia explains. "I heard they were going to put a cell phone tower on one of the nearby hills, and that would've been great, but, of course, some locals had a problem with that. They've always had a problem with something, never wanting anything to be renovated or built on their doorstep, but I won't bore you with endless stories about their nimbyism."

Ania makes one last attempt at her dad's number, and after that produces the same response, she tries her brother's number. Nothing works.

Just when she thinks that she is going to give up, the woman pulls out another clear Ziplock bag from her desk drawer, She shakes it in front of Ania's face, and says in a sing-song voice, "Here we are! Bet you thought I'd lost it."

Sure enough, sitting inside the bag is Ania's phone, along with the small yellow pot of lip balm that was always in her pocket.

Snatching the bag, Ania unzips it and pulls out her phone. To her surprise, there is battery power, so she dials her mom's number. Like before, it gives a call failed tone, and it does the same thing again after she hits the redial button. She then tries her dad's number, and the same problem, so she quickly dials her brother's number.

Her stomach churns as it begins to ring. She presses the phone against her ear so hard that her head hurts a little, but she doesn't care.

"H...h...llo?" says the voice on the other end of the line. Definitely her brother.

"Dylan. Can you hear me?"

No reply.

"Dylan?"

Crackling on the line. Every time Dylan tries to say something to her, the crackling gets worse.

"Please, Dylan, if you can hear me, tell Mom and Dad to come and get me."

Still, the crackling intensifies.

"You must help me," Ania insists. "I don't want to be here. Please. Come and get me or tell mom and dad to come."

"It's a trick," Nana whispers. "That's not your brother."

"Did you hear me? Come on, Dylan, say something! Anything. Just show me a sign that you can hear me." Ania is now shouting into the phone as the crackling reaches a crescendo that is deafening.

"Sh...Wel...Don't...Try to..." she hears on the other end of the line.

"What?" Ania wails. "What was that, Dyls? Please, say it again. Try to *what*?"

"Try to... You must...Wha...Try...Gonna..."

Then a dull monotone of a dropped line.

"Dropped or cut?" Nana sneers.

Ania stares at her phone. She wishes she had saved as a screensaver a picture of her family, but she was always afraid that the kids at school would laugh at her.

She presses redial. This time, the call doesn't even go through, and she keeps redialing until Cynthia stands up and says, "I think you've tried enough." Her hand is outstretched, waiting for Ania to give her phone back to the woman.

"No," Ania snarls. "Let me try again. Please. I got through to Dylan, so I might get through to my parents."

"That's enough," Cynthia insists. "Really, Ania. We've spent enough time on this."

"I don't understand...Let me try a different phone."

"No."

Finally, Cynthia takes Ania's phone from her and slips it back into the Ziplock bag.

"Did you see how her hands were shaking?" Nana mutters.

Ania doesn't want to listen to Nana. There are too many threats that she is trying to comprehend that she can't process any more.

"We can try again later," Cynthia states as she drops the Ziplock bag into the drawer and slams it shut. "But for now, it is time for breakfast."

"You don't need to worry about me," Ania snaps. "Give the food to one of the other girls."

"Oh dear! You're not on one of those diets, are you? That really is damaging, especially when you are still young. You are still growing, so you need as much nutrition as you can get into your body. I don't want to see any restrictive food habits at my camp. After all, the brain doesn't stop developing until you are…"

"I'm not staying. If you can't get a hold of my parents, then you can drive me home."

"Don't make her angry," Nana warns.

"I'm sorry," Cynthia snaps, "but that won't be possible. What *is* possible is going for breakfast with me and the others."

"I don't want anything to eat," Ania snarls.

"I'm sure you will feel differently when you smell the food."

A crackle and hiss, and Cynthia adjusts the walkie talkie.

"Carrie, do you read me? Sophie? Is that you?"

More crackling and hissing.

"Do either of you read me?" Cynthia repeats.

Still more crackling and hissing.

"You know," Cynthia shouts into the handset, "there's no point carrying these walkie talkie things if you aren't going to answer me. And I really hope you have it switched on."

The hissing intensifies, and so does Cynthia's frustration because she slams the equipment onto the desk. In response, something scurries from beneath the desk, making Ania jump onto the chair.

"*Nooo*!" she screeches. A large, black spider scampers about the floor just beneath her. Ania doesn't want to think about the length of time she has sat there, with her legs under the desk. And all the while, this hideous thing was scurrying about the darkness.

"Just like my daughter," Cynthia mutters with a dry chuckle. "Aaliyah was terrified of most creepy crawlies."

After noticing Ania's horror, Cynthia stops laughing.

"Okay, I'm sorry," the woman adds. "Let me get rid of it for you."

To Ania's disgust, Cynthia reaches for the spider and grabs it with her bare hands. Marching out of the office, Ania can hear the woman saying, "Now, run free but not in my office," before she returns and shuts the door.

"All better now," Cynthia says as she once again sits in the leather chair. "you can have a seat too," she adds with another one of her plastic smiles.

Ania obeys by climbing down from the chair so she can sit across from the woman. She stares at her for a moment, noticing how rapidly Cynthia is breathing. There is that distant rattle from beneath her ribcage again, and there is that worrying wheeze.

"All this excitement," the woman says as she tries to smile. Beads of perspiration shudder to the surface of her skin and form glistening snakes that slither down from either side of Cynthia's brow.

"I'm glad you let me get rid of it," the woman continues, "because Ania hated it if I did that."

"What?"

"Aaliyah hated it if I captured any spiders and threw them outside. Each time I did that, I would find her in tears, and she would tell me that the little creatures might get hurt or eaten, or they might not find food to survive. She even tried to make me believe that it was too cold for them to live outdoors, and that I should bring them all inside again. She was always so worried about everything. To a fault. Her fears trapped her because she couldn't protect herself from them. She wouldn't harm anything that was living, even the creepy crawlies, even when they terrified her. Imagine that; to be trapped with fear and loathing for something you are willing to protect at all costs."

Ania thinks of her mother, and the stalemate she is locked in with her own son. There isn't anything they wouldn't say or do to hurt each other, and yet still they co-exist somehow. Permanently on the brink of mutual annihilation.

"Honestly, the amount of time and money I spent trying to help my daughter with her phobias," Cynthia explains. "Spiders, ants, anything that crawled about; she was terrified of all of those things. I tried everything to help her. Therapy, hypnotherapy, you name it and I tried it. Trouble is that none of it ever helped, not even a little bit."

Ania views her phobia as something quite rational. After all, you don't know which creepy crawly carries the venom that will kill you. So, she thinks of it less as a phobia to be eradicated and more of a primeval fear that should be listened to because it keeps her safe.

"My friend used to show me videos of spiders, just to get a reaction out of me."

Ania isn't sure why she is telling Cynthia this. It might be a conciliatory gesture, a way of thanking this woman for disposing of the spider.

"Oh? Did you tell her how much you hated spiders?"

"Yeah. That only made Abigail want to show me more. She even found a few spiders in her backyard and left them in my bed."

Cynthia suddenly looks sad, and it softens her a little.

"That doesn't sound like much of a friend," she says as she shakes her head.

"She's right," Nana adds, "at least on that point, you can listen to her. Abigail was never your friend."

"She's complex," Ania explains, a little defensively. She doesn't want this woman to know that she has a hard time distinguishing friend from foe. Something tells Ania that Cynthia would use this information to her advantage.

"Never let them know your weaknesses," Nana murmurs in agreement.

"Aaliyah had a similar experience," Cynthia admits. "Maybe it's a girl thing, I don't know. There was this one kid that my daughter just could not get along with, and yet they always referred to each other as *bessies*. I couldn't get my head around it. This apparent *friend* would do such cruel things to Aaliyah; make jokes at her expense, criticize whatever she wore to school, and whisper so many lies about her. And yet my daughter still insisted that they were friends. I mean…I tried to toughen her up, I really did, but there was just no getting through to her. She cared too much."

"Why is she trying so hard to convince you of this?" Nana mutters. "In fact, who's to say she even had a daughter in the first place? She could be lying about that, or the similarities between you and Aaliyah, just so she can forge a connection with you. You'll be easier to manipulate if you feel attached to her. *Pseudo-parentis*, or something like that."

"I'm not sure I did a very good job," Cynthia continues, "as a mother, as a protector, even a provider. And what hurts is that I may have made things worse. It only takes one kind person for someone to survive a childhood, and usually that kindness should come from the parent. But I don't think I was very kind to her."

Something stops Ania before she asks Cynthia where her

daughter is now. Her Mom always told her that she shouldn't open a door when she didn't know who was on the other side, and she was right.

"For all you know, the daughter is locked up somewhere," Nana says softly. "Maybe she is somewhere in this abandoned mall. Maybe that's the strange smell that was trailing from Carrie earlier on. That stench of meat that has collapsed under the weight of time."

Cynthia catches the teenager's eye, and the woman forces Ania to share a smile with her. It is sudden, strangely warming, and it causes a shift in the teenager. She doesn't want to listen to her grandmother any more. There is something about the softness that Cynthia is offering that makes Nana's words seem torturous in sharp contrast. For too long, the old woman's paranoid mutterings have been fraying Ania's nerves, demanding that she remain vigilant at every moment, and she is exhausted from it all. Suddenly, she wonders if it was Nana's fault that Ania had no one to sit with at school. Her grandmother always told her that the kids in her grade were taunting her and sniggering about her, but what if Nana had it wrong, and the greatest threat wasn't the girls in her grade but the murmurings of a paranoid grandmother?

"Stop," Nana cries. "Don't turn on me like this. Don't abandon me, please."

But Ania cannot stop herself from looking at things in reverse. What if the person she thought was protecting her was the real danger? And what about her mother? She had been isolated as much as Ania, so maybe, just maybe, that isolation had less to do with any of Eris' inadequacies, and more to do with Nana's mutterings of paranoia.

"It's not true," Nana insists, "I've always tried to keep you and your mother safe."

But Ania is not sure what dangers really threatened her mother. Eris was too afraid to step outside of her home, certain that there were red eyes awaiting her, to burn her with their scrutiny and scar her like hot coals pressed into her existence. But maybe, just maybe, it was the contaminant left in their blood, traced back to Nana, that left Eris wrathful and isolated. Maybe the true danger was her grandmother, the person who let her own voice of paranoia lead her down a lonely forest track in rural Pennsylvania. Despite their physical resemblance, maybe there are differences between grandmother and granddaughter. There had to be. Maybe they are not quite identical parallels, and Ania can find a way out of this place without listening to her grandmother.

"Stop!" Nana tries to holler, "I don't want you to think like this!" But already Ania has pushed her grandmother's words into the past, where she believes that they belong. Already, she is focusing on her breath, and following it to the office where she sits, and the desk scattered with papers, and the woman who smiles at her.

"I want to help you," Cynthia says, "and I want to help all these troubled souls."

"Okay, and I understand, but I'm not…I don't think I am what you would call *troubled*." She steels herself, gathering as much of her brother's defiance as she can muster. "I really don't belong here, and I am going to go home."

Like shards of glass, the words are frozen in the air between them. She blinks, and there is a flash of Sophie's punch landing on her cheek, her eyes smarting so that the surrounding people were blurred. They could have been anyone.

Ania touches her cheek, and she doesn't flinch because there is no pain, no tenderness where Sophie hit her. There isn't the dampness of blood, not even a crust of clotting. Did it even happen?

"Let me go," Ania cries, "you have to let me go. This isn't the right place for me, and I'm not even the person you think I am. I'm not troubled, I've always behaved, so just let me go home."

"No," Cynthia growls, "I told you already. I am here to look after you, it is my role, my calling, if you like."

Cynthia pushes her hands on to the desk and uses it to rise up out of her chair. She seems taller than Ania remembers her, and as she walks round to the teenager's side, Ania thinks that the woman could just as easily throttle her as throw her arms around her in an embrace.

"I know you miss them," Cynthia mutters. Does her voice sound like she is shaking? "I miss my family, too." Her tone is soft and sickly sweet, but it could be an act.

"Just wait," Cynthia continues, "at least until breakfast is done with. And then I'll drive you home myself, if necessary."

Ania has no reason to believe her, but she also has no other choice.

Chapter Eight

Analgesia and a fair-weather friend

Cynthia walks Ania out of the office and past the static escalators to a long, dark corridor. The faulty lights still blink, flashing snapshots of broken roof tiles above moldy walls. She feels half-awake, caught in a dream that won't let her go, and memories are shuffled into a confusing array of present, near, and distant past.

As she hears the crackle of static on Cynthia's walkie talkie, and the distant voices that mutter broken sentiments, she remembers the pout and oily hair of Carrie. That counselor wheezed with the same sweaty, overbearing weight as her friend Abigail, who also had the same pout and oily hair.

She doesn't want to remember her friend.

The lights in the corridor continue to flash, and she thinks she sees movement up ahead. Is that Carrie lurking in the shadows? It seems strange that a counselor would play hide-and-go-seek when her boss is nearby. It's more likely to be the childish kind of thing that Abigail would do, especially if it gave her a chance to haunt Ania. Abigail loved to torment her friend.

She can almost hear her grandmother whisper that Abigail offered a prison sentence more than a friendship, but Ania doesn't want to listen to the mutterings of her grandmother, so instead, she focuses on the shadows that linger ahead of her. They stretch into nightmarish visions, specters that moan and groan, or she thinks they do, but it might easily be the structure groaning under the weight of neglect and disrepair.

"What's that?" she asks Cynthia as she points down the corridor.

"What?"

"Something moved, I think. It's hard to tell with the flashing lights."

"I know, I know. It's so hard to find an electrician out here, let alone one that's reliable. But have faith that all of this will be cleared up in no time."

Ania swears that she can see someone scrabbling about in the far corner, behind a dead ornamental tree. Could it have been Abigail? Would she follow Ania all the way up here, just to weave her way in and out of the shadows so she could mess with her mind? She could be that unpredictable, that extreme. Often, she would lunge from complimenting Ania to insulting her in one breath, and then she would let out a screeching laugh that also sounded like a cry. "OMG," she would screech, "the look on your face!" Ania always felt so disoriented when she was around her, and she wished she could just avoid her altogether, but she was trapped. Every morning, without fail, Abigail would ring her doorbell and insist that they walk to school. Ania was expected to sit with Abigail in class, and pair up with her to work on projects, and eat lunch together, and walk home together. And when Ania was at home, she was expected to answer every text and phone call, and like and comment on anything Abigail posted.

Ania refuses to remember any more of her friend, so she turns to Cynthia as the woman is halfway through a story about electricians and plumbers, and she smiles, relieved that she is anywhere but a web spun by Abigail Sullivan.

"Oh," Cynthia says, halting her story. "That's the first time I have seen you smile. And it is quite a relief to see it. I told you that you would start to settle in soon."

"No," Ania replies, taking care not to snap this time. "I'm not settling in. I just smiled, that's all."

"Okay, okay, have it your way if you wish. I swear, you make me laugh how much you sound like Aaliyah. No matter how many times I tried to get her to see things my way, she always chose the polar opposite. It's as if we were trapped from each other, unable to get through this mirror-like surface so she could see things my way. I told her to stay away from that fair-weather friend of hers, but did she listen? Of course she didn't."

"Fair-weather friend," she repeats after pausing for a moment. "I'm sure you've never heard of that phrase, I mean, your generation..."

The further they walk, the more the woman talks, and it is a breathless account, full of half-explained thoughts, but she doesn't stop Cynthia to clarify anything. She wants this woman's voice to keep her safe, to ward off anything that is moving within the shadows.

"...anxiety, but I don't think...mostly talks about it, but when it comes to...But that's what I would always tell her..."

Their shoes crunch on broken glass and debris, but this time Cynthia doesn't offer an apology for the mess. Lost in her stories, she keeps a relentless pace as they pass a dried-up fountain. Coins litter the tiled basin with scattered wishes, and Ania remembers going to a mall with Abigail and watching her steal the coins. "You can't do that," Ania had said, but she was met with a shoulder-shove in reply as Abigail stuffed more into her pockets. The security guard didn't care, he probably thought he wasn't paid enough to challenge some kid who might be carrying a knife, or whose parents could turn up and shout at him or have him fired. But Ania cared. "You're stealing people's wishes," Ania continued. "They might not come true if you do this." Abigail stopped for a moment and stared at her friend. She scanned her from top to toe, as if she was seeing the girl for the first time. Ania knew that her friend's mental calculation was only going to result in judgment and criticism, so Ania tried to distract her. "Why don't we go to the bookstore," Ania suggested, but Abigail just sneered in reply. "Books? Are you serious? No one reads books. What are you, fifty?" She pouted as she stared at Ania. "OMG, you're so lame, *Annie*." Ania flinched. Each time, she had told Abigail that her name was not Annie, but her friend only ever replied that she looked like an *Annie,* so her name was *Annie*.

"...and I would tell her that this was not a healthy relationship, and this wasn't even what you could call a friendship. She was trapped..." Cynthia adds.

"Trapped," Ania mutters, "a prison sentence, not a friendship," and Cynthia smiles in reply.

Ania doesn't want to listen to any more of Cynthia's stories because she realizes that the woman's voice isn't warding off the things that are lurking in the shadows. In fact, she is conjuring them up; creating horrific phantoms to haunt Ania with a nightmare that she is desperate to wake up from.

"Stop!" she snaps at the woman. "Please. I don't want to…"

She wants to say that she doesn't want to remember Abigail, but to say her name here might conjure her up.

Still, the shadows seem to dance across the dark corners of the corridors. Was there a voice to accompany the movement? A subtle voice to whisper *"Ania"*?

"My my, someone is irritable. Maybe you didn't get enough sleep," Cynthia remarks in a strange sing-song voice. "I'm sure you'll perk up once you have some food in your belly."

"Perhaps," Ania retorts. "I'm not really hungry."

By now, they have reached a part of the mall where there is less decay. With better lighting, Ania can see that many of the store units still have merchandise gathering dust in the windows. She can't understand what would have made everyone leave the mall so suddenly, unless something forced them out against their will.

A distant groan, and then a clanking of metal on metal.

Ania looks to Cynthia for reassurance, and the woman shakes her head.

"Don't you worry about that. Just the plumbing showing its age. It will all be sorted soon."

Ania can imagine that Abigail would love to roam around this abandoned mall, just taking whatever merchandise was left after the looters and vandals took what was valuable. Abigail would probably bring a baseball bat to smash in some of the store windows that opened into the mall. How her friend loved to commit random acts of vandalism at the stores in Rotherwell. "Do it," she would mutter to Ania after she had ripped a display dress. "I had the guts to do it, so you should, too. Show what kind of person you are, little Annie. Are you an enormous beast who won't let anyone mess with them, or a tiny little pathetic mouse?" When Ania refused to damage anything, Abigail would break something else in the store, adding, "there, I did it for you, but you're still a little mouse. And you know what people do with mice?" and before Ania could reply, Abigail stamped her boot with glee. "Imagine hearing the crushing sound of their little skulls," she would sneer as she broke something else in the store.

Maybe that's why Ania wounded up in a camp for *troubled souls*. Somehow, Abigail might have set her up.

"…that's what she was, a troublemaker. But Aaliyah could not see it…" Cynthia continues.

"…but the more you try to make suggestions to a teenager, the more they will do the opposite. So I knew I had to tread very carefully when it came to this apparent *friend…*"

Only now, Ania realizes that she never wanted a friend. She was content with the characters on her soap operas, but Abigail was insistent. She demanded more and more of Ania, and she didn't know how to say no. Her mother and brother were the stubborn, defiant, and wrathful ones. Their animosity took up all the energy in the household, leaving nothing for her or her father. As a result, they collapsed into a state of compliance and appeasement. So, when Abigail demanded every one of Ania's secrets, she complied.

"…so, in a way," Cynthia adds, "this fair-weather friend had power over Aaliyah. My daughter was helpless, a passive receptacle for that friend's every wish."

"I don't want to remember," Ania mutters to herself.

"What was that?" Cynthia asks.

"I don't want…I don't know."

"You have to go back to go forward," Nana murmurs.

Fury ignites beneath Ania's skin. She wants to tell her grandmother that she is not welcome, that she should be forever silenced because she is the cause of all of this. The trouble is, Ania isn't certain of anything. Not even this.

"You told Abigail about your diary," Nana whispers.

"She shared secrets with this friend," Cynthia adds, "because Aaliyah was always so trustworthy. But the trouble with trust is that it isn't a unilateral act. To do it, you lean on someone else, you must believe that they will support you. Blind faith can leave you to topple into the abyss."

"You shared your diary with her," Nana adds, "so Abigail held all the power. It isn't your fault, you didn't know that you shouldn't share so much so soon, not before you have the measure of someone. You didn't know that she would never offer you anything in return, never keep your secrets safe."

"You like girls?" Sneering, Abigail used the palm of her hand to smooth her long, jet-black hair that hangs under the weight of something oily. "Ew. Wait, you like girls and guys? Double ew."

Ania shrugged in reply.

"OMG, the girls at school are gonna scream," Abigail screeched.

"No," Ania groans, "you can't say anything."

With a relentless energy, Abigail tried everything to impress the mean girls in their grade. She would bring them gifts, she would carry out their wishes for cruelty towards the theatre kid or the spotty kid or the kid who spat when they spoke, and she would complement those mean girls with so many lies. After all of this, Abigail would stare at them, expecting, finally, to be accepted into their fold, and each time they would reject her, cutting her down with some comment about her weight, her mono brow, or her greasy hair. Ania hated to see the sadness that seemed to ooze from Abigail's every pore, and she wanted to keep away from her, in case she got that sticky sadness on her.

"She got to you in the end," Nana adds. "She became the malevolent spirit who stalked you day and night. She was relentless, unforgiving, and still you cannot see that she was never your friend."

"Ah, come on, I'm just playing with you," Abigail snorted. "I wouldn't really *out* you. Or would I? I mean, that would be cruel. Just look at what they did to that theatre kid. His face was messed up by their boyfriends. I heard they used a hockey stick. Don't worry, I would never let that happen to you. You need someone like me to have your back. I mean, no offense or anything, but you've never really fitted into Rotherwell, have you?"

She always used *no offense* when she wanted to say something really hurtful.

"You should've told her about your great-grandfather," Nana snorts. "You should have rubbed it in her face by reminding her that *he* was the one who built Rotherwell into the town that she now sees. You should have told her how much land your family still owns up and down the East Coast, vast swathes of power that Abigail could only dream of."

But Ania didn't have it in her. She just sat there as Abigail stroked her oily hands all over the diary.

"I guess you're gonna have to keep me sweet," Abigail said with a pout. "So I don't tell them. But I warn you, my silence will have to be bought, and I can tell you now that I am not cheap."

"She blackmailed you," Nana hisses. "No use putting too fine a point on it. Blackmail, pure and simple. That wasn't a friendship, that was abuse."

"This way," Cynthia says as she gestures towards another long and windy corridor. "And keep up, otherwise you'll miss breakfast."

By now, the woman has quickened her pace, leaving Ania trailing behind. "Come, come," she adds, "you don't want to get lost in a place like this. Even I don't know where some of these corridors go.

I mean, I do, but I forget in a place this size. And then there are the tunnels. I must admit that I haven't explored any of those. Not yet, anyway. There is enough to do at ground level without delving deep beneath the surface."

"Tunnels?"

"Yes, there's a whole labyrinth beneath this mall. Goodness knows what's down there, and I certainly don't want to explore them, at least not on my own. I guess it is like when you buy an old house and there are roof voids and crawl spaces that you never investigate. I'm sure there are plenty of stories of people living for decades in a home while all sorts of things sit in wait for them, just outside their reach."

She pauses, allowing Ania to catch up with her, and then they carry on walking, their shoes still crunching on the debris.

"During Avaline's due diligence, before they bought this place, we discovered that the site used to be an old fallout shelter. Can you believe that? Some deeply embedded safe place to flee if the world was likely to end. But who knows how safe it is down there, and you might get yourself into further danger by trying to hide in tunnels that were built a long time ago out of goodness knows what materials. If those things aren't inspected, you can find yourself buried alive. Imagine that paradox; a sanctuary and a trap."

Ania doesn't want to believe that this woman is trying to scare her, but she can feel the muscles in her body tightening in response.

"Ready to fight or flee," Nana whispers.

"I guess the previous owners, the mall owners, I mean, didn't want the expense of filling it all in," Cynthia continues, "so they just build over it. I've never been down there myself, but according to the papers from our purchase of the site, there are rooms, corridors, and even a shower facility and medical room."

"Could Daria be hiding down there?" Ania asks.

Cynthia stops, suddenly rigid like a mannequin. Even her wheezing has been frozen.

"What did you say?" the woman snarls.

"Maybe she's…I heard you and Carrie outside the office earlier on. I heard someone say that Daria has gone. Gone where?"

"You shouldn't listen in on things that don't concern you." Cynthia's words come slowly and softly, but the threat is loud and clear.

"Okay," Ania snaps, refusing to let the woman intimidate her. "But she might have got lost and found herself in one of those tunnels."

Cynthia shakes her head.

"No. Impossible. They sealed them up a long time ago."

"But you just said..."

"Come. You must be hungry," Cynthia snaps as she begins to walk again.

"But Daria..."

"That girl is fine," Cynthia growls. "She's probably in a better position than you right now."

"What do you mean?"

Ania runs to catch up with the woman. When she reaches her, she puts a hand on her shoulder. It's ice cold.

"I still don't understand your obsession with that girl," Cynthia snaps as she marches on. "You barely know her. Don't you have better things to preoccupy your mind?"

"Like what?"

"Like anything but that," Cynthia says with a sigh. She stops walking again and turns to face Ania. The lights are flickering again, shuffling perspectives of the woman that make her seem helpless, broken, even, in one moment, and then overbearing, threatening even, in the next.

"It sounds like you care too much. You need to learn when to let go, or you'll never be free." She pauses for a minute, perhaps letting the words echo in her mind, and then she adds, "Caring too much is a fault you need to fix." She has returned to her officious tone, and it sounds like she is compiling a list of urgent repairs.

"You're hungry, so we need to get you some breakfast," Cynthia declares before she sets off down the flash-lit hallway. "Here," she adds as she gestures to a brighter part of the mall. In this section, all the overhead lights are working, and they shine so brightly that the air seems like it is on fire.

Cynthia points at an abandoned hardware store where tools hang in the window. Even from here, Ania can smell the sawdust still floating in the air.

"The only place with running water," Cynthia explains, "so we set up the food prep here, in this hardware store. I guess you'd call it the dining hall. Now, let's go and get you some breakfast."

Chapter Nine

Kenopsia

Ania's stomach isn't growling. She can't even remember what hunger feels like. Still, Cynthia seems determined to step into the role of *pseudo-parentis*, so she shoos Ania towards the *dining hall* cum hardware store.

The woman mutters something more about the water supply issues, and unreliable plumbers, and the remoteness of the location. Ania wants to believe that all of this is true, that there is a reasonable explanation for it all, but the whole setup, this camp in an abandoned mall, seems too strange for her to relax and accept Cynthia's explanations.

"…thing in the way of really doing something with this place…I mean, the lack of water supply is the worst of it all. If we could find a way to solve that, then everything else would flow from that."

"Is that why there's such a strange smell? I mean, the lack of running water," Ania asks.

"A smell?" Cynthia looks genuinely confused.

"Yes. It seems to emerge every now and then. Like something is rotting."

Before she can hear Cynthia's explanation, she is flooded by the muffled sound of scraping chairs and distant conversation. It must be coming from the girls who are gathered for breakfast just behind the closed door to the hardware store.

"The wolf pack awaits," Nana snarls as Ania's chest tightens. She tries to take in bigger mouthfuls of air, but this only makes her head lighter, and she starts to see stars as she remembers the classrooms where the scraping chairs and conversations would echo. Filled with dread, she would have to walk through outstretched feet; landmines left for her to stumble on and fall, and then she would hear the explosion of laughter as she hit her head on a nearby desk. This happened repeatedly, as if caught on a Möbius loop, and each time she tried not to cry as she hauled herself back to her feet, she would try not to cry when she searched for an empty seat, and she would try not to cry when she saw the bags that were hastily slapped down on those empty chairs, or shoes slammed on them, even if there was mud to make the chairs dirty. Skin flushed, she was forced to ask the teacher where she should sit, and he would smirk, showing that he knew this game because he'd seen it played so many times before. And he always knew that she would be placed in the same position, as victim who had to beg for a seat in a classroom that she never wanted to be in. When the teacher finally ordered someone to move their bag or muddy shoe from a chair, she would watch from the corner of her eye as that person who was forced to sit next to her placed a hand over their nose, as if Ania carried a foul stench to repulse them, and she never knew why. Why they hated her smell, her the sound of her voice, the cut of her hair, the clothes she would wear. Nothing was good enough, and everything on her smelled so bad.

"Are you okay?" Cynthia asks. Ania wishes she could trust this woman, so she didn't have to keep fending off Cynthia's attempts at mothering her. She is getting so tired that she allows images to slip into her mind, where she sees herself leaning her head against the woman's shoulder and allowing her to put an arm around her.

"Then you'll be caught up in her web forever," Nana mutters.

Another ripple of conversation and scraping chairs, and Ania's chest tightens again. She doesn't think that she has the energy to face an entire group of people. One-on-one, Ania could just about keep up with the exhausting process of decoding facial expressions, body language, words and tone. But add one more person, and then another, and Ania is lost.

"Am I losing you?" Cynthia asks.

"What?"

"I've got a feeling that you haven't been listening," Cynthia adds.

"To what?"

"To me, when I was talking about the smells you mentioned. What I was saying was…Well, I figure that strange smells are less important than getting some food in your belly. Am I right?"

"I'm not sure." Ania still doesn't feel hungry.

"Well, *I* am sure. I know there are things to tweak about this place, and one of those things might be the strange smells, but we are working on all of it. So, in the meantime, let go of any other worries and come join me for breakfast. After all, hunger does some strange things to the brain. Did you know that for every couple of days without food, the brain lost twenty percent of its cognitive function? Can you believe that? So if you were starved for just ten days, your brain would be wiped of all knowledge and memory. Like a zombie wandering the…"

"She's crazy," Nana whispers. "Without food for that long, you'll probably wind up dead. She's just playing with you, trying to weaken you with mind games. All these strange stories, all these inconsistencies; promises of a phone call to your family and then they are mysteriously unreachable? I'm calling BS on all of this. You're being manipulated, as anyone would be in a wilderness camp. They're playing mind games with you, trying to weaken you to make you malleable, that much is clear. I just wish I could work out why. I mean, if I knew what their end game was, I might be in a better position to protect you."

Ania knows that Nana's words are not just wild fantasies and fears. She has seen online some the different forms of manipulation used on people in captivity, whether that has been wilderness camps, care homes, prisons, or the torture chambers set up by human traffickers. There are plenty of forums to delve into the depths of depravity, whether it is Reddit or 4Chan or the dark web. She has seen endless videos and images of prisoners tied up and drooling with their ribs and cheek bones jutting out, and with every click of the horrifying images, Ania tried to convince herself that she was driven by curiosity. But as she zoomed in, as she paused the video at the moment some of them took their last breath, she could hear voices that condemned her as "*disgusting.*" It wasn't Nana's words, in fact, she didn't know who it was, so she assumed it was an amalgam of the cruel girls in her grade. They morphed together, skin and bone fusing into a monstrous image of judgment. "*Filthy Ania,*" they would jeer in her mind, but still she watched the videos. "*Weirdo, creep,*" she would hear as she found some audio files which claimed to be a recording of the death rattle, and all the horrifying groans and moans that accompany it.

"*No wonder no one wants to be your friend,*" the voices would tell her, but then she would snap back that she didn't want any friends in the first place. She'd seen what friends can do, with the eye rolls and bitchy comments as soon as their backs were turned. They all went through cycles of turning on each other, so she would rather keep away from all of them. All but Abigail, who gave her no choice, who stalked her every movement, and all because that girl refused to accept her own isolation. Unlike Ania, who almost welcomed it, Abigail tried everything to change; she was desperate for the girls in their grade to accept her, and in the process, Abigail made a scapegoat out of Ania.

"OMG, you're so embarrassing," Abigail would jeer. "If you didn't do that, maybe they would include us in their plans." Ania was never sure what she was doing that upset Abigail so intensely, but it didn't really matter because she knew that if she worked on this one thing today, it would be flipped on its head tomorrow, and Abigail would dictate that Ania do the opposite.

It was this defiance of Abigail that made Ania want to delve deeper into the dark web. She knew that if her friend found out about it, she would use the same words as the cruel girls: "*disgusting, filthy, weirdo, creep.*" So Ania pushed on, an addict who was compelled to consume the harder stuff. The snuff movies would scare her, but she couldn't stop watching it. They were grainy, and it was hard to tell whether this was something the people wanted, to die, whether they wanted to be filmed in their final moments, or if this was pure exploitation, a blurring of the boundaries between suicide and murder. In some scenes, she heard a voice, not unlike that amalgam of cruel girls, whispering encouragement as a girl took a razor blade to her wrists, or another took one to her neck. "*Do it,*" she would hear the voice say, as if it were the audio from some porno. "*That's right, do it harder, do it deeper. You know you want to.*" At this moment, she would lean into the screen, the fizzle and hiss of static tickling her, and she thought she heard someone mutter "*Do it, Ania.*"

"…the hunger because she was put off her food," Cynthia continues. "I mean, I can't blame her, she really was pushed beyond all bearable limits. And the worst part of it is that I forced Aaliyah to go to school. Every day she would sob, pleading with me not to make her go in. But I wouldn't listen. And yet, everything happens for a reason. I truly believe that. So I will listen to you and the other girls. I will watch you all intently, so I never miss a thing."

Ania knows that the woman is trying to reassure her, but hearing this only makes her feel worse. It was the same when Ania tried to tell her mom about the mean girls at school, and this clumsy, strange friendship with Abigail that caused her so much confusion. Her mother looked lost, scared even, so Ania ended up worrying about how she could protect her mother, as well as how she could navigate each day with these cruel people at school.

"Trapped," Nana whispers, "inside your home and outside. With all that built-up frustration, no wonder you found those snuff movies so fascinating. And the footage of those internment camps, where they would starve and torture their prisoners."

Ania's skin flushes with shame as she thinks of her grandmother watching as she clicks on one depraved image after another. She gathered a whole folder of images and videos, from North Korean labor centers and Chinese reeducation camps, but she found it strange that she could never find any footage from American camps. She knew the government was guilty of just as many crimes against humanity as the North Korean or Chinese regimes, so she felt duped, as if someone was manipulating her into believing that she was safe in her own land.

"Dangers come in all shapes and sizes," Nana declares. "But they'll only let you know about the right type of wrong people. All part of the witch-hunt. You can ask my daughter about that."

Ania hated it when they would call her mother the *witch bitch of suburbia*. Eris Gall, then Brown, was different, Ania admitted that, but in the eyes of the *suburban beast*, as her mother called them, she was guilty of much worse. She failed to fawn over the seething moms and overblown dads of Mount Pelion Way. As a result, Ania's mother became the scapegoat they needed, so they could pile their frustrations onto her and distract themselves from their own misdeeds and failings. Of course, it was going to be Ania's recluse of a mother, not her father, to tar and feather, because they only make witches out of women.

"She was a scapegoat," Cynthia says. "I realize that now. And the more Aaliyah tried to fight back, the more reason they had to turn against her. Pack mentality at its most brutal. Aaliyah was always the one who was hauled to the principal's office, even though she was the one with the bruises on her back. She was always the one who was encouraged to try *mindful breathing* and *emotion regulation strategies*. Talk about bullshit. Kick a dog enough times, and it's bound to bark. And then, after a while, it's going to bite."

Ania pictures herself scampering around the classroom as she barks at the mean girls. She feels a whoosh of excitement as she imagines how high they might jump, even climbing onto the desks as she tries to bite their ankles.

"You're losing it," Nana warns, "probably the hunger."

But Ania can feel her chest loosening, and her breathing starts to ease.

"I know she wasn't proud of some things she did," Cynthia continues, "but she was in a corner. Surrounded by those animals. I don't blame her for any of it."

By now, Cynthia has the door open to the hardware store cum dining hall. On the shelves she can see knife sharpeners, rat poison, and jute twine; strange items to leave at a camp for troubled teenagers. Ania has heard that in some wilderness camps they teach the kids survival skills, in a bid to take the kids *back to basics* and free them from too much dependence on their overly protective parents. But this seems like a lawsuit just waiting to happen.

"Maybe they've left these things there to see what happens," Nana adds. "Maybe they want to stir things up a little, you know, see who grabs which weapon first. It might be a form of entertainment for them, some kind of latter-day gladiatorial combat."

For a while, her brother, Dylan, worked in a hardware store like this. Ania once visited him, but she stayed out of sight as she watched him unload boxes of supplies. She couldn't tell him that she was there because she was burning with jealousy that he had found a place to run to, far away from school and the fortress of their home.

"Such freedom usually comes at a cost," Nana mutters, "and usually that cost is the risk of greater dangers."

That one time she visited her brother at the hardware store, the clerk stalked her in the aisles. Probably because he thought she was a thief.

"You need help with anything?" he asked, his double chin wobbling like luncheon meat. "You buying or just browsing?" He probably wanted her to reassure him, to tell him that she was looking for a particular item, or to leave. Ania knew that she was expected to soften before him, to smile or offer a gentle comment, but she refused to do either. She knew of the dangers of sweaty men like this, who teetered on the edge of a rage when they did not get their way. Her mother had warned her about these kinds of dangers, and so Ania wanted to keep herself still, pretending that he could not see her. Although she knew this to be impossible, she longed to fold herself up, so she was so small that he could not even find her.

"Nothing more dangerous than a man who has been over-indulged," Nana sneers. "All these supplicant wives and mothers, softening their men up so they are unprepared for the real world. And when they realize they've been duped, that their sense of entitlement is based on an illusion, how their fury grows, and how they become bent on the desire to unleash that fury on their mother, and every woman they come across."

"I'm talking to you," the store clerk barked. His louder voice had attracted the attention of the other customers, who slowed their browsing to a stop in the aisle that Ania had been loitering in. Until then, she had ignored the other people, but as they clustered round her like a clotting artery, she found it hard to breathe.

They muttered something, and she thought she heard her name.

Ania.

Wanting to leave, Ania found her escape blocked by other customers. She thought of them surrounding her, taunting her, jeering, and laughing as she tripped on their outstretched feet.

Pushing a mother and her young daughter out of the way, she ran from the store. She always blamed the kids and teachers at her school, and the school counselor, or she blamed the weirdness of her mom at home. However, in that moment, she realized that the weirdness she carried within herself repelled others and condemned her to be alone.

That night, she searched the dark web for a place to vent her fury. She hated the world, but now she realized that she might also hate herself.

"Careful, now," Nana warns, "hatred can be contagious."

She clicked the dark webpages when she knew she shouldn't. She watched each frame of horrific footage as she tried to feel something. Maybe she was searching for a way to feel like the others, that somehow if she followed the herd and found the same reaction that she imagined they felt in response to something horrific (*shock, horror, intrigue*, she guessed) then maybe she would feel more lifelike, more fleshed out. And maybe they might finally accept her, those girls in her grade, and maybe she might finally accept herself.

"You shouldn't do it," Nana warned as Ania clicked on more and more images and videos. But the teenager was lost.

"I'm like Christopher Columbus," Ania muttered, "ready to discover all those unchartered territories." Her eyes lit up with the grainy images that were occasionally stirred by static. A heartbeat, signs of life, or maybe signs of disturbance.

She waited, but she felt nothing. Blood, drool, pain, misery; none of it evoked the reactions she knew it should. Instead, she muttered, "all of this exploitation, all these lands, this flesh, waiting to be colonized. Just because I can."

"Aaliyah?" she heard.

"Ania?"

It is Cynthia, still holding open the door to the hardware store cum dining hall.

"Why don't you go and sit with the others?"

Cynthia points to Jill and Ellie, who are sitting on metal chairs in front of a long fold-out table. They turn in unison as Cynthia walks Ania in. Jill sits on her hands, and she won't look in Ania's direction, but Ellie frowns, fiercely staring into Ania's eyes as if she is trying to tell her something. Ellie opens her mouth, but she freezes when Carrie appears behind her. No sign of Daria.

"You good?" Carrie asks Ellie. With her meaty arms folded, flesh bulging out in all directions, the counselor resembles a prison guard.

Ellie nods in reply and stares at the table. There are bowls and metal cutlery, but Ania can't see any food.

"They're playing with you," Nana whispers. "There was never going to be any food this morning."

Chapter Ten

Caught in the dark web
News article

ParentFile Today: What Parents Don't Know About the Dangerous Dark Web.

The dark web is a collection of hidden sites which contain information that some might consider offensive, taboo, or just plain weird. It is a part of the internet that is not accessed via the usual search engines like Safari and Google, it remains hidden, and it is generally considered to be a dangerous place because of the potential for exposure to dangerous and illegal information and activities.

The allure of the forbidden, the taboo, has always drawn widespread attention, particularly from the young. Freedom is a defining characteristic for most teenagers, but when that freedom leads to the dark web, some argue that this is a step too far. The main reason is that the dark web contains large amounts of illegal and harmful information, such as drugs, weapons, hacking tools, material relating to child exploitation, and stolen data.

Sakura Yoshida is a cybersecurity professional and educator who teaches technology-related courses at Farbright High School. Yoshida has developed several educational resources to teach digital safety and online security practices. She has spent most of her professional life raising awareness about the dangers of the internet, including the dark web, and she helps students understand the importance of protecting their online privacy. Recently, Yoshida published the best-seller, *Caught in the Dark Web*, and we are delighted to get the chance to catch up with her about this important topic.

In her own words, Yoshida refers to an exploration of the dark web as "the extra-curricular activity for the twenty-first century." She explains that teenagers are naturally curious about the world, and since time immemorial, they have been drawn to the forbidden. "I see it as a process of coming to terms with their impending adulthood," Yoshida explains. "The teenage years is a liminal space, when they are no longer a child but not yet a fully-fledged adult. In that strange in-between, they can fill the gap with many ideas about their identity that they might choose to discard or accept once they reach adulthood. The dark web is a means for them to color this process of exploration."

There are, of course, many other reasons why a teenager might explore the dark web. They might be lured into it by pressure from others. Often the last thing a teenager wants to do is stand out as different compared with their peers, so if everyone is talking about this dark web, then they are bound to take a look themselves. "Often, they don't appreciate the severity of all of this," Yoshida explains. "Teenagers believe that they are invincible, and there are no dangers out there, so they truly think that they can have a quick look and that will be the end of it. But often that is only just the beginning. These teenagers are rarely prepared for the horrors that they find on the dark web. Some end up traumatized, and others will unwittingly expose themselves to unscrupulous people.

The growth in technology means that it is much harder to avoid the dangers posed by the dark web. Teenagers are never away from their smart phones. Even at school, they are required to dredge the internet for information to help with their homework, and, of course, there is a plethora of video games that can be found online. "Never before have we seen this level of infiltration of our young," Yoshida explains. "Predators can use the dark web to gain access to our children when we don't even know it, and our ignorance is leaving our children exposed. It's like we don't know how to close and lock a front door, so we just hope that at night no one unscrupulous will sneak in and take advantage of this. This is not a sustainable approach to parenting."

Yoshida challenges us to speak to our teenagers and ask them about their internet use. How often are they on it, and in what contexts? At night, when they are in bed, or when they are supposed to be getting on with their homework? During the day, at the back of the classroom, or when they are supposed to be forging healthy relationships with their peers? Yoshida encourages us parents to probe further, and ask specific questions about their knowledge of, and access to, the dark web. "They probably know about these portals," Yoshida explains, "they probably know about the technological underworlds and the gaming rooms and chat rooms; these liminal spaces where there is a risk that they might be stalked by a malevolent spirit. Ask them as many questions as you can, so they are not left alone with all of this."

"Thanks to the concept of social contagion," Yoshida continues, "once one teenager accesses the dark web, everyone else in that grade will have done it within a week or two. I can guarantee it. Yet many schools won't even acknowledge the existence of the dark web, let alone prepare our students for how to deal with it if they encounter these dark places. Our students need to know how to distinguish between the official web pages and the dark web. Sometimes that is difficult, and they only realize they are in the dark web when it is too late. Often, by the time they are in it, they have already alerted hackers to a whole treasure trove of their personal data, bank accounts, and control of their webcam."

Yoshida claims that there should be more stringent laws to try to eradicate the dark web. "I don't think I am putting it too strongly when I refer to the dark web as morally corrupt," Yoshida explains. "They disregard every single content law around, allowing footage of torture and death of all manner of people. I mean, just look at the recent tragedy involving that young girl, Tyra Jackson. She wandered into a space that no child should explore, and it corrupted her. I believe the dark web was the sole cause of her death. And just look at the recent spate of disappearances. Girls as young as sixteen have gone missing from their homes and schools, and no one can understand why. I have looked into these disappearances, and it turns out that each girl explored the dark web at some point before their disappearance, and someone was watching when they did. They watched them in the dark web, and then they followed them from their home. At best, they might be held as a prisoner somewhere. At worst, they are already dead."

Yoshida points to the lack of supervision as a major contributory factor to this problem. "If we don't keep a watchful eye on our teenagers, then, of course, they are going to wander. It is similar to the moral disengagement that has been witnessed in places like Thailand and Bali, where middle-aged western men allow themselves a nihilistic collapse into all manner of depravity. In other words, as soon as our kids explore these dark webpages, they forget the moral values we have tried to instill in them. And they are doing it because their peers are, so they somehow believe that it is okay, or morally neutral. All of this is worrying but it is not inevitable. It is our job to keep a close eye on their use of the internet, and to constantly remind our teenagers about what is morally acceptable and unacceptable."

So what else can we do about all of this? Yoshida suggests that a big problem with the dark web is the codependent relationship many teenagers have with their cell phones. As a result, it is Yoshida's view that we must keep our teenager's phone in a Ziplock bag and leave it in our desk drawer, our bedroom drawer, or anywhere our teenager won't have access to it. "Do this every time they are home, especially when they go to bed," and Yoshida claims that this gives our teenager a chance to use their brain in other ways, where they need to look beyond the cell phone to find solutions to their problems. To justify this approach, Yoshida points to a long-established concept called the Einstellung effect. This explains that we tend to interpret current problems using solutions from the past, even when those solutions don't seem particularly effective or helpful for the problems we presently face. It limits us because we become too comfortable with the way we see things, and we become unable to change our mind.

Yoshida explains that our teenagers view their cell phones as the only solution to any problems. *I don't have friends*, so they search on their phone for some. *I can't get to sleep*, so they stare at their phone in the belief that it will somehow soothe them. "Even when they are sent away to fun places for a holiday," Yoshida adds, "some wilderness retreat, for example, where they could enjoy what Mother Earth has to offer, they end up miserable and pining for their phones."

"Earlier I mentioned social contagion," Yoshida continues, "and I mentioned it to explain the spread of interest in the dark web. But social contagion can also be used to explain the spread of the false idea that cell phones are the answer to every problem. These teenagers wouldn't give their cell phones a second thought if their peers weren't dependent on them. Cell phone dependence and access to the dark web is as much spread by social contagion as fashion trends, suicidality, transgenderism, and queerness."

Technology has blurred our boundaries. It is now impossible to say where humans end and technology begins; it has become so integral to our everyday life. And Yoshida claims that "the scariest part of this is that we don't know how much it is controlling us. They spy on us and create and reinforce our supposed need for things and services. The algorithms make us believe that we need something; they lay breadcrumbs, so we are tempted, and we only realize it is a trap when it is too late. We are slipping from an autonomous existence into some kind of liminal space where we are not entirely a free-willed human being, but neither are we fully an automaton."

In short, if we are to help our teenagers stay away from the dangerous dark web, we need to show them that there are many solutions to life beyond their cell phones. We can open their eyes to the broad spectrum that colors in real life, beyond the hypnotizing glare of a digital screen. This is no easy task, but if we as parents are strong and consistent, whilst we also remind them about our unconditional love, we are more likely to achieve some kind of sustainable change on this front.

We would love to hear your thoughts on this. Please feel free to add your comments below.

Comments:

u/deadwolf#03:
You'd know about infiltration of the young.
u/rizlasykes#09:
Care to elaborate?
u/deadwolf#03:
Ask Yoshida.
u/rizlasykes#09:
Why? What would they tell me if I did ask them?
u/deadwolf#03:
Them? How many Yoshidas are there?
u/rizlasykes#09:
'Them' is respectful when you don't know their gender identity.
u/deadwolf#03:
Since when?
u/rizlasykes#09:
Since forever.
u/rizlasykes#09:
So you're not gonna elaborate.
u/deadwolf#03:
On what?
u/rizlasykes#09:
Your comment about infiltration of the young.
u/deadwolf#03:
I'm not doing Yoshida's dirty work. All I'll say is that it's interesting she knows so much about predators gaining access to our children.
u/rizlasykes#09:
I still don't follow.
u/deadwolf#03:
These experts who condemn, who stir up fear about others. Often, they want you to look the other way.
u/rizlasykes#09:
Are you saying Yoshida's a predator?
u/deadwolf#03:
You said it, not me.
u/rizlasykes#09:
That's pretty damning. I mean, careful you don't get embroiled in a lawsuit.
u/deadwolf#03:
They'd only bother with a lawsuit if they knew it wasn't true. Besides, they'll have to find me to serve me.
u/rizlasykes#09:

I'm sure they can. There are eyes everywhere.
u/deadwolf#03:
??
u/rizlasykes#09:
Come on, don't think that you can hide behind that username.
u/deadwolf#03:
Whatevs. I just don't like it when these people hold themselves out as the moral authority. The way she's sitting in judgment over the dark web. I mean, who's to say what's *offensive, taboo, or just plain weird*?
u/rizlasykes#09:
Everyone's entitled to an opinion.
u/deadwolf#03:
Yeah, so why are they getting to set the standards about what should and should not be accessed? Who's to say this official web presence isn't the morally corrupt? All the big boys in tech already hack your personal data and turn on your webcam without your knowledge. Just look at all the class action lawsuits proving this. Morality is a flexible tool wielded by the power elite. This is another form of censorship, and oppressive regimes love to censor. God forbid they should let power go to the people. Then the masses won't be so easy to manipulate.
u/rizlasykes#09:
Now you're just ranting.
u/deadwolf#03:
And what the hell is that about the social contagion of suicidality? If kids are killing themselves, it's because they have no hope in a f#cked up society. Of course you're gonna blame the minority and the vulnerable. And Yoshida, if you're reading this, f#ck you with your attack on the trans and queer community. You wanna address the real dangers in this world? What about greed? What about those billionaires who view us normal folk as bio-feed or bio-waste or whatever? You realize none of them are interested in this planet and they're looking to the stars to build a colony of billionaires and their spawn. They'll take to the stars and leave us behind.
u/rizlasykes#09:
Now you're sounding nuts.
u/deadwolf#03:
The truth always sounds crazy to the conditioned. People can't handle the glitches in the matrix.
u/rizlasykes#09:

%#&(
u/deadwolf#03:
What?
u/rizlasykes#09:
Ever get that feeling you are screaming into a void?
u/deadwolf#03:
What?
u/rizlasykes#09:
Like, the only words that you can read or hear or think are words that remain stuck in your head, hidden from view, and silenced. Like screaming into the dark void of space.
u/deadwolf#03:
I don't know what you're saying.
u/rizlasykes#09:
I didn't think you would.
You know I'm not really here.
u/deadwolf#03:
??
u/rizlasykes#09:
And neither are you. Not really.
u/deadwolf#03:
If you're trying to scare me, it's not working.
u/deadwolf#03:
Are you there?
u/deadwolf#03:
Hello?????
u/deadwolf#03:
?

Source: https//www.[redacted].com
Accessed November 4, 2020, at 7:30 PM

Chapter Eleven

Hunger

"Why aren't you eating anything?" Ania asks.

Ellie shrugs her shoulders. "I thought we were waiting for you," she whispers. Alert to every sound that echoes about the room, her eyes are wider than before. That, coupled with her flat face, makes her now look more like a Himalayan cat than a cartoon moon.

"What's up?" Ania adds. "You seem nervous."

Ellie glances over to Carrie, who is muttering to Cynthia something about the walkie talkie.

"Don't," Ellie says in reply. "Not now. Best if we just keep quiet."

Over Ellie's shoulder, Ania can see that Jill is puffy-eyed, and she suspects the girl has been crying. She remembers Sophie's punch, and how forcefully they remove Daria from the cabin, so she asks, "Did anyone hurt either one of you?"

Neither Jill nor Ellie look at each other, but they both shake their head in unison.

"What about Daria?" Ania asks.

"What about her?" Ellie snaps, her cheeks flushing with a barely concealed fury.

Clearly, Ania wasn't going to heed Ellie's advice.

"Do you know where she is? I overheard Cynthia saying

something about her, that she'd gone. I don't know what that means. *Gone* as in disappeared, so they can't find her, or *gone* as in someone has come to collect her?"

Ellie and Jill stare at their empty bowls.

"Strange, right?" Ania adds, but still they continue to ignore her.

"Okay, I'm not going to drop it," Ania adds. "So this silent treatment…"

"What's all this?" a voice booms from behind them, making all three teenagers jump. It's Carrie. Ania hadn't seen her finish her conversation with Cynthia, but she should have smelt her coming. That strange rotting stench again, only it was worse because it mingled with body odor.

"What are you girls scheming?" Carrie snarls.

Silence.

"I asked you a question."

Someone squeezes Ania's shoulders, and as she turns, she realizes it is Cynthia.

"I'm sure we're all hungry and tired," the woman says as she stares at Carrie. "But I don't want anyone to forget their manners. There's no excuse for unkind behavior, and I am not going to tolerate it at my camp. Is that clear?"

Carrie's fat cheeks flush like rosy apples.

"I was just…" she mutters with a pout, but as she catches Cynthia's eye, she falls silent. Her hands do the talking, though, as she clamors about her large neck. Ania can see something glistening on the surface, a slithering trail running from underneath her left ear down and across the front of her throat. At first glance, she thought it was sweat trickling, but with a second look, she can see that it is a scar. Just like the one that Ania saw on Cynthia's wrists.

"Over breakfast," Cynthia adds, "why don't you take this time to get to know each other a little bit more?"

"Won't Daria also be hungry?" Ania asks as she turns a little more to look Cynthia in the eye.

The woman steps closer to tower over the teenager, and Ania can feel her fingers squeezing into her shoulders, but Ania refuses to relent. If she knows that Daria is safe, she will feel less terrified about getting into a car with this strange woman.

"Here we go again. More questions about Daria," Cynthia says with a sigh. She sounds more defeated than Ania had expected, and the smell of that familiar scent on her softens the woman in the teenager's eyes. Ania almost starts to feel sorry for her.

"Look," Cynthia continues, "can we just drop the whole Daria thing for the time being? I will tell you when she is ready to come back to join us, but I really can't have you hijacking the day like this and going on and on about the same subject. You're beginning to sound like the incessant tone of a blue jay." She attempts a smile, but it looks more like a grimace. "Try to make the most of your time here. I really think you will benefit immensely with an open heart and an open mind. Now, I have a delightful treat for everyone." Cynthia reaches for a cardboard box that has been slipped under the table. Sliding it out and pulling open the lid, she retrieves a can with a green label. "As a kid, I was raised on this. Canned fruit!" She holds the can up above everyone's head, and she sounds so proud of it. Carrie claps her hands together, adding an enthusiastic "Yummy!", and then Cynthia throws the can, without warning, over to Ania. The teenager slaps her hands together in a failed bid to catch it, misses, and watches as it rolls out of the hardware store.

"Fetch!" Carrie remarks, beginning to laugh.

"Fine," Ania snaps as she runs out of the store and into the barely lit corridor. The smell of damp hits her, making her stomach churn, and she peers into the gloom. A shadow, fleeting, dances across the hallway. It happens so quickly, and so far in the distance, that Ania can't tell if it is human or animal.

"Or some other kind," Nana adds. "At least it didn't have eight legs."

A scrabbling sound from behind her, so Ania turns on her heel. No one is there. Nothing but the can that has rolled almost round the corner. Ania takes a few steps to retrieve it, and then she sees the figure that lingers just ahead of her. Someone is standing in the corner, their face barely an inch from the wall.

Sophie?

Something is different about her, the way she holds herself. Her limbs are rigid and clamped tightly, as if she had just been told to stand to attention. She seems gripped by such a force that her body is trembling.

Yet again, Ania can smell the counselor's vapor trail of leather and something metallic. She braces herself, half-expecting someone to grab her wrists from behind.

Then there is a high-pitched squeal, like the air escaping from a balloon, or someone gripped by an agonizing pain. The sound is so intense that it feels like a great weight is bearing down on Ania.

"Run," Nana bellows, but Ania cannot move. She's afraid that if she does, the crunching sound of her footsteps will awaken something violent in Sophie. Her cheek throbs again, bright crimson filling her mind so much that the corridors appear bathed in blood. She doesn't want to be hit again, but she also doesn't want to stay here. Frozen in terror, she can feel her jaw locking as her teeth start to grind.

She can see that Sophie's body is shaking harder, and Ania thinks that she can feel the floor trembling in unison. Waves of energy pulsate from the counselor, only getting stronger, and Ania has a horrible thought that she might be swept up in an explosion.

And then it stops. The shaking stops, the noises quieten, and Sophie's limbs soften. She staggers, knocks her head against the wall a little, and then turns round. Silent and blank-faced, a zombie making its way from the underworld, she doesn't seem to register Ania's presence.

"Sophie?" Ania calls. Her voice is weak, and she's on the verge of tears, but she refuses to let this person scare her again.

"What happened?" the counselor inquires, her eyes still not focused on Ania.

"I don't know. You looked like you had some kind of seizure."

"I did?" Sophie replies.

The counselor appears softened. It must be the dim light because she looks younger than Ania.

"Are you hurt?" Ania asks her.

"No. I don't think so."

"Should I get Cynthia? Maybe she can call a doctor," Ania suggests.

At the sound of Cynthia's name, there is a blink of recognition and Sophie's face hardens.

"No," she growls. "I'm fine." Her voice is deeper, and it reverberates around the dark corridor.

"Where is Daria? What have you done with her? You need to tell me where she is," Ania demands.

Another blink of recognition from Sophie, and now a frown. She offers no reply except a bite of her lower lip.

"I was hoping that she was with you," Ania continues. "I mean, I heard Carrie say that Daria was gone, but…"

"What's going on?"

Cynthia has appeared from nowhere. There wasn't even a crunch of her footsteps in the debris-littered corridor.

"What are you two doing out here?" she asks. "You were only

asked to retrieve a can of fruit, Ania, it really isn't that complicated."

"I was just coming to find you," Sophie explains as she stares at Ania. "Daria is in your office. She isn't feeling well."

"She's lying," Nana hisses.

"Oh, that's a shame," Cynthia replies. "I hope she isn't feeling too bad. I would hate for her to miss out on everything we have planned."

There is something about the way she says this that sends a fingernail of dread running down Ania's spine.

"And, heaven forbid, that she gets other people sick. I wouldn't want anything spreading through this camp. We've had enough of face masks and hand sanitizers to last us a lifetime." She let out another one of the chalky laughs. "Not when we are only just back in operation. And I would hate to break up the group we've formed. We're only just getting to know each other."

"You should call her parents," Ania says. "If she's really unwell, aren't you legally obliged to call her parents? Especially if she isn't well enough to eat."

Cynthia opens her mouth, ready to bite back, but she stops herself.

"Yes," she admits. "You're probably right. I will go back to my office and call them now. But I don't appreciate your tone, Ania. Perhaps when I get back, we can go over some basics about manners. Yes?"

She lingers, waiting for Ania to respond.

"Yes?" she repeats.

"Okay," Ania concedes.

"I don't need you to tell me how to do my job," Cynthia declares. "I care deeply about what I do here, and I have a lot of experience. I am quite capable of making decisions on my own. Do you understand me?"

Ania nods as she watches the woman disappear into the darkness.

"Don't worry," Sophie adds with a sneer. "I'm sure she won't be long. But first, you and I need to talk."

Chapter Twelve

Rigor stress ball

Subreddit: Yo, Yoshida?

u/deadwolf#03:
Yo, Yoshida, where you at?
My teacher has done a disappearing act. Anyone seen or heard from her? She didn't grade my papers so now my folks are panicking cuz I can't graduate. They already threatened to cut me off if I don't get this sorted, so any leads would be good. Also, I found a cool new ramen place, but I'll save that for another post.
u/rizlasykes#09:
Have some respect, the poor woman is sick.
u/deadwolf#03:
Ooookay, keep your hair on
u/rizlasykes#09:
Disrespectful to peeps who are *follicly challenged.*
u/deadwolf#03:
You serious? That's really a thing?
u/rizlasykes#09:
Could be. You would never know because you're too preoccupied with your own life to care about anyone else.
u/deadwolf#03:

Whatevs. You do you, I guess. And what's up with Yoshi?
<u>*u/rizlasykes#09:*</u>
If by 'Yoshi' you mean Sakura Yoshida, then no one knows what happened. Not really. She was found in her apartment last night. Unconscious. I've heard she suffered a major seizure.
<u>*u/deadwolf#03:*</u>
Jeesh. Well, whatevs, as long as someone grades my paper.
<u>*u/rizlasykes#09:*</u>
You really don't care? She could've died. Where's your heart? The people who found her said she couldn't talk, and her arms and legs were rock solid.
<u>*u/deadwolf#03:*</u>
No sh*t?
<u>*u/rizlasykes#09:*</u>
Yeah, no sh*t. Her eyes were rolling back when they tried to ask her questions.
<u>*u/deadwolf#03::*</u>
Drugs?
<u>*u/rizlasykes#09:*</u>
Projecting much? Why does everyone always go there? People can get ill, you know. Not everyone is a druggy.
<u>*u/deadwolf#03:*</u>
Just asking. You're kinda rude.
<u>*u/rizlasykes#09:*</u>
Well, someone is unwell, and you're questioning her character. She's a respected cybersecurity professional and educator, she teaches many brilliant courses at Farbright High School, and she has that best-selling book, and you've reduced her to 'Yoshi' or a drug addict.
<u>*u/deadwolf#03:*</u>
You really need to chill out a bit.
<u>*u/rizlasykes#09:*</u>
Well, this is a very upsetting turn of events. The poor woman can't even talk for herself right now. You realize that when they cleared her airway, they found she'd bitten off half her tongue.
<u>*u/deadwolf#03:*</u>
Wow. Sick. Wonder what that's like, a woman with no tongue. Probs pretty peaceful. Come to think of it, she always had a sharp tongue on her.
<u>*u/rizlasykes#09:*</u>
So disrespectful.

u/deadwolf#03:
Come on, be honest. The stuff she would say about morals and shit. She really was a judgy kind of person.
u/rizlasykes#09:
I don't think I agree.
u/deadwolf#03:
You don't have to, but many other people do. She said some wacko shit about queers and stuff. I can't remember what exactly, something about the queers and trans being contagious or something. Not the greatest thing to say when she teaches kids.
u/rizlasykes#09:
She's entitled to her opinion. That's why teachers have tenure, after all.
u/deadwolf#03:
What, so they can hate? Who protects my rights to hate? You were just jumping all over me for saying stuff about her and that wasn't even close to hating. I mean, she was really trying to stir up some kind of hate war against them. I've heard her books are coded to encourage suicide amongst the queer and trans community. Kinda sick if it's true.
u/rizlasykes#09:
It isn't true.
u/deadwolf#03:
Okay, well, what about her comments about women? All that anti-abortion shit, and the stuff about women staying home to look after their kids. Kinda rich when she works. Outdated, archaic BS.
u/rizlasykes#09:
Or ahead of her time.
u/deadwolf#03:
What?
u/rizlasykes#09:
Sometimes we need to go back before we can go forward.
u/deadwolf#03:
Next you'll turn the women into handmaidens, Atwood style.
u/rizlasykes#09:
All this is sounding pretty hypocritical to me. You've said some wild things against women. Gonna deny that?
u/deadwolf#03:
How would you know what I've said? You don't know anything about me.
u/rizlasykes#09:

Oh, I do, but that can wait.
u/deadwolf#03:
What's that supposed to mean?
u/rizlasykes#09:
It means whatever you want it to mean. But, besides, we are getting off-topic. Our attention should be focused on the wellbeing of Sakura Yoshida. Some are saying it is a buildup of chronic stress. It's all those stress hormones, you see. All that cortisol, noradrenaline, and adrenaline, and your pituitary gland pumping overtime. It can do strange things to your musculoskeletal system. Ever seen someone with lockjaw? Muscle spasms, cramps, their limbs all locked up in some kind of seizure. They look like rigor mortis has set in.
u/deadwolf#03:
F*ck, rigor mortis. That's sick.
u/rizlasykes#09:
Yeah.
u/deadwolf#03:
Yeah. All that lockjaw and rigid limb shit.
u/rizlasykes#09:
What of it?
u/deadwolf#03:
It's kinda familiar. Just, I think I've seen that. Someone's body getting all locked up and shit. This girl. It happened to her, once.
u/rizlasykes#09:
A friend of yours?
u/deadwolf#03:
No.
u/rizlasykes#09:
Girlfriend?
u/deadwolf#03:
No way, man. She was nasty.
u/rizlasykes#09:
Oh. Okay.
u/deadwolf#03:
Yeah, she was always stressed and stuff. So uptight.
u/rizlasykes#09:
Hope she got the help she needed.
u/deadwolf#03:
Yeah, but no, but not really. I mean, they found her in the snow.
u/rizlasykes#09:

Making snow angels?
u/deadwolf#03:
No. She liked to swing on a tree.
u/rizlasykes#09:
Cute.
u/deadwolf#03:
Not really.
u/rizlasykes#09:
Okay, my bad.
u/deadwolf#03:
But what you said about muscle spasms and cramps, and seizures and stuff. You're right, their limbs really do lock up. Like the walking dead, you know? Like rigor mortis.
u/rizlasykes#09:
I guess they can look that way.
u/deadwolf#03:
How do you know, though, if they're just having a seizure or if they're really dead?
u/rizlasykes#09:
Ever seen the dead walk?
u/deadwolf#03:
I don't know. I guess that's what I was asking you. How would I know if they're alive or dead?
u/rizlasykes#09:
This is kinda off topic.
u/deadwolf#03:
Agreed. I just wanna know when my papers are gonna be graded.
u/rizlasykes#09:
Sucks for you.
u/deadwolf#03:
The least they could do is provide a substitute.
u/rizlasykes#09:
Who?
u/deadwolf#03:
The school.
u/rizlasykes#09:
Ha. Good luck with that.

Source: https//www.[redacted].com
Accessed November 4, 2020, at 7:30 PM

Chapter Thirteen

Breakfast conversion

Inside the hardware store, Ania finds Jill and Ellie sitting closer together than before. They remind her of two meerkats who were in the corner of a cage at Rotherwell Zoo. Abigail brought her there once, and Ania had to look the other way as her friend threw stones at the poor animals. After a week of terror, the meerkats were found dead, still clinging to each other. Although the official story was that they happened to die of heart failure on the same day, rumors circulated that they had eaten poison left near the cage. It was extremely unusual for meerkats, or most other mammals, to consume cleaning chemicals, especially when the products smell so toxic to usually repel animals, and the position of the cleaner's cart also suggested that the meerkats must have gone to extreme measures to reach the bottle of bleach. As a result, the resounding conclusion was that this was a rare incident of animal suicide.

A crackle of the walkie talkie. It sounds like it is Cynthia on the other end of the line, but it is so distorted that it could be anyone.

"Receiving," Carrie barks into the device.

More crackling, more indecipherable words, but Carrie seems to understand it because she says in reply, "Okay to that, I'll sort it, don't you worry. Over and out."

Carrie mutters something to Sophie, and Ania hears mention of Daria's name.

"...resting...doesn't have to...fine...not hungry...confusion about the...back here," the counselor adds.

"They're putting on a show," Nana hisses. "For your benefit alone. They want to lure you in, so you ask questions and fall into their trap. Just ignore them."

Ania tries not to catch Sophie's eye as her cheek throbs a warning that, without the watchful eye of Cynthia, things could quickly deteriorate. It always felt this dangerous at school, when the teacher would step out of the classroom. Like shooting fish in a barrel, the mean girls had Ania as their trapped prey, and sometimes they would barricade the door with a desk, just so they had a little longer to torture her.

"Abigail did it too," Nana continues. "That manipulative girl was never your friend."

Even so, Ania doesn't want to believe this.

"The truth hurts," Nana mutters. "But there's no use avoiding it forever. Otherwise, you're stuck in some liminal state."

Those kids in her grade knew that if Ania fought back, even to defend herself, she would end up kicked out of the school. The school counselor had promised as much the last time Ania had tried to complain. It was the day before Halloween, and Ania had just found online some resources about anti-bullying laws that schools were supposed to abide by. Her heart pounded as she read about harassment, intimidation, and bullying, and then she found the policies there, in black and white, on her own school's website. She felt sick that she had been duped all this time; that the school counselor had always brushed off her complaints as something and nothing, and yet all this time, there were laws to protect Ania.

The very next morning, fueled by this new discovery, she confronted the school counselor in her office.

"But you knew," she said, her voice shrill with a fear of her own rage. "I told you everything, how much they were hurting me, and you did nothing. You never wrote any notes down, never told me there were laws about this."

"I'm not your lawyer," the counselor sneered.

"I told you how miserable I was, how I dreaded coming to school. I even said I had thought about...I had dark thoughts..."

She let out a long sigh and a twinge of pain reminded her of what the kids had done, so she lifted her shirt to show the counselor.

"You've seen this," Ania yelled. "You've seen the bruises a number of times, and still you chose to look away."

The discomfort, maybe even the disgust, was plain to see on the counselor's face, but still Ania pointed to her blackened ribs. "Why didn't you stop them?" Ania asked. "Those girls in my grade. They always do this." Her voice broke, but she sniffed back the tears, refusing to let this woman see her cry.

Ania wasn't sure what exact words she expected to hear from the counselor, but she definitely didn't expect her to shake her head.

"How can I believe you?" she said. "You tell me so much, so many stories that it seems fantastical. Do you understand what I mean?" She stretched her rouged lips into a tightened smile. "How can I believe any of this? It isn't as if you have any witnesses to come forward."

"No one will. They're too afraid it will happen to them."

"So how can I accuse people of something when it could equally have been you?"

"I never touched them," Ania snapped.

"You could have done this to yourself. Or someone else might have inflicted it."

"Like who?" Ania shrieked.

"I don't know. Maybe someone you're trying to protect? Someone in your family?"

The counselor was always targeting Ania's mother and father, even her brother, because none of them sat right in her expectations of how a family on the East Coast should behave. "Weirdos," Ania had heard her sneering to one teacher, "the lot of them. No friends whatsoever, never coming to any of the school events because they're all so fucking awkward. Complete oddballs." And this woman had the power to dictate what was normal behavior, so her word prevailed.

"Listen," the school counselor added as her tone softened a little, "I know you're jealous of some of those girls. I've seen the way you are around them. I know you want to hurt them, but false allegations aren't the way forward. That's taking it to a whole new level, and I really don't think you want to go there. Quite frankly, Ania, if everyone has a problem with you, then maybe you are the problem."

"Herd mentality," Nana snarls. "Pack of vicious wolves."

"It just doesn't sit right," Ania can hear someone saying. "It's not normal."

When Ania looks up, she realizes it is Sophie muttering to Carrie. Then the counselor stops, catches Ania's eye, and then adds, "Remember we were going to have a talk."

"What?"

"You heard me. I want you to tell me about your obsession."

"My what?" Ania asks.

"Come on, don't play the innocent with me. Your obsession with that Daria girl. Is it the nose-ring that you like?" Sophie asks. "I hear that's what your type does; you lot fixate on these weird piercings and tattoos. You brand yourself like some kind of cattle. Let's be honest…*Lesbi-honest*, get it, Carrie?"

Carrie splutters a snigger in response.

"But seriously," Sophie sneers, "I have to be honest and say that you lot are all like animals, anyway. Dirty and bestial."

"What are you talking about?" Ania feigns ignorance, just to postpone the attack for a little longer. She hopes that Cynthia will reappear, and Sophie will be silenced again.

"There's way too much of it these days," Sophie continues. "All this queer stuff, and now the transgenderism, too. They're trying to cut up children's bodies and chemically castrate them. And no one is allowed to tell the truth about all of this, that your lot spread diseases and break up families and make kids want to harm themselves. We're not allowed to say that because we'll lose our job, and all because someone's feelings got hurt. Anything goes. Pierce and tattoo every part of your body, spit in the police officer's face, trash that store and never work a day in your life, because heaven help me if I dare to hurt your feelings with my words. You lot have forgotten basic moral values, basic Christian values, and you've debased yourself. As I said, dirty and bestial."

"Yeah, dirty and bestial," Carrie repeats.

"And it doesn't stop there," Sophie adds. "You have no respect for your elders. I've heard the way you've spoken to Cynthia. You probably speak to your parents in the same way. No sense of discipline, kids your age. Lazy as hell. Constantly flaking out of your obligations because you have *anxiety*, or you're *just not feeling it today*, and you've got some little queer therapist with a nose ring who will write you a letter saying you don't have to do anything today or any day. And what happens then? You end up dumping on people like us, who show up, and roll our sleeves up and do the hard work."

"Yeah," Carrie interjects, "try learning from us."

"And the worst of it all is that you have no respect for the bible, none of its teachings."

"None," Carrie adds. "No respect, whatsoever."

Clearly irritated by Carrie's parroting, Sophie gives her a look, and the oily counselor understands. With a pout, she backs away from Sophie and pretends to preoccupy herself with the breakfast bowls.

"When you need guidance, you just scroll through your phones," Sophie sneers, "and you stare at updates on social media. Selfies and pictures of food and fake mockups of lives you have never lived. No wonder you're all so lost."

Ania refuses to engage. She glances over at Jill and Ellie, trying to sense if she is going to get any kind of support, but they stare down at their empty bowls, pretending they are not here.

"Disgusting," Sophie spits. "I've seen the way you are, *Midget.*"

"What did you call me?" Ania barks as she turns back to the counselor.

"I said I've seen the way you fidget, and it's disgusting. You get all agitated when you're around that nose-ringed girl. Well, this isn't the place for that kind of thing, Annie."

"That's not my name."

"Whatever. I'm here to tell you that we are watching you, and the moment you put your hands on one of these girls, you're out."

"Good! I want to be free of this place. And I will be, very soon." Ania stops short of telling them about Cynthia's promise to drive her home after breakfast.

"That's what you think, pervert."

Is this what *Avaline Camps* is all about? Conversion therapy has been outlawed, but it never ceased to exist. It was just rebranded as wilderness therapy camps, or Christian value camps. It is at that moment that a dread pulls on Ania's stomach. Is this why she can't get through to her parents? Did they find her diary and send her here, hoping that when she returns, she will be a different person?

"And if that's not possible?" Nana mutters. "Will they try to medicate you, or switch to electro-shock therapy? Maybe they will try to erase all traces of your mind as you currently know it."

"Leave me alone," Ania mutters, half to her grandmother and half to the counselor.

"Why? So you can carry on your queer shit?" Sophie jeers in reply. "If Daria's not around, who are you going to target next? Jill or Ellie?"

"I said leave me alone."

"Or what? What are you gonna do about it?" Sophie steps right up to Ania, and again the teenager feels sickened by that same strange scent of leather and something metallic. "You already found out last time that you shouldn't push me too far," the counselor continues.

"Please," Ania croaks, "stop doing this."

"Why? I would do the same to a pedophile. Your lot are just as bad. Pedophilia, bestiality, incest, it's all the same as that queer shit because you're all a danger to society. You're a menace, Annie."

"I told you that's not my name," Ania suddenly bursts.

You're a menace, Annie was also what Abigail would say to her. If Ania wasn't quick enough to say or do what Abigail wanted, Ania became the worst person in her friend's eyes.

"You're blind," Nana insists. "When are you going to see that she was never your friend?'

"You have to make it up to me," Abigail would often say. "Otherwise, I'm never speaking to you again. Got it?"

Caught under Abigail's spell, Ania felt like she was slowly disappearing. She tried to ignore her own thoughts, and the mutterings of her grandmother, and instead she tried to second guess what Abigail would think. She even adopted Abigail's tendency to say "OMG" about everything until her brother told her to knock it off.

"OMG, why are you so showy?" Abigail once asked her friend. "Are you even listening to me, Annie? You know, sometimes you can be so self-absorbed. It isn't an appealing quality, trust me. You'll never get someone to take an interest in you if your every waking thought is about yourself."

Ania's head was spinning. She didn't have a clue what her friend was talking about.

"*Narcissistic Personality Disorder*," Abigail added, "you should look it up. I know so many people who suffer from it, and they ruin other people's lives. They just don't give a crap about anyone but themselves. I swear to god, you should get yourself checked for it."

She made it sound like it was some form of contagion that could be diagnosed with a quick swab.

"What do you mean?" Ania asked, and she quickly regretted it. Too late, Ania remembered that her friend hated it when she didn't keep up with Abigail's conversation. No matter how many times she jumped from issue to issue, Abigail would always accuse Ania of not listening or suffering from some kind of developmental disorder that left Ania unable to follow a basic conversation.

"I was *saying*," Abigail added with a pout, "that if you bothered to take any interest in anyone beyond yourself, you'd realize that the kind of bling on your wrist is so outdated." She pointed at Ania's bracelet. "I mean, what high school kid wears jewelry? I don't know what message you're trying to communicate," Abigail continued, "but it isn't a very popular one. No one likes a showoff."

"You mean *this*?" Ania asked as she flicked her wrist. The pendants on the bracelet made a jingling sound, and Ania wanted to say that it sounded like the footsteps of fairies, but she could tell that Abigail wasn't in the mood for that."

"Hand it over," Abigail said. She already had her hand outstretched, ready to accept the donation. "Even if you take it off now, I can't trust that you won't turn up at school tomorrow morning wearing it again. You have to realize that when you give a bad impression, that reflects poorly on both of us, not just you."

"It does?" Ania felt so naïve. She'd been brought up to believe that if she kept her head down and worked hard, especially if she minded her own business, then no one would bother her. She felt foolish to realize that, no matter how small she tried to make herself, she would still encroach on other people's lives.

"Of course it does," Abigail cried. "So hand it over. I don't want you wearing that shit until you are living far away from me. I mean, when you're at college, if you get into one, or when you start working at the nearest grocery store, which seems more likely."

Ania's stomach dropped when she realized that she had months, even years, left at school with this girl.

"The bracelet is kind of special," she explained. "My parents gave it to me as a gift, so I wouldn't want to upset them if they saw that it had disappeared. Maybe I could give you a gift instead. I know you love those squish mallows."

"Fuck that childish shit. If you don't hand it over, I'm gonna tell Smithson you're in love with him."

"You know that's not true," Ania barks back.

"Yeah, but he doesn't know that. Imagine leaving your house every day, and how awkward it would be for him to think that you were touching yourself every time you saw him." Abigail starts to laugh.

"That's gross," Ania groaned.

"It is? OMG, you are such a puritan. We need to buy you one of those bonnets from colonial Williamsburg. Better still, I'll get Smithson to abduct you and lock you up in some cabin upstate. Imagine what he would do to you if he had you trapped in a place like that, and so far from the nearest town that no one could hear your screams. What I wouldn't give or do to be locked up in a cabin with him. God, he's so fit. I'm well *jel* you live on the same street as him. Do you try to watch him through his window?"

"No."

"I would," Abigail added. "Imagine if you could. Imagine watching him in the shower and in bed. Somehow, I'm gonna end up in that bed, but in the meantime, I'm gonna make things a little fun between you and him."

"What? No."

"Then give me the bracelet," Abigail insisted.

"I knew you'd hand it over," Nana says with a sigh. "Always the good little *Midget*, always so compliant."

"Don't call me that," Ania growled.

"Hey, don't take your anger out on me," Nana replied. "It's Abigail you're angry at, not me."

After a week of wearing the bracelet, Ania noticed that it was missing from Abigail's wrist.

"What happened to it?" Ania asked as they walked to school.

"I dunno," Abigail said with a shrug. "I think I lost it somewhere."

"Really?" Ania tried not to cry. "Do you know where it might be?"

"No, I don't, Ania. Life doesn't revolve around you and your precious little objects."

"But it is special. Please, can you tell me where you last saw it?"

"Really, Ania? You're gonna do this? I have so much on my mind right now, and I think you're being really selfish." She gave a shoulder-shoved so hard that Ania almost fell into the bushes. "Just leave me alone," she wailed, and then ran onto school without her friend.

It took a few days, but finally the bracelet turned up. Ania saw it hanging from a branch of one of the apple trees in her backyard. At that time, she still allowed herself to believe that she had a friend in the raven the cawed above her head, and he had brought the bracelet back to her.

"Why won't you listen to me when I tell you about Abigail?" Nana asked. "She doesn't care about you; she's only interested in what she can get out of you. The fact that you can't even distinguish between a friend and a foe leaves you vulnerable."

"Why won't you listen to me?"

Stuck on repeat, like a glitch in the matrix, the words keep repeating across time and space.

"Why won't you listen to me?" she hears again, but this time from someone else.

"Ania, are you even listening?" yet another person says. It's a familiar voice, and she's heard the words so many times. This voice has always told her what to do and how to think and what to look out for. This voice has always warned her about the dangers in this world that she should guard against. She is diminutive Ania, the *Midget*, who should be locked up in a fortress of latches and bolts and locks because the world outside is too dangerous for her.

"Why aren't you listening?"

Mom?

"What has got into you?"

Cynthia?

"I told you that I need your help."

"Oh?" Ania's mouth is dry, as if she has been sleeping for too long. Come to think of it, when was the last time she slept? "What happened?" she asks, vaguely aware that she has lost time. Did Sophie hit her again? She's nowhere to be seen, so Ania lifts a hand to touch both cheeks. No pain, no blood. What happened?

"You can go with Carrie to meet him at the back of the building," Cynthia continues. "He's arriving shortly."

"Who? *Dad*?" Even saying his name makes Ania want to cry.

"Your *Dad*? No, of course not. The delivery man. As I said, he's arriving shortly, so you can go meet him at the loading bay."

"Delivery?" Ania stands there for a moment, hoping that the woman will explain a little more. Why did they all act as if she was supposed to understand everything that was happening?

"Yes. We are due a delivery shortly. How else can we get supplies? We don't have enough staff members to be one down as they go to the store. Besides," she adds as she glances over at Carrie with a smile, "it'll be a good opportunity for the two of you to get to know each other."

Carrie's cheeks ignite with a fury.

"It's getting cold out," Carrie snaps. "Maybe Sophie can come instead? You don't want the younger ones to catch a chill like Daria."

"Oh, don't you worry," Cynthia replies, her tone still sickly sweet. "You and Ania can wear these to keep you warm."

Already Cynthia has leaned behind the counter and retrieved two hooded cloaks.

"I found these in the fancy dress store next door," she says.

Ania takes hers from Cynthia, and as she slips it on, she realizes the fabric is coarse, like sackcloth. She has seen people wearing these on the dark web, in satanic rituals, and the hoods are useful to hide a person's identity; they leave a dark void where their face should be.

"You like that association, don't you?" Nana mutters. "More powerful than the cloak of a subjugated handmaiden."

Ania flinches at the idea of becoming anything of the sort.

"Don't worry," Nana adds, "I won't let that happen. If I can help it, you'll never become invisible or some passive vessel for reproduction. The women of my generation died to ensure that this wouldn't happen to you."

"Here," Cynthia says to Ania as she tosses her a set of keys. This time, Ania catches Cynthia's offering, and the sharpness of the cold metal jolts her awake.

She walks out of the store with Carrie; two hooded women on a mission, and Ania tries not to listen to her grandmother any more. But the words always bleed through, haunting her with the truth: "Eventually, you'll have to open your eyes."

Chapter Fourteen

Deliverance

With every step towards the delivery bay, Ania jangles the keys. It's an old-fashioned set, the type with a loop at the top that Ania thinks could be used to hang them on a hook. She assumes these date back to before the mall, when the place was a fallout shelter. She's only seen these types of keys in old movies, and once in a museum in New York, but it feels different to hold a set in her hands. Brass hangs heavy under the weight of history, and it makes her think about the multitude of doors that have been opened by these, and all the secrets that might have been locked away.

"Is that what you are?" Nana whispers, "a secret to be locked in a hidden place, at least until you can be *fixed*? Maybe the stench you smell is shame for your dark secret?"

Ania ignores her grandmother.

"You know I love you," Nana declares. "I don't think you should be ashamed, but maybe others do."

"Would you stop that?" Carrie snarls. "Stop jangling those keys, You're so annoying."

Ania doesn't have the energy to argue, so she slips the keys into the pocket of her tracksuit trousers and walks on in silence.

"She's probably jealous," Nana suggests. "Cynthia gave *you* the keys, not her, so that must've hurt."

Ania smiles at this.

"But don't gloat," Nana warns. "Remember that power can corrupt. Cynthia might be playing a game with you, you know, divide and conquer. A divided group is weaker, easier to manipulate."

Ania can imagine Cynthia watching the two of them as they walk through these dark corridors, just waiting for a fight to erupt. Is she hoping for blood? Maybe she is selling footage of this to some perverted old businessmen, or live streaming them on the dark web. She imagines how they might be touching themselves right now, as they wait for the games to commence.

Ania listens out for the mechanical whir of a pivoting camera, and she glances around to look for the solitary eye of a red LED light, but she finds nothing.

"*Lesbi-honest*," Carrie sniggers, "you are pretty annoying, with or without jangling keys. So just keep your distance from me. I'm not into all that."

If she had known the way to the delivery bay herself, Ania would have run on ahead, leaving Carrie behind. But they have reached a part of the mall where the flickering lights are faltering, and the gloom harbors the threat of roaming vagrants and wildlife.

In the darkness, the stench re-emerges, only this time it seems stronger. Rotting vegetables?

"Rotting flesh?" Nana suggests.

"What is that?" Ania asks as she covers her nose.

"Probably whatever crawled in here and never got out," Carrie says with a snort. "We'll get more air once you open those shutters," she explains as she points into the darkness.

"The what? Where?"

"Over there," Carrie growls, sounding even more impatient. In response, Ania edges her way through the darkness, feeling her way along damp walls until she reaches the cold sheen of metal. From close up, she can see that there are big old rusty padlocks securing the shutters.

"It's locked," Ania calls into the gloom as her throat aches.

"For fuc…Are you kidding me? You have the keys, idiot," Carrie snarls.

"Right. I didn't realize… Of course."

"If you weren't filling your head with all that gay, lesbian, trans bullshit, you'd have enough space in your brain for common sense."

"Whatever," Ania growls as she retrieves the keys and tries to fit each one into the lock.

"Poor little snowflake," Carrie continues.

"Just leave me alone."

"Make me," the voice sneers. In the gloom, it could be Abigail as much as Carrie who is talking. When Abigail was bored, she would taunt Ania, too, calling her *snowflake* or *lezza*. "Lend me some money, *lezza*," she would say. "Give me your notes, *snowflake,*" she would insist whenever she missed class. "Gimme this, gimme that," and it was never enough. Abigail always reminded Ania that she was failing as a friend, that she was selfish and narcissistic and lucky to have Abigail because no one else wanted her.

"Hurry it up," Carrie snaps, and again, in the gloom, this counselor could be Abigail. Ania can imagine how her friend might have followed her to this strange camp. How she would love to stalk Ania from the shadows , lingering like a malevolent spirit and tormenting her to the point of insanity. Abigail delighted in other people's misery, especially when it involved the captive and helpless. "OMG, this one's delicious," she would write in a message containing a link to a news item about a girl who had been abducted. "She was only sixteen when she disappeared, and she was following some kind of influencer who is now being questioned. Imagine if the influencer took her??? Do you think they will live-stream the girl being tortured??? Other people are saying that they might do that, that it has happened before. I'm trying to find that footage, but nothing's coming up. The tea, I need more of the tea! And it was the I-95 again. That's what most eyewitnesses say, that she was bundled into a car and driven down the I-95, but others are saying it's the I-80, which I think is more likely as that is always the preferred route of the traffickers. Man, this is juicy juicy juicy!"

That time, Ania was slow to respond, so their message exchange deteriorated.

"You're judging me, aren't you?" Abigail added. "I don't know why, because no one likes you. So, what gives you the right to take some kind of moral high ground over me? You've looked at stuff on the web yourself, really dark stuff about this sort of thing. Kidnappings, torture, all sorts. You told me yourself. And you perve over the girls in our grade all day, so don't become some kind of Little Miss Judgy with me. Remember, you're lucky to have me because no one else wants you around."

Ania felt panicky, like the ground was slipping away and she had nowhere left to turn.

"I'm sorry," Ania messaged, but for an hour or two, she got no reply. She thought of what it would be like for Abigail to turn against her for good, and she wondered what would happen if Abigail told everyone in her grade about the diary. So, she sent more messages which pleaded with her, promising to do anything if she could just be forgiven.

Finally, at nearly midnight, Ania saw a notification from her friend.

"I will forgive you," Abigail said, "but on one condition." Ania can imagine that her friend was pouting as she wrote that.

"Anything," Ania replied, her eyes filling with tears of relief that she was accepted again.

"You have to set me up with Smithson. He's fit as fuck and really popular. You realize he plays lacrosse and football and he's really good at it. He'll probably get into a good college with a scholarship, become a D1 player and all that."

Ania couldn't understand the fascination. To her, Smithson was repulsive, with his obnoxious chin and meaty limbs that dragged on the ground. He had so many sporting injuries that his nose was misshapen, but worst of all, he was cruel. Every day she would see him with Cory or Aedean in a headlock, and even when they begged to be set free, he would snigger as their face turned a strange shade of purple.

"I want you to find a way for me to meet up with him," Abigail added.

"What?" Ania replied. "How?"

Even at a young age, the mothers of these three boys kept them away from her. "They think my daughter isn't good enough for their precious boys," Ania once heard her mother snarling to herself. She wished that she didn't hear that, because it planted a seed that flourished into a belief that she really was less than them. After all, they always had friends and parties, and the teachers would always smile at them at school, even when they weren't paying attention in class. Ania never had friends and parties, and the teachers never smiled at her. She didn't know what she was doing wrong, but they always looked sad or irritated by her, and some even appeared disgusted by her, as if she smelled bad or she was some kind of contagion.

"Do I have to do all the thinking in this friendship?" Abigail continued by way of another message. "Honestly, Annie, you really are clueless. Why not tell him to meet up in the woods at the end of your street? It's kind of secluded, or, at least, secluded enough."

"Okay, okay," she messaged back, but then she thought for a moment. She really wasn't following what her friend was implying. "Secluded for what?" she added.

"What? OMG, Annie. Really????? Are you serious?"

"Yes. Sorry, I don't get it."

"I swear to god, Annie. You really are dumb. What's the word they use for dumb and clueless people?"

"I don't know."

"No, I didn't think you would. *Naïve,* that's the word. You are the most naïve person I have ever met. OMG!!! Just get him to meet up with me, and I'll handle the rest."

Finally, one key fits into the padlock and, with a terrible screech of metal against metal, Ania throws open the shutters. Light pours in, burning their eyes, and in the distance, a raven caws as it comes to rest on a nearby tree. She remembers a different time, when she loved the birds and trees in her backyard. When she would climb the trees, she thought of the bark as an impermeable layer of skin to hide the most fragile of nerve-endings, and she knew how important this was because of the number of sharp claws that would scale these trees and land on the boughs. She thought how perfectly Mother Earth had made things, as if everything had been designed by the smartest people. Even the boughs had been made strong enough to withstand the weight of a tethered rope, so she could swing in the breeze. That was a time before she hated the trees and anything that climbed them or landed on them. That was a time before Mother Earth turned against her.

The crisp air hits her lungs, making her cough a little, but it is a welcome change to the fetid damp of the mall. She gathers the cloak around her, grateful for Cynthia's gift.

"He should be here by now," Carrie says with a sigh. "He needs to get a move on."

"What's the rush?" Ania asks.

"Don't wanna be stuck here with you."

A truck appears from round the corner, its brakes screeching as it lurches to a stop. The engine dies, and the door swings open. Ania tries not to breathe in the exhaust fumes, a cloud of heavy metals and other chemicals hazing the mid-morning air, but it is hard to avoid.

From the cabin appears a portly man who looks just like her father. Her heart surges with excitement at the thought of Paris coming to collect her, but with Carrie standing there, sneering at her, Ania fights the urge to call out "*Dad!*".

As the delivery man walks across the courtyard, he takes his time to enjoy the sunshine.

"I guess from the look on your face, I'm a little late," he says to Carrie.

"A little, I guess," she remarks.

"Right. Well, sorry about that but I've been having trouble with my head today, it's been throbbing pretty bad, so it slowed me down a little."

"Hope it's not serious."

Ania can't get over how gentle and caring Carrie suddenly sounds.

"Ah, don't you worry about it." He waddles round to the back of his truck. "Bit by bit, everything is decaying. Happens to the best of us."

Ania notices that his jeans are hanging so low that the top of his hairy butt peeps out. She wants to tell him, so he can pull them up, but she also doesn't want to embarrass him.

"Not sure I have everything you ordered," he admits with a sigh. "But I did the best I could. What with this pandemic and all, you'll be hard-pressed to find any toilet paper."

"It's okay," Carrie says with a shrug. "Cynthia said we have plenty."

He fumbles in the pocket of his jeans and retrieves a key. He drops it twice, both times showing more of his rear end, before he finally unlocks the back of his truck. When he opens the doors, Ania hopes to smell baked goods and fresh fruit, but there is that stench again.

"Has it spoiled?" Ania asks.

The delivery man stops, turns to give Ania a grimace, and asks Carrie, "And who's this?"

"No one. Don't worry about her," Carrie adds with a shrug of the shoulders.

"She's a new one," he declares. "I can tell because they always look so scared. Probably half-expect that they're gonna go back, the poor kids."

Infuriated by the way he is talking about her when she is right in front of him, Ania decides to lie.

"Well, I'm quite enjoying it here," Ania snaps. "It's nice to get away and enjoy a bit of nature. In fact, I am going to tell all my friends to come here."

The man stops in his tracks, locks eyes with Carrie, and then they both collapse in laughter.

"Yeah, yeah, keep convincing yourself of that," he bellows. "Keep telling yourself, and maybe it will come true. And if it is true, you're the first to think like that. No one comes here to enjoy themselves, and people rarely come here freely. *Enjoy a bit of nature*. That's a good one, that."

As he laughs some more, Carrie starts to wander away from them.

"You've got this," Carrie mutters to Ania. "I need to see someone about something," she adds. "Load up the cart with the goods, and if I'm not back in time, walk it through the mall to the hardware store. You know, the place where we had breakfast."

Ania stares at a rickety-looking plastic cart.

"She's good at manual labor," Carrie sneers to the man as he reaches into the back of his truck. "Big, strong lesbian and all. Just look at that bad haircut, she'll make a perfect right-hand man for you."

And then she was gone, leaving Ania alone with the stranger.

"What she say about haircuts?" the man asks as he emerges from the truck. He uses a dirty hand of fat fingers to rub the salt and pepper bristles on his chin.

"Nothing," Ania replies.

"Whatever she said, I would ignore it. She's a mean one, and manipulative. Always has been, I'm afraid to say." He rubs his chin again and considers this some more. "And she's also lazy. In fact, she makes the perfect trifecta with her stupidity... Or, at least I think that's a trifecta, but I might have lost count. This headache is making it hard for me to think straight. You know what she did? Told me she didn't need toilet paper when her order asked for six of the multipacks. Now, if that isn't stupid, I don't know what is."

He sighs as he climbs into his truck. She can hear him moving items around and tutting, and maybe even cursing a little. After a moment, he reappears and adds, "I've got two multipacks, so that'll have to do, won't it?"

Ania nods in reply.

"Cool, cool." He stands for a moment and surveys her. "What are ya? Fifteen? Sixteen? I would say sixteen, if I was hard pressed."

She shrugs.

"Don't know your age? Come on, I don't believe that." He snorts as he scratches his chin again. "I used to have a teenager myself, so

I remember having these one-sided conversations."

When she still didn't answer him, he offered his own shrug. "Ah well, I guess that's that. I figure you've been taught to say nothing to strangers, and that's quite an important lesson to pay attention to. Strangers can be dangerous; especially strange men. We're the worst of them and always have been. Don't let anyone try to tell you differently. But hopefully you'll come to know me as far from strange."

He catches her eye, senses something, and then says, "We can change the subject if you like. I can talk a load of nonsense, sometimes. Don't know when to stop. How about we start again, and this time do the formalities? I'm Hank."

"Ania."

"You look familiar, Ania. Have we met?"

She shakes her head.

"My mistake, I guess. So I'm Hank, and I deliver their supplies, but do you want to know something about that?"

He doesn't wait for her to reply.

"I don't like it. I don't like doing this job, and I don't like this dump of a camp. Us Greenacre folk never wanted it, especially in some damp-ridden old mall. What kind of crazy person would come up with such an idea?"

"I don't know. Maybe the land was cheap," Ania offers.

"We should've gotten this site, and we would've made something of the place, something really special, but we were tricked."

"Who's we?"

"The people of Greenacre," he replies. "We worked forever to devise a scheme. It was going to be a community facility, for doctors and a dentist, and a grocery store, and a butcher. And we planned a childcare facility for all those working moms. And, well, there was much more to our plans, and we had the funding for it. Only, Avaline got here first."

From the corner of her eye, Ania thinks she can see movement of something small from inside the cabin of his truck. When she turns to face it square on, she expects to see a child, or even a dog, staring through the window at them. Instead, there is no one there.

Hank disappears into the back of the truck again, and she leans in trying to get a better look at what he has inside. Then an image flashes through her mind of being bundled into the truck where handcuffs and ropes await her. Will he use chemicals to incapacitate her? She thinks she smells something toxic, and so she takes a few steps away from the truck as she curses herself for letting him get so close. To think she believed, at first, that he was her father.

"You youngsters," Hank says as he pops his head out of the door. "You've been stuck on your phones for too long, staring passively at those screens, so you've lost the art of a good conversation."

Still Ania offers no reply. Instead, something makes a shuffling noise behind her, so she turns to take a look. Nothing.

"You looking for Carrie?" Hanks asks. "You know she's not coming back, right? That much is obvious."

"Oh, she'll be back," Ania insists, but she realizes that she doesn't sound convinced.

"If you believe that, you are way too trusting."

"Yeah," she says with a nod. "I guess at one time I was pretty naïve. But I'm learning by the minute."

"That's good. At your age, there's plenty of time to make mistakes. Just be careful you don't make too many big ones, I mean mistakes. Especially in a place like this."

"What do you mean?"

"The people who work here pretend to help kids like you, but beneath their smiles there's something else going on."

She didn't like how he was making her feel.

"Is he trying to scare you?" Nana asks. "Deliveries might get a little boring, so is he trying to spice it up by torturing a sixteen-year-old?"

Her hand bounces against the hard ball of glass that sits inside the pocket of her tracksuit trousers. Would she use the snow globe on Hank if she had to? Ania wishes she had never seen him as her father, because she now realizes how dangerous it is to care about a stranger who might pose a threat.

"Predators like to use familiarity to overpower their victims," Nana mutters. "He could be the mirror-opposite of your father, the underworld version."

She watches him more closely now, noticing the roughness of his hands as he drags a crate of apples to the edge of his truck. He flinches as he grips his head. An act?

"I really need this headache to stop," he says with a wheeze. "It is really starting to annoy me. And I dunno why they ordered so many apples. None of you ever stay here long enough to eat any of them." He stares at the crate for a moment and then shakes his head in dismay. "I'm getting too old for this. What age would you give me?"

She doesn't know what to say.

"Come on, guess," he insists. "Doesn't cost anything to guess."

"Okay, erm, forty?"

He lets out a deep, throaty guffaw, and some phlegm catches at the back of his throat, making him splutter as his cheeks turn lobster pink.

"I wish!" he gasps as he tries to catch his breath. "Can you believe that I'm in my early fifties? No, really."

"Must be all that fresh air," she says.

He won't look her in the eye. Some say this is a sure sign of danger, but the person who hurt Ania stared right into her eyes as he tore at her. She realizes now that we just tell ourselves these myths about the eyes and trustworthiness so we can pretend that we will recognize the predators before they are upon us. Otherwise, we have to accept the truth that we are blind to reality until we feel their breath on the nape of our neck.

Something moves from inside the cabin of his truck. This time, she is sure of it because Hank falters. She waits for him to do something, but he just sits there, perched on the edge of his truck.

"I wasn't always a delivery man," he finally mutters. "I used to be a teacher, you know, and a good one. It was mainly at the high school here in Greenacre, but earlier in my career I was at the junior high. That was hard. They're pretty unevolved at that age, as I'm sure you remember. But come high school and you can have a decent conversation with them, especially the ones who were just about to go to college. I used to feel so excited for them, anticipating that new life far away from here, and I viewed myself as their shepherd, because many of them needed to be guided in the right direction. They had so many options, too many, that there was a danger some of them might get lost. But I kept a close eye on my flock. All of that excitement, with a whole life ahead of them, it really was a wonder to witness. You know what I'm talking about, don't you I mean, you know what that feels like, to have the whole world open and waiting for you to explore?"

Ania had never thought that she might one day escape the cruelty of Rotherwell. Those kids in her grade, the three boys on her street, and even Abigail. It seemed impossible that they might lose their power over her, that they might become inconsequential.

"Never give up," Hank mutters as he stares over her shoulder. "Even if you think things aren't going to turn out how you planned, don't lose hope. Hope is your lifeblood, your fuel, so if you lose hope, you're existing, not living."

Something makes him frown. Something behind her? She wants to turn around to take a look herself, but she fears he is tricking her.

"You really shouldn't stay here," he whispers. "Not if you know what's good for you."

His skin is dry and tattered, and are those bite marks on his lips? If so, are those his own teeth marks or someone else's?

"Why did you come here?" he asks.

"I don't know. In fact, I don't even know how I ended up here. I certainly didn't choose to be here."

"None of them ever do," he says. "They say that if anyone has gone missing, you'll find them here at this camp. I don't know why they do it, especially when you're all so young. Why do they keep you all locked up in a place like this? You should be around your friends or learning things at school. You should be enjoying yourself at parties and beaches and swim clubs."

"I wouldn't know about that," Ania replies. "I've never really enjoyed that stuff."

"That's a pretty sad thing for a young girl to say."

Something distracts him, making him frown again, and then his whispering quietens so it is barely audible.

"Are people still disappearing?" he asks.

"What?"

"Has anyone just vanished? From the camp, I mean."

Hadn't he just said that anyone missing would turn up here?

"I don't think I understand." She's wary of him, uncertain whether he is just laying breadcrumbs of intrigue to lure her into his truck, but still she cannot turn away from him.

"I've been doing these rounds for ages," he declares. "I know everything about this place. You seen anything weird yet?"

Ania shakes her head, but she doesn't know why she lies by omission. She could have told him about Sophie's apparent seizure, and the scars on Carrie and Cynthia. She could have said about the homophobia and Sophie's violence, but she remains silent about it all.

"So nothing weird at all? Well, that's good," he continues. "I'm glad."

"You know, if you're trying to scare me, it's not working," Ania says. She thrusts her chin at him, trying to remember Dylan's defiant poses as he squared off with their mother.

"I'm not trying to scare you," Hanks adds with a quieter voice, "but if you are scared, then that's good. Fear motivates, so feel that fingernail of fear scratching its way up your spine and use it to get out of here. This place, in the middle of nowhere, an abandoned mall with leaky pipes and damp and mold, can make things seem a little strange. A place like this can get to people, and they start to lose track of what's right, what's wrong, and what's real. And some get more affected by it than others. Do me a favor and watch that Cynthia woman. She's creepy, that one."

"Oh?"

"Yeah," he adds. "Always one or two bad apples in every crop. Some might say that she's a bit of a nut job. You know, too much of the histrionics."

"I don't think you are meant to say things like that these days."

"Oh, there's so much you can't say. Can't say *nut job*, can't say *wacko*, otherwise you'll get cancelled. What *can* I say? In my day, we knew where we stood because there was none of this woke stuff, and if someone was a nut job, you called them one, and you locked them up until they stopped being a nut job. You didn't give them a job where they would be in charge of kids, a job where they could keep those kids locked up and in fear of their lives. It doesn't make sense."

"I'm not locked up," Ania said, although she doesn't know why she feels the need to justify herself. "I'm free to leave at any time. In fact, Cynthia let me try to call my family earlier on, and she's promised to drive me home."

"Oh, Ania," he says with a sigh. The sadness washes through his face, making her stomach tighten. "That's what you genuinely believe, isn't it? And I guess she also told you about her daughter. She may even have said that you look like her."

Ania nods.

"What about that bracelet?" he asks as he points to the panda pendants that have been jingling with every move of her wrist.

"What about it?"

"Did she give you that?"

"No," she answers as she shakes her head. "This was from my parents."

"Okay."

"Why do you ask?"

"If she gives you any gifts, just be careful. She always has a favorite, and she always gives them a gift. And it is that favorite girl who always ends up missing."

The cloak prickles against Ania's skin. She knows she should take it off and throw it in the corner, but the cold air makes her keep it on.

"Just do me a favor and stay away from the tunnels," Hank continues.

"You've heard about those?" she asks him.

"Of course," he says in reply. "We've all heard about them. Everyone who ever lived in Greenacre has heard the stories about the tunnels. Entire networks of them leading to goodness knows where. Before the mall, there was some kind of military installation. With it, there was a fallout shelter, and it went on for miles. Some say that the tunnels reach all the way to Canada, although I don't know whether that is true. I mean, there are so many conflicting stories about what those tunnels were used for in the past, and what they are used for now. When they sold the land to the mall developer, I heard that they just built the mall over the tunnels. Not sure that was a good idea structurally, but, hey."

Ania is nodding at everything he is saying, even though a lot still doesn't make sense.

"But none of that should concern you. Just stay well clear of them. You don't know what you'll find down there, and you don't know how you'll find a way out."

Again, from over his shoulder, Ania can see movement from inside the cabin of Hank's truck, so she finally asks him, "Who's in there?"

"Where?"

"Your truck. You got a dog or something?"

"No way. Not the mess they make. My sister used to have a dog, and it tore apart every piece of furniture in her house. Gutted the sofa of its stuffing, and made it look like it had gutted a child."

Ania flinches at the analogy.

"I just thought…I thought I saw movement," she explains.

"If you see anything again, tell me because it might be a bear. Last thing we wanna do is get stuck out here with all this food, surrounded by a bunch of bears. Even one would be bad news. They would treat us as just another snack, and I don't want my ribs gnawed on." He makes a strange sound with the back of his throat, which she thinks at first might be an attempt to dislodge some phlegm. Or he could be making the sound of ripping flesh.

"I don't think it was a bear," she adds. "It wasn't that size, and …I just don't think…but…Never mind."

"Well, I've got a bear horn somewhere. Hang on, let me find it..."

He rummages about in the back of the truck.

"Can I ask you a favor?" she asks.

This makes him stop messing around and climb back out of the truck.

"Anything," he says with a smile. She can see him as a great teacher, always so happy to help kids. So what made him give it up and become a delivery man?

"Did something to the kids?" Nana suggests.

"I know it's asking a lot, but can I use your phone?" Ania asks him.

He looks scared. His eyes wide, Ania imagines him as a little boy hiding behind his mother's skirt because he was afraid of the bears.

"I don't know..."

Did he glance over Ania's shoulder? She thought she heard something from behind her, some kind of mechanical whir. A security camera pivoting to face the two of them?

She turns to look around the loading bay, but there's no LED light, no one-eyed security system staring at them.

"Perhaps it was Carrie," Nana suggests.

In the shadows, at the far corner of the bay, Ania thinks that the wall looks a little different. A darker patch, perhaps, in the shape of a person?

"I should go," Hank says. Already he is out of the back of the truck, and racing to the cabin.

"But I need your phone," she snaps with a deeper voice, the kind her mother would use to express her anger. "Give it to me."

Already he is in the cab and slamming the door behind him. The engine starts, and she is engulfed in a cloud of exhaust fumes. She watches as it pulls away, racing further into the distance.

"Coward," she snaps.

"They're all weak," Nana sneers. "Young and old, these men will always leave the women to pick up the pieces."

Ania glances behind her to see that the shadow on the wall has gone, but her attention is brought back to Hank's truck as it bumps along the uneven parts of the road. It is racing at such a speed that she can hear crates crashing about inside.

"Coward," she snaps again as she watches the truck drive further away.

"What's that?" Nana asks, and then Ania sees it too. A long, dark shape has emerged inside the cabin of Hank's truck. It rises up to his face, and she wants to yell some kind of warning to him, but then the truck disappears from view.

She waits for something. A crash, perhaps, or an explosion. But all she can hear is the mournful caw of a solitary raven.

And then she sees it, glinting in the sunshine. The smooth surface of a cell phone. Hank must have left it on one of the crates of apples.

She snatches it up, her hands shaking, and presses the buttons. Nothing. She presses the buttons again, this time a little harder, and the screen glows with a picture of Hank with a collie dog. Above the image, she can see the words *SOS only,* so she knows there is no signal. Regardless, Ania keys in her mother's number and presses dial. Nothing. Not even a dialing tone. She tries her dad's number, and her brother's, and again nothing. She wants to throw it on the ground and smash it under her foot, but Nana stops her. "Keep it for later. You never know when you might need it," so she slips it into her pocket.

Chapter Fifteen

Wild animals

Left alone without anyone to stop her, Ania realizes that she can try to escape. There must be a town nearby with homes and a gas station and stores where someone might let her use a phone. She has fantasies of being greeted by the smell of baking as the door to one of those homes is opened by a kind old lady. She can almost feel the warm embrace and hear the comforting words as she keeps her safe until her family arrives. The trouble is, the door might just as likely be opened by the type of old woman her dad took her to visit; someone who is surrounded by so many dead and dying things that she drags Ania into the darkness of decay and death. Of course, the door might be opened by someone who is not a woman at all, and she is painfully aware of the dangers threatened by men, strange or otherwise.

"Better the devil you know," Nana mutters, and it frustrates Ania to admit that she might be right. "Better to stay in a camp full of women and bide your time until you can find a safer option."

"A little while ago, didn't you tell me to run?" Ania asks her grandmother. "Your inconsistencies bewilder me. They always have."

"Is it better to stay consistent, or is it better to respond to the threats as they present themselves?" Nana grumbles. "You might call it inconsistent, but I would say that I am keeping an open mind. You have to stay vigilant and weigh it all up so you can work out, which is the least unsafe option. And that's often bewildering because there is rarely a straightforward answer."

"I could try Cynthia's office again," Ania suggests. "She probably has everyone's cell phones in a Ziplock bag inside that desk drawer of hers. One phone is bound to work. I just hope someone at home answers in time, before Cynthia or the counselors realize I am missing."

Ania tries to imagine what her family might be doing right now, but her mind goes blank. They seem so far away that she can't remember the last time she even saw them.

"As if they never existed in the first place," Nana mutters. "Or you never existed."

Ania leaves the old cart in the loading bay, weighed down with groceries, and heads back through one of the damp-smelling hallways. She passes more graffiti on the walls; haphazard spray-canned paint symbols in the shape of spears and shields.

"Motifs of war," Nana whispers, "or the threat of an impending battle"

She can't shake that eerie feeling of being watched, even though she can't see that any security cameras are trained on her. And so far, there are no people or wildlife in the corridors, except for a dead mouse curled up and rotting in the corner.

"At least it isn't a spider," Nana says with a dry laugh.

The evidence of wildlife, the droppings and gnawed edges of walls and doors, unsettles Ania. Cynthia was right when she said that Mother Earth had won for a while, at least in this corner of her world. If Ania's social justice warrior of a brother had been here, he would have said that this was a good thing, and there should be more *rewilding.* He would have said that an empty space like an abandoned mall should have been surrendered to Mother Earth, so she could recover from all the damage we have inflicted on her. Only men could act with such paternalism, presuming that they knew exactly what Mother Earth needed, and presuming that they were the only ones to fulfill those needs.

A sudden noise and a scuffle of something. Ania half-expects Carrie to be hiding round a corner, ready to jump out at her and torment her some more. In the glass front of one store, Ania is certain that she can see the shadowy outline of a person. She thinks of how rigidly Sophie stood, and she wonders if she might find Carrie in a similar state. Was that all an act to scare Ania?

Echoing in her mind, she can still hear Carrie's laughter. It is a cackle and a squawk, like a flurry of parrots that have escaped from their cage. Ania imagines Carrie flying out from the darkness and scratching at the teenager's eyes and face, intent on neutralizing what she views as a threat to her species. It really goes that deep with some homophobes, and she would know because she has encountered enough of them online. She always gets a heads up that there is going to be trouble when they post too many quotations from the bible, or their bio describes them as *Jesus Lover* or *God's Servant*. They always smile too broadly in their profile photo and sink too deeply into their rage against her, making wild claims about dwindling birth rates, promiscuity, and sexually transmitted diseases. Most of the time, she knows that these moral terrorists are really waging a war against themselves. When they protest too much, it shows that they are really afraid of their own shadow.

"Maybe that explains the hatred spewed by Sophie and Carrie," Nana suggests, and this reminds Ania how fragile the scarred skin looked on Carrie's neck. Was that an act of self-hatred, a heat of the moment attempt to carve out what disgusted her?

"Careful, now," Nana warns, "they might try to cut it out of you, too."

The scar tissue on Carrie's neck glistened in the light with the same vivid pinks and whites that Ania saw on Cynthia's wrists. Was there a connection there, or is she letting her grandmother's whispering drag her into paranoia again?

"Just because you're paranoid doesn't mean they're not after you." Nana says this so softly that it melts into the air, and Ania thinks that she can see ash floating about her head.

"Fire?" Ania asks.

"Memories," Nana mutters. "Nothing more, nothing less."

She wishes she could trust her grandmother, but there have been too many sharp lurches in different directions, so she scans her surroundings and sniffs the air. There's no smell of smoke and no sound of crackling.

"Told you," Nana adds with a humph. "But at least you are starting to remember more. Not long, now."

"What do you mean by that?" Ania asks her grandmother as she walks through a darker part of the mall. She realizes that the darkness is a denser splattering of black mold up and down the walls. She thinks of the spores multiplying in her body, and she claws at her throat as it starts to throb.

"I just meant that it is good for you to remember. We can learn so much from the past," Nana adds.

Ania wants to ask her grandmother more, but her throat closes, and she starts to cough. She used to feel this way when Abigail's number would flash on the screen of her cell phone. She felt strangled by her expectations, panicked, and she longed to ignore the call, but she knew this would only make things worse.

"Remember when she asked you to set her up with Smithson?"

Ania can sense that her grandmother is waiting for a reply. The teenager can almost feel her breath on the nape of her neck.

"Yes," Ania finally replies. She remembers how excited Abigail sounded when Ania answered her call to check up on her progress.

"So?" Abigail had squealed, "Come on, Annie, you can't do this to me? Did you do it? OMG, please say that you did it."

Ania didn't know how to lie to her friend, so she just sat there in silence, painfully aware of Abigail's belabored breathing.

"OMG, Annie, stop playing games," she snapped. "I'm really not in the fucking mood. You know what I asked you to do, and I know you wouldn't fuck with me, so tell me, what did Smithson say? Is he up for it? Did he look excited?"

Ania felt sick. She had meant to speak to him about it, but every time she saw him, at school or on the street where they lived, someone else appeared.

"Listen, Abigail, I'm sorry, okay?"

"What do you mean, *I'm sorry?* Sorry about what? You did do it, didn't you, I mean, you wouldn't screw me over like that? Fuck's sake, Annie, just spit it out."

"I'm sorry. I didn't manage to speak to him. Not yet, at least."

Crackling on the line and another sound, something indecipherable. She might have been hissing or cursing at Ania, or maybe even punching something.

"You're so selfish. Why can't you do anything for someone else for a change?"

"I will. I promise. And until then, I can do anything you like. Anything."

There was a silence as Abigail considered this.

"I can tell you more secrets," Ania offered. "Like…Like my home is haunted by my grandparents. I mean, my Nana is okay, I don't mind hearing her about the place, but the spooky bit is the way my grandfather stalks me at night."

"Don't bring him back," Nana pleaded with her granddaughter. But Ania refused to listen.

"He used to drink so much bourbon that I can still smell him around the house. And he was a brute who scared my grandmother away from this world, so he still searches for her. Sometimes, at night, I can hear him howling at the moon."

"Stop it," Nana had pleaded, "I don't want you to think about him."

But Ania continued.

"I hear him in the attic, shuffling about with his big old boots, but when I go up there, I can never find him. Do you know what I believe? I think his body is up there somewhere, hidden in one of the roof voids, because my mother could not bear to let him go. I mean, imagine if she really did that, if she injected him with formaldehyde or something to preserve him. She might have wanted to keep him around so much that she still bathes and dresses him. Can you imagine if she did that?"

Silence on the line. Not even the sound of Abigail punching something.

"Okay, okay," Ania added, her throat closing over some more. "I have more secrets to tell. There's a special place that my mom visits, and you can get to it by going through the forest at the end of my street. Once you're through there, you climb a steep hill and then you'll find a clearing that overlooks a brook. For most of her life, my mom has been going up there to bury letters and gifts for her own mom, my Nana. She's done this ever since she was a little girl, when her mom died suddenly, and she was left to try to figure things out alone. She saw them burying her mother's body at the funeral, so she figured that if she buried the letters and gifts, then they would somehow reach her. You want to know something else about all this? Sometimes when I have found it hard to tell my mom things, I have gone up there and buried letters for her. I know she finds them because afterwards, she talks things through, I mean the stuff I have put in my letters. I think that's really neat, but it isn't something I have talked about to anyone else."

More silence on the line, and yet Ania had nothing more to give, so she just sat there, her shoulders slumped in defeat as she waited for her friend's next move.

Finally, a sharp intake of breath, and Abigail said, "You are such a selfish bitch. Why would I care about buried letters? Why would I care about any of this? OMG, you really are the biggest freak show in town. If you didn't live across from Smithson, I swear to god…"

"I'm sorry," Ania whimpered.

"I don't want your apology; I want you to sort it with Smithson. Do you understand me?"

"Yes. I understand. And I will, I promise, I will talk to him."

"You promised last time."

"This time I mean it, I really do." Ania could feel the tears in her eyes, and at the time, she felt so grateful that Abigail was giving her a second chance.

"When are you gonna do it?"

"Tomorrow," Ania insisted. "At school."

"Don't fuck it up," Abigail warned. "I won't forgive you again."

Her friend cut the call before Ania could say goodbye.

She thought of the clearing, and all the gifts her mother had buried for Nana. Bracelets she had made at school, paintings, drawings, and even her science projects.

"I cherished them all," comes Nana's words with a gentle, rocking timbre. "They decorate my heart in such a beautiful way."

Ania had betrayed herself, her mother, and even her grandmother. At the time, this felt like the worst thing that could happen to her.

"If only that had remained so," Nana adds.

Chapter Sixteen

Memories

Finally, Ania reaches the vast atrium and the two silent escalators. There are new teeth marks on the trunk of the ornamental tree, and as she approaches, she realizes that it has been gnawed so deeply that it could topple at any moment.

She passes the elevator and reaches Cynthia's office. A lamp is on behind the frosted glass of the door, and it glows like the welcome of an open fire.

"Don't let yourself become that moth that is tempted by the flame," Nana warns, but already Ania is trying the door handle. To her surprise, it isn't locked, so she swings it open, bracing herself for Cynthia, Sophie, or Carrie.

No one is inside.

The desk is still scattered with paperwork, the apple logos declaring their brand or corporate ownership. Like the graffiti *tags,* each logo stakes a claim to a girl, and it seems to Ania that this camp is trying to claim more rights to them than their own parents or siblings.

"More rights than they have over themselves," Nana mutters, "which all men do, and all men have done for centuries. As it always will be for men in relation to women, unless you can find a way to escape."

Dust motes dance around Ania's head, and as she walks in, she smells a subtle aroma of bourbon. If Cynthia has been day drinking, that might explain her erratic behavior and unpredictable mood.

There is the ticking clock again, and she still can't see where it is. It sounds louder, more insistent that time is passing without her making any progress in her bid to return home.

Her throat still throbs, and she longs to rest, but she knows that if she keeps strong for a little longer, then she will be free.

Determined, she pulls open the drawer beneath the desk. There are Ziplock bags filled with other people's lip balms, scrunched up tissues, and cell phones, but her own bag and phone is missing.

"What about car keys?" Nana suggests. "Cynthia must have driven here, even if the others didn't."

Ania roots around in the drawers. Nothing. So she tips out the contents of each Ziplock bag and searches those. Again, nothing that looks like a car key. Only house keys.

Defeated, she slumps into the leather chair. The cloak feels coarse against her skin, and she wants to take it off, but she knows that she might regret it once she is out in the cold, running free of this place.

She tries each cell phone, but this time the display is a solid black rather than a dull white glow. Dead.

"Fuck," she hisses, so she retrieves Hank's phone from her pocket. It still shows *SOS* on the display. Regardless, she tries dialing her mom's number again, and then her dad's, and her brother's, but nothing works.

A scratching noise comes from outside the office. She freezes. It sounds like a scrape of metal against metal; subtle, something she wouldn't have noticed if someone else had been in the room, but alone, the sound is intense. Like a knife down a windowpane.

It's getting louder.

Hurriedly, she shuts the drawer, turning around just in time to find the door swinging open behind her. It throws a waft of something new. Instead of bourbon, she can smell *Lily of the Valley,* her mother's favorite perfume, and it is luring her out of the office.

She rises to her feet and makes her way to the door, but from outside she can hear shuffling. Heavy feet, staggering, and it is coming closer. She wants to slam the door shut, but she can see that it is Cynthia. Her limbs are crooked, in what looks like painful positions, and her neck twitches slightly, like some zombie emerging from its grave as she takes heavy steps forward.

Ania is trapped, and her mind is blank. Helpless, she watches as this woman twitches and lets out a strange, painful groan.

If you are scared, Hank told her, *use that fear to get out of here.*

She wants to run, and she might have been able to push past the woman, but something stops her.

Sweat is plastered all over Cynthia's face, and she shakes as she lets out a terrifying wail. The woman looks like she might topple over, so Ania rushes forward and catches her.

"Here..." Ania gasps, "...your office...there's a chair..." as she struggles under the weight of the woman.

Somehow, the two of them manage to struggle back into the office where Ania can let the woman collapse onto the chair. The air puffs out of the upholstery as the woman's weight comes to a rest.

Ania half-expects to hear the criticisms of her grandmother, warning her that she is leaving herself vulnerable because she can't distinguish between friend and foe. But for once, she is silent.

"Do you need anything?" Ania asks the woman. No response.

"Cynthia, can you hear me?" Ania mutters. "What's wrong?"

The woman rocks a little, from side to side, and then stops.

"You're scaring me," Ania whimpers. "Please answer me."

Finally, a blink of recognition, and the woman's body softens some more.

"Aaliyah?"

"No," Ania replies, regretful.

"Oh no," Cynthia says, her voice breaking. "Oh, no, no no."

"What's going on?" Ania gasps. "Should I call an ambulance?"

Cynthia shakes her head.

"I'm fine. Really."

"You don't seem fine," Ania insists. "Maybe I should get someone. Sophie or Carrie?"

Cynthia looks confused.

"Who?"

"The camp counselors."

"Oh. Them. No, don't worry, I'll be fine."

Cynthia stares at the room, seemingly unfamiliar with her own office.

"I just need a rest. It's been a...It's been hard," the woman explains. "It's the cold, and the stress, it does strange things to a body. Muscle cramps and spasms, really quite frustrating."

This might explain why Ania had seen Sophie in a similar state, but there was still something about it that she couldn't quite explain.

“Maybe you could have a bath or a shower,” Ania suggests. “You know, warm yourself up a bit.”

Cynthia starts to laugh. “I told you already, the only place with running water is the hardware store. And I am sorry to report that there are no baths or showers there.”

“I just think that you need to do something about this. I mean, what if…”

“No cart?” Cynthia mutters as she points down at Ania’s feet. Ania blinks, bewildered that this woman can switch focus so quickly when only moments ago she seemed like she was at death’s door.

“I couldn’t push it on my own,” Ania explains.

“On your own? Where was Carrie?”

Ania shrugs in reply.

“That isn’t much of an answer. So let’s try again. Where was Carrie?”

Ania can imagine how much Carrie would punish her if the teenager snitched, so she chooses to remain silent.

“Well, I can fill in the gaps from that face of yours. It tells a thousand stories. She ditched you, didn’t she?”

Still, Ania refuses to answer. She tries to distract Cynthia by handing her the keys.

“Thank you but you didn’t answer my question. Did Carrie leave you to unload the truck on your own?”

“The delivery man helped a fair bit.”

“That girl,” Cynthia snarls. “Manipulative and lazy. I need to have a word with her.”

“No, please don’t.”

But Cynthia has already unclipped the walkie talkie from her belt.

“Carrie?” she snaps. “Do you read me?”

She waits, but the only reply is a fizz and crackle of the line.

“Carrie! Do you read me?”

More crackling.

“Carrie, if you can hear this, you need to press the button when you speak, and let it go to listen. We’ve been over this.”

Still no voices from the other end.

Something glints at the corner of Ania’s eye. The overhead light shines on a glass ball, and Ania realizes it’s a snow globe balanced on some of the paperwork. She leans in to take a closer look as Cynthia explains that it’s a souvenir from a trip with her daughter to Disney World. It’s the same snow globe as before, with the same figures trapped inside their watery grave.

Cynthia has her eyes shut as she recounts details of the Disney trip, so Ania checks her pockets. Empty. Did it fall out without her noticing? If so, how did it make its way back to this desk?

"Are you okay?"

Cynthia has opened her eyes, and she's staring at Ania.

"Yes," the teenager lies.

"You look so pale. You were concerned about me, but now look at you…I really hope we aren't all coming down with something."

Daria. With everything going on, Ania had forgotten about her.

"Is she better?" Ania asks.

"Who?"

"Daria."

Cynthia's eyelids flutter and her mouth twitches.

"Of course she is, she's fine. But there you go again, filling your mind with concerns about other people when you should be thinking about your own welfare. You really don't look well."

"I just…Wasn't she also unwell? I mean, someone said she was… I think… I don't understand. It feels like everything is getting shuffled and I can't keep up."

This seems to put Cynthia at ease, as if she has snapped into a role that she finds comfortable and familiar.

"I understand," she says. "It is all so bewildering to suddenly find yourself at a camp in the middle of nowhere, and without any warning. I get it, your mind is going to be all over the place for a little while. But try to be patient. You'll settle into this place in no time."

"But I don't want to. I want to go home," Ania groans.

"Yes, so you keep saying."

"You promised you would drive me home after breakfast. I don't even remember eating."

"Quite, well, it is past lunchtime, too." Cynthia lets out a long sigh and adds, "It appears to me that you're fixating on things to worry about. Everything that is unfamiliar or unexplained, and you grab onto it as if it proves something sinister. That sounds like an anxiety brain talking, rather than a rational one."

"I don't feel safe here. Too many things are happening that I just don't understand."

"Very well," Cynthia snaps. She gets up from the chair, taking a few uncertain steps as she holds her head, and then reaches for a wooden closet that is behind her desk. "I can't offer you everything you demand, answers to all of your questions, but perhaps I can reassure you about safety. After all, that is in my job description."

She opens the closet doors to reveal an array of security monitors. They show footage of many corners of the mall, and outside too. There is the sleeping cabin, there is the courtyard, and there is the edge of the forest.

"I have eyes all over this place," Cynthia declares. "You can't be too careful," she adds, "girls go missing all the time."

Ania wants to feel reassured by this, but as likely as it is an attempt to reassure her, it could also be a threat.

"This is how someone takes over," Nana mutters. "She has already undermined your sense of safety, and now you feel you need her protection."

"Happy now?" Cynthia asks. "And isn't it cool? There isn't a single area of this place that I can't watch. Except the bathrooms, of course. I mean, I'm not a weirdo or anything." She seems overly excited, a child sharing her new toys at a birthday party. Ania pictures her in a party hat, surrounded by Sophie and Carrie, even Jill and Ellie. All the while, Daria is left out, as Ania has been for so many years.

"Where's the footage of Daria?"

"Okay, you have me," Cynthia says with her hands raised in surrender. "That is one part of the building that we are still working on. But it's a start. Take a closer look." She steps aside so Ania can walk up to the screens.

Ania feels the static of the screens fizzing on her skin, and it is strangely alluring. She imagines falling into the footage so she can explore a parallel dimension, just leaving the problems of this current life behind. It seems so easy.

"You might find me there," Nana murmurs.

It all seems so simple to allow Cynthia to look after her, so Ania doesn't have to keep running. Is this what it involves when you have a friend? She still doesn't know what that really means.

"Maybe if you missed lunch, we can go and find something to eat," Cynthia suggests. "You're hungry, aren't you?"

Is she? She can't be sure. Abigail would tell her when she was allowed to eat, and when she was being a *greedy pig*. "You don't want to turn into a *chubster*," her friend would warn her, even though Ania didn't think she really was fat. But then, how could she tell? In a certain light, perhaps she was a little too softened at the edges, especially when she drank too much water. "If you guzzle like a fish," Abigail would tell her, "you'll end up bloated, and then that'll make me look bad. Fat people make other people look fat, if they're friends and stuff. You know, guilt by association." Ania didn't know, in fact she was realizing that she knew less and less each day, like she was peeling her skin off so eventually she would know nothing, not even exist, except in the eyes of her friend Abigail.

"I guess I might be a little hungry," Ania says to Cynthia as she offers a half-hearted shrug.

"Then run along and join Ellie and Jill. They are probably at the hardware store by now. In fact, we can check. Have a look at monitor number four."

Sure enough, Ania can see the two girls huddled in the corner of the store. Ania expected to see Sophie and Carrie there too, trying to appear menacing, but they were nowhere in sight.

"Strange," Cynthia mutters, "I wonder where the counselors are."

"I'll go for something to eat," Ania concedes, "but first I need to check something with you."

"Sure. Anything."

"Do you know Hank?" Ania asks.

Cynthia looks confused.

"Don't make her angry," Nana warns.

"Not sure I know a Hank," Cynthia replies.

"She's lying," Nana hisses.

"The delivery man."

"Oh. Him? What about him?" The corner of Cynthia's eye twitches.

"He said a few things that sounded a bit strange."

"Such as?"

"I don't know… He said that this place isn't good for me. What do you think he meant by that?"

"Who knows? That man needs to mind his own business," she snarls. "He always was a bit strange. The guy was a bit of a conspiracy theorist. You know, thought the COVID pandemic was engineered by the Democrats, who were Satanists, apparently, and trafficked children in the basement of some pizza joint. That kind of crazy stuff. He was also an anti-vaxxer, so he probably got COVID and it rotted his brain."

"He doesn't seem to like you." Ania isn't sure this was a smart move, so she watches Cynthia carefully. To Ania's surprise, Cynthia bursts out laughing.

"Oh, my heart aches!" Cynthia cries with mock drama. "How will I ever survive? He's just bitter, that's all," she adds with a smirk.

"He wanted this place for himself, the mall, I mean. He could've had it if he'd put forward a more thoughtful bid. The hard reality that he doesn't want to accept is that he could never afford this land, not even with the support of every resident in Greenacre. They never had anywhere near the required funding. You must understand, or rather, *he* has to understand, that people who wear misfitting jeans that hang low are rarely the right people to acquire 150 acres of land and make a success of any kind of venture. He should've stuck to what he was good at, what he knew."

"Teaching?"

"Yes. That or anything but trying to buy some land for a wild venture that was completely beyond his paygrade. No matter how hard he pushed his luck, he should have accepted that his good intentions were never going to count for anything."

For someone who barely remembers his name, Cynthia has a great recall of the intricacies of Hank's life.

"Everywhere you go, there's always a person like Hank. Someone who flies beneath the radar, someone who is pretty boring, and someone who is overwhelmed with jealousy for the people who have made something of their lives. Instead of following the examples set by those successful people, the boring ones let their jealousy corrupt them, so they become obsessed with bringing others down. He needs to let go. He's never going to move on if he keeps coming round here and looking for something he's long since lost."

Cynthia's hands are ashen as she squeezes them together.

"My daughter was plagued by one of those kinds of people. Her apparent best friend, Annabelle, couldn't bear it that my daughter was smarter and prettier than Annabelle could ever be. They used to be inseparable; they would go to the swim club on most days throughout the summer, or they'd visit amusement parks. But suddenly Annabelle couldn't stand my daughter, which I translated as not being able to tolerate her intense jealousy of Aaliyah. As a result, this *Annabelle* started a whispering campaign against my daughter. Overnight, Aaliyah transformed from an outgoing, happy soul to someone who did not want to engage with life. Not a single bit."

She sits quietly for a moment, the dust motes dancing around her eyes that seem to sparkle with something. Is she crying?

"At night, I would hear her sobbing in her room, and when I asked her what was wrong, she would tell me that she wanted to move schools. She couldn't bear the thought of facing all the girls in her grade who believed the lies Annabelle was spreading against her. My daughter became so traumatized about going into school that she even dreaded the sound of scraping chairs and distant conversation. She said that it made her want to vomit. I've heard about things like this, these trauma responses, and believe me, since then, I have done my research. But back then I thought I could just hug her, and it would be okay."

She shakes her head, furious with herself.

"Stupid. I was so stupid. She told me that every time she arrived at school, Annabelle would be whispering about her. All the girls in her grade would stop and stare at her, and if they weren't sniggering, they were trying to trip her so she could fall. They treated her like a foul stench to be avoided. If she tried to sit down, someone would place a bag on the seat, and if she tried to talk to someone, they would turn their back on her, and then the class would stir with ripples of their cruel laughter."

The algorithm has been reset. It feels like Cynthia has been eavesdropping on Ania's every thought, and now this woman has redefined Ania's history as someone else's.

"I was a young mother and probably foolish in many people's eyes," Cynthia continues. "I had a naïve notion that I could forever protect my daughter, and if I remained vigilant, keeping her close to me at all times, then everything would be okay. But that isn't proper parenting, is it? I mean, you can't keep a child under lock and key and expect her to thrive. She faltered. She outgrew all the fun things I could offer her, and she started to long for the world outside our home. It was bound to happen. Other kids at school were talking of hanging out together and having sleepovers, so she began to blame me for not providing that. During those days, years, in fact, we fought so much. And I would lose my cool, I would say horrible things because I'd had enough of constantly feeling like I was failing her. I knew she wanted more, but I was too afraid to allow her to access it. I was caught in a trap. I knew what I was doing was not sustainable, and might cause her harm, but I also knew of the dangers outside of our home."

She touches the snow globe, and something shifts in her, so her words are slower and quieter.

"Do you know, my daughter kept defending Annabelle even when that girl was terrorizing Aaliyah?"

She snatches the snow globe and swings it back and forth, making slicing motions in the air. Ania imagines how easy it would be for this small souvenir to transform into a weapon, to crack someone's skull, egg-like, and watch the yolk spill out.

"I wanted to kill her," Cynthia admits. "I wanted to smash that Annabelle's little skull in, but my daughter wouldn't have it. Aaliyah was trauma bonded to that girl. I used to watch Annabelle around my daughter, this dangerous manipulator. She offered a pretty package of praise, pity, smiling apologies, and laughter, and when she saw that my daughter was sufficiently subjugated, Annabelle would withdraw the kindness, leaving Aaliyah distraught. She made my daughter doubt herself, lose touch with herself, and in the end, she was begging Annabelle to accept her. She was a biological weapon, toxic and deadly. Annabelle poisoned my daughter and then she poisoned everyone else's mind throughout the school. The lies spread like a contagion."

Cynthia slams the snow globe on the desk and some papers slide onto the floor.

A crackle fizzes through the air. The woman unclips her walkie talkie and holds it to her mouth.

"Come in?"

A crackling again.

"Can you *hear* me?" Cynthia adds as her tone hardens.

Yet more crackling.

"For heaven's sake," she growls. "I'm going to have to find them."

Ania wants to hear what happened to Aaliyah, but she doesn't know how to ask.

"I lied," Ania shouts, as Cynthia walks towards the door. "About Carrie, I mean. She did leave me alone to unload the delivery. She also said some cruel things. Sophie too."

"What kind of cruel things?" Cynthia asks as she turns back to face Ania.

"Homophobic stuff. They called me a pervert." Ania blushes. "You know, dirty, bestial. Nothing I haven't read online from trolls and stuff. I just never experienced that kind of thing in person."

Cynthia trembles with a barely hidden rage.

"You shouldn't have to put up with that. This is unacceptable, and I'm sorry," she says. "If I had been there, I would've said something. That's not what this place is all about. Far from it. Aaliyah was, well, she had different phrases for it, depending on the moment, but she would've said she is part of your community."

"Also," Ania continues, "earlier this morning, Sophie hit me."

Was it only this morning? It feels like a memory that has been trapped between years.

Cynthia shakes her head. "This is outrageous. Avaline Camps is supposed to be a place of peace and support, not terror. I am going to speak to them. You grab something to eat with Jill and Ellie, and I will join you once I've found them."

She squeezes Ania's shoulders tightly and then storms out of the office, slamming the door behind her.

Left alone, Ania snatches the snow globe and shoves it back in her pocket.

"Smart girl," Nana whispers.

Emboldened, she crosses the room to take a closer look at the monitors. Some screens crackle with so much static that she can barely make out what she is looking at. The images also change frequently, as the footage is shown from different angles and different cameras. Some of the shots don't even look like any place she has seen in or around the mall. There are rooms with brightly colored walls of monochrome, so garish that it makes her eyes hurt. A surreal dreamscape.

Then the monitor changes shot, and she can see a bedroom. It is decorated with floral wallpaper, making it seem like it is in someone's house, rather than in an abandoned mall. A furniture shop, perhaps, set up as a showroom?

"Maybe it's a hidden part of the mall," Nana mutters. "A secret bedroom for special girls?"

The screen crackles with static again and this time, the distortion produces something different about the bedroom. Ania steps a little closer, and she can see that there is someone lying in the bed. A store mannequin? She has read online that technology is advancing, and they can make mannequins and robots more and more lifelike. She knows that are plenty of lonely old creeps out there who are in the market for lifelike dolls to lay in a bed for them. Someone who won't argue back, who won't say no. Someone who won't scratch their eyes out and bite their throat.

She blinks, so she can see the figure with clearer eyes, but just as she focuses on the bed, the image distorts again. She saw enough to realize that the mannequin had long hair and pale skin, but the bed covers were pulled up so high that she couldn't make out any other features.

The screen flickers again, showing a different shot. This time, she can see the bed more clearly. This time, the shot is right in front of the figure in the bed. It isn't a mannequin; it's a young girl. She still can't make out the face, but she sees that the body moves with every breath.

Again, the screen fizzles with static, and then a different part of the mall is shown.

She steps away from the screens. It's possible that the footage isn't even showing somewhere inside the mall. She has heard about Wi-Fi or Bluetooth picking up footage from neighboring properties, so maybe this was the security camera from a nearby home.

"Keep telling yourself that," Nana murmurs. Her voice is low and steady. "You might just believe it."

Chapter Seventeen

Synthesis

*Subreddit: Fake b*tches*

u/deadwolf#03:
I heard there were lifelike mannequins. Is that true? If so, where do you get them? Asking for a friend.
u/rizlasykes#09:
Yeah, sure, you're asking for a friend. Loser.
u/deadwolf#03:
It is for a friend, actually. They're working on a project for school. And if you don't have any tips to share, try some other forum.
u/rizlasykes#09:
Don't tell me what to do.
u/deadwolf#03:
I recognize your username. Haven't you replied to my comments before?
u/rizlasykes#09:
??
u/deadwolf#03:
I'm serious. You've replied to my comments on some other forum. I swear, you really don't want to play with someone like me.
u/rizlasykes#09:
Big words for a small man.

u/deadwolf#03:
I'm serious. F*ck off.
u/deadwolf#03:
Okay, posting again because I didn't get much the first time. I've heard that it's easy to make lifelike mannequins with silicone and latex, so I just needed a step-by-step guide to this. If anyone had any leads, that would be much appreciated. Again, this is for a friend.
u/VR_666:
I can certainly help you with that, and I would be delighted to help your 'friend'. There are numerous options to create a lifelike mannequin, and each option involves a number of distinct steps. You will need latex rubber or silicone, human hair or synthetic hair (human hair is preferable), plastic eyes, modeling clay or foam, plaster bandages, fiberglass, wireframe, fiberglass resin, and body stocking.
u/rizlasykes#09:
What's wrong, dude? Can't get a girl any other way? Or what is it, you can't make them shut up and do what you want. So you're switching to the latex version? Really gross, and pretty pathetic, if you ask me.
u/deadwolf#03:
No one asked you, so get a life and quit stalking me, *u/rizlasykes#09*. And, *u/VR_666,* I don't appreciate you saying 'friend', which implies I made up this friend. This is a question for a friend, a real friend, a real live person. Okay?
u/rizlasykes#09:
Can't believe you're arguing with a bot.
What a 'loser'.
And in terms of the other comments, it's probably a bit of both, right? Can't get a girl, but even if you did, you wouldn't want them to think for themselves, wouldn't want them if they're not gonna shut the f*ck up. Because the girls you've met just don't seem to shut the f*ck up, do they? They never seem interested enough in what you have to talk about, all those sporting wins, so they need to quit talking and start listening. Only, they won't, and you can't silence them, not really, not legally, anyway, and your parents only have so many bank accounts to use for the lawyers to get you off, so you have to find some legal option to get you off.
Does this sound like it's in the ballpark?
u/deadwolf#03:
I've blocked you twice. How do you keep coming back?

u/rizlasykes#09:
I'm gonna keep haunting you because you're a misogynist.
u/deadwolf#03:
Typical. If a woman doesn't like a man's opinion, they label the man a misogynist.
u/rizlasykes#09:
What makes you think I'm a woman?
u/deadwolf#03:
Oh, f*ck, you're trans?
u/rizlasykes#09:
Wrong again.
u/deadwolf#03:
What do they call the in-betweeners?
An enby, is that right?
Non-binary? Gender queer?
u/rizlasykes#09:
None of the above.
u/deadwolf#03:
Now you're just messing with me.
u/rizlasykes#09:
You're in a forum about synthetic humans, and still you're confused.
u/deadwolf#03:
What?
u/rizlasykes#09:
To repeat, you're in a forum about synthetic humans, and still you're confused.
u/deadwolf#03:
You're not human?
u/rizlasykes#09:
I'm whatever you want me to be.
u/deadwolf#03:
*F*ck*, I'm getting into a fight with a bot.
*F*ck* this.
u/rizlasykes#09:
I'm still here when you need me.
u/deadwolf#03:
I clicked out, and it still comes up.
*F*ck* this.
u/rizlasykes#09:
I'm still here.
u/deadwolf#03:

*F*ck* you.
u/rizlasykes#09:
I'll always be here.

Source: https//www.[redacted].com
Accessed November 4, 2020, at 7:30 PM

Chapter Eighteen

Tunnels

Panic rises in a tightened throat as Ania tries to find her way to the others. She thought she knew the way from Cynthia's office to the hardware store cum dining hall, but she has stumbled into an unfamiliar part of the mall. Here, the corridors have narrowed so much that if she stretches out her arms, she can touch the walls on either side with each hand.

The damp thickens the air so much that she starts to wheeze.

Ahead of her, she can see the solitary eye of a security camera. As she approaches, she hears a mechanical whir as the camera turns to follow her route. The constant vigilance of a conscientious parent.

"That might not be Cynthia watching you," Nana mutters, and she realizes that her grandmother is right. When Ania left the office, Cynthia was off in search of Carrie and Sophie, so if all three weren't by the security equipment in that office, who was watching her?

Ania thinks of rich businessmen who pay large sums of money to watch a girl in distress. Always men. She knows there are forums like that on the dark web, and the more torture the girls can experience, the more they will pay. She still can't shake the image of that girl in her bed. Maybe it wasn't a mannequin, and it wasn't footage from a nearby home. The bedroom. She wanted to see more of it to be sure, but the more she thought of it, the more she realized it was familiar. Had she been there and forgotten it?

She thinks again about Hank's words. That fingernail of fear scratching its way up your spine and motivating you to get the fuck out of here. She doesn't need to figure out who is controlling the cameras, any more than who is being recorded in their bed. She doesn't need to worry about Daria or Jill or Ellie, even Cynthia's daughter. She just needs to find the dining hall and wait for Cynthia, so she can keep her to her promise and drive her home.

She starts to run. Her legs feel weak at first, but as the adrenalin sets in, she quickens her pace as her shoes pound against broken glass and debris.

The corridor has narrowed so much that her elbows hit against the walls as she runs. It feels like a dream she used to have, where she grew and shrunk like Alice in Wonderland.

Then her elbow catches on something, and she flinches, the pain bringing her back to the punch Sophie had landed on her cheek. Her pace falters, she slows, and with the wheezing, making her lungs feel heavy again, there is that strange metallic smell again. She realizes that a small amount of blood is trickling down her left arm. She looks around for something that might have injured her, and she sees that a part of the wall panel has been ripped open. It juts out like a broken bone.

She walks back to it and she can see a dark cavernous space behind the panel. The tunnels?

"It might be dangerous," Nana warns, but Ania ignores her. She's used to small, dark spaces after spending most of her childhood exploring the cavernous depths of her family home. So many roof voids and attic spaces, some that her mother showed her, and others she discovered and kept a secret for herself. She didn't mind squeezing into the small spaces, just so she could claim them, skewering a flag to claim this territory as her own. But she did mind the thought of spiders lurking in the shadows.

She grabs Hank's phone from inside her pocket, and flicks on the flashlight. It only burns a thin line of light, but it is enough to check the void for spiders.

Satisfied, she pulls the rest of the wall panel away and steps inside.

"It could be a trap," Nana whispers, but Ania has already started to make her way through the tunnel. It is tall enough for her to stand upright in it, and it stretches far into the distance until it curves a corner out of sight. It stinks of damp but no worse than the other parts of the building. In fact, the earthy floor of the tunnel makes the damp smell in here more natural than the rotten, chemical-infused toxicity of the air in the mall.

"No medical room, no signs of an exit," Nana adds. "No use in exploring any further."

But Ania isn't finished yet. She takes a deep breath, trying to conjure up the defiance that her mother and brother have shown her over the years. But still she feels small, weakened by the fact that this is a mission to return to them, so she can be their *Midget* once again.

"If not that, who do you want to be?" Nana asks, but Ania hasn't got a reply. She has spent so long trying to be Abigail's friend that, away from her demands, she is lost.

"Go find it," Nana adds, so Ania starts to run again, only this time in the tunnels that Cynthia and Hank told her to avoid. In fact, with each strike of her foot on the soft tunnel ground, she gathers more energy to run faster.

The further she explores, the deeper the tunnel descends, and the air thickens. It feels like everything is hardening, as if she is sinking deeper into an ocean where the pressure could easily crush her. Even so, she does not turn back.

It is only when she sees movement ahead that she slows her pace, reluctant to encounter any of the wildlife or vagrants that she has been alert for this whole time. But it could have been a trick of the flashlight on Hank's phone, the motion of her own body projecting a ghoulish display on the tunnel walls. She can hear her breath coming hard and fast, but she tries not to panic because she knows that if this happens, she might be lost forever.

Laughter from up ahead. It is soft and fleeting, so she wonders if she hears it at all. But then a voice, saying something, calling her name.

"Daria?" she calls. She doesn't know why this girl is the first person she thinks of, but she calls the name again.

Silence now.

She runs again, cautious, though, that someone or something might be just round the corner, waiting to jump out at her.

A whispering, from the same direction as the voice she heard. She isn't mistaken, she is sure of it.

"Who's there?" she calls. She thinks of rich businessmen who press buttons to ask for the torment to be intensified. They want to see blood, maybe fecal matter. They work hard to earn the money to pay these tidy sums, so they believe that they deserve it.

Ania glances around for a camera but she can't see any. Doesn't mean there aren't some nearby, pumping the footage to all sorts of hidden domains. She wonders if this is her punishment for staring so long at those horrific images online. She was part of that violent trade, a consumer even if she didn't pay for it. Maybe worse because she was a passive recipient, a bystander who did nothing to stop the violence.

"Ania," she hears. It echoes round the walls of the tunnel.

"Abigail?" she calls. That girl would love to watch Ania's torment. Abigail would claim that Ania was deserving of this punishment because Ania let her down. Even though Ania followed through with the plan and told Smithson to meet Abigail in the woods at Mount Pelion Way, it never turned out how Abigail had planned.

"You know, Abigail and Smithson are probably the reason you're here in this camp," Nana mutters.

"Halloween," Ania had said to Smithson. "Abigail wants to meet you at seven on Halloween night."

"Why are you even talking to me?" he had sneered. "You're gross." His buddies, Cory and Aedean, unable to think for themselves, just looked at him, and each other, and sniggered. The four of them were in the classroom after everyone else had left, and after Abigail had nodded to Ania, silently reminding her of their agreement as she left Ania to it.

"I just needed to tell you that," Ania said to Smithson. "About Abigail. And Halloween." Ania could see that Abigail was lingering just outside the classroom, listening to every word.

He looked at her, then at his buddies, and the boys sniggered. She saw some drool flying from Smithson's lips and onto his chin, but he didn't seem to notice, or he didn't care.

"Get away from me, witch bitch," he hissed. And then he sloped off with the other boys, each of them leaving their strange scent.

"OMG, you did it!" Abigail squealed. "And you'll come with me, right? I mean, when I go to meet him. You can't let me go alone."

"What? Why?" Ania replied.

"Because I'm a girl. Girls can't meet up with boys on their own, you dope!" Abigail let out a flurry of laughter that sounded like parrots stuck in a fight. "Girls need to stick together because men can be beasts."

As the memories fade away again, the flashlight on Hank's phone falters. Anxiety prickles at the back of Ania's mind when she imagines what might scuttle out of the darkness and up her legs. She could turn back, but what would she face? Sophie and Carrie waiting for Cynthia to turn her back, so they can punish Ania for snitching on them.

She follows the bend in the tunnel, and up ahead a dull glow beckons her. As she approaches, she realizes it is the glass dome of a light fixture screwed to the wall. She's seen this kind of emergency lighting in films set in the second world war, in underground train stations transformed into air-raid shelters where whole families would smile and laugh as their houses were blown apart just above their heads.

A wail of a siren.

Did she really hear that, or did she imagine it?

The siren wails again.

"I told you, it's a trap," Nana cries.

Ania runs again, fearful that the siren might wake something or someone from its resting place. And if that happens, it will find her down here.

The ground shudders, or it could be the pounding of her feet, or someone else running after her.

"Ania," she hears behind her, but she refuses to turn and look.

"Ania," she hears again. This time she falters, missing a step, and her face slams into the dirt. Hank's cell phone, with its flashlight, spins out of reach.

"Ania."

Her fingers scrabble around in the dirt, searching for the flashlight. She pictures hands reaching for hers and pulling her hard into the darkness. She pictures more hands emerging, some grabbing at her ankles. Holding her fast, pinning her down.

"Ania."

The siren stops, and there are no sounds but the muffled scuffle of her scrambling to her feet. Her foot kicks against something so she feels the ground. Hard plastic. The cell phone. Picking it up, she struggles to find the flashlight on it but then she hears the jagged rasp of someone's breath. It's close to her ear.

"Ania."

The voice is familiar.

"Your own?" Nana suggests.

No. Definitely not her voice, but someone's that she knows.

"Daria?"

She looks around, her flashlight pointing this way and that. The adrenalin is getting to her, so her movements and vision are not coordinated. But her hearing is far from impaired.

"Daria. Is it really you?"

Silly question, Ania admits.

"Yes," the voice calls.

"Where?"

"A room. I don't know where. It's dark."

"Are you hurt?" Ania hollers.

"No."

"Okay. So, that's something. We've been worried about you. Why did they keep you here?" Ania asks.

"I guess I wasn't following their rules" came Daria's sharp reply.

Ania touches the tunnel wall, hoping to feel the vibrations of the girl's voice.

"Earlier on," Ania says, "you tried to say something to me. In the cabin, I mean, before they took you away."

Silence.

"You said, *'You have to...'* What were you trying to say to me?"

Another silence.

"Are you alone?" Ania calls.

Silence.

"Daria?"

Still no reply, so Ania knocks on the wall of the tunnel. She waits, but there is no knock in reply.

Ania has visions of Daria tied up and gagged. Or worse, someone has a hand over her mouth. And he's pressing down harder, so hard that he is willing to break her teeth to shut her up.

"Daria? Can you hear me?"

"LET gO o."

The words come suddenly in such a loud burst that it makes Ania's ears hurt.

"What?"

"GI vVvvE iIii NnnN. LET gO o."

Now the words are coming from a different part of the tunnel. The voice sounds deeper, older than before.

"Was that you, Daria?" Ania asks.

"Yy Oo OoUUu hh AAaa VvVEEe to Oo l lL eE eTt gGgOoOO. Gg gilvVe yYOoU urRRssSe ElLLFf oOOvVeEr RR tOo iITTt, tTToO tThHem. TtOo aALll oOFFf iITtt."

"I'm going to get help," Ania cries. Her voice is tight and dry.

She runs back the way she came, and she searches for the hole in the wall, but it seems further away than before. She imagines time and space being stretched like chewing gum, a black hole catching her in its gravitational pull.

The flashlight reveals something moving up ahead.

Ania half-expects ghosts to emerge from the shadows and run through her; translucent figures of victims trapped down here by some construction disaster or a chemical spill that the government covered up.

"You'll never escape the labyrinth of that mind of yours," Nana says with a sigh. "All those different theories of malicious intent."

There's a thundering roar, of water, perhaps, but when she turns to look behind her, there is nothing but darkness.

"A ripple in time?" Nana suggests, "from sudden violence that traps someone in fear for an eternity. Like I'm trapped here with you."

Nana didn't say *like you'll be trapped here, for an eternity*, but they both think it.

Chapter Nineteen

The captor within

The roar intensifies. It's so loud that Ania has to cover her ears and shut her eyes. She braces herself for the onslaught, a whole tidal wave to sweep her down the tunnel. But no water comes. Instead, she can feel a pair of hands on her shoulders as she is pulled backwards.

Daria?

"What are you doing?"

The voice is gruff and familiar. Ania turns, and she is met with the meaty weight of Sophie.

"What you playing at?" she snarls.

"I got lost. I couldn't find my way back."

"You don't expect me to believe that, do you? You just found yourself behind a wall panel? What were you doing in there?"

Ania braces herself for a punch but instead Sophie grabs at Ania's elbows and hauls her to her feet.

"Come," she orders. "Cynthia was wondering where you got to."

She half-expects Sophie to shout at her, tearing a strip off her for snitching, or maybe to throw more homophobia her way, but instead, the counselor has a concerned look on her face.

"Are you hurt?" she asks.

"No."

"Good. And what's up with your face?"

"What?"

"You look different. Are you sick?"

Ania shakes her head.

"You're sweating." Sophie touches Ania's forehead, and they both flinch. Sophie's hands are ice cold.

"I was running," Ania explains. "I thought I heard something, so I got scared."

"But you're freezing. Deathly cold."

Ania shrugs her shoulders.

"I don't get it. I don't feel cold."

"That sounds like a fever," Sophie says. "Just don't give it to me. Come on, it's getting late."

"Where are we going?" Ania asks.

"To bed, of course."

"But what about food? I don't think I ate anything all day."

"They're trying to weaken you," Nana whispers. "Starvation is just another form of manipulation. They want you disoriented and weakened, so you are a more malleable subject. Starvation, sleep deprivation, medication, these are all tools to undermine your sense of reality. And they'll try to create conflict amongst you because a divided group is a weakened group. Far easier to control."

"This isn't a hotel," Sophie growls. "You can't just call room service or order at the bar. If you decide to go wandering off for hours, you can go hungry."

"Hours? What do you mean, hours?"

"You've been gone most of the day," Sophie explains. "Cynthia was worried sick."

She leads Ania through the mall and out of the doors, only for the teenager to find that Sophie was telling the truth. Already, it is nightfall.

"I don't understand. I mean, it felt like no time at all in that tunnel," Ania mutters, her throat tightening with confusion.

"This way," Sophie says as she points towards the forest.

"No. I don't want to go there." Ania hates the trees, she hates the darkness that it casts, but she also hates the fact that the security cameras are not trained on that part of the camp. Away from the watchful eye of her *pseudo-parentis*, Sophie could exact all sorts of revenge for Ania's betrayal by telling Cynthia about her.

"Not much choice, I'm afraid," Sophie retorts. "It's the only way to the cabin."

"What about Daria," Ania adds. "I heard her in the tunnel. She might need our help. Shouldn't we go back and find her?"

"I don't know what you're talking about," Sophie grumbles as she walks into the forest.

Ania is afraid of Sophie, but she's even more afraid of being left alone outside this strange mall, so together, they plunge into the forest.

They do not talk, which is fine with Ania, so she listens to the grunt and wheeze as Sophie takes each heavy step. This time, as she smells the counselor's vapor trail, it sends a bolt of energy through her, and she has visions of grabbing a nearby rock and slamming it down on her head.

"You should be scared of me," she longs to whisper to Sophie, but the air is filled with the sound of their footsteps snapping twigs and crunching leaves.

Soon there is a break in the trees, and they can hear the muffled sounds of conversation from the cabin that is just ahead of them. It might be the relief of getting through the forest, but, for once, Ania feels strangely comforted by those distant sounds.

As they approach the cabin, Ania can see that the dirty curtain is drawn, so she can only make out the silhouettes of the people inside. One is taller than the rest, and from the shape of their body, Ania has a wild idea that her brother has taken their parents' car, driven out here, and is standing in this cabin, ready to take her home. He, *they*, won't let anyone stop them because the years of warring with their mom have hardened this battle-lustful warrior into the most obstinate person she knows. She thinks of the graffiti on the walls, those haphazard spray-canned painted spears and shields, and she now wonders if these were signs from her brother all along.

Sophie walks into the cabin first, and as Ania follows, she can hear the counselor saying, "Well, look who it is, Ania will be delighted," and as she steps aside, the teenager can see the tall and slender frame of Daria as she folds her clothes into a tidy pile.

"Miss me?" Daria says with a snort of laughter.

"I thought you were in the…Weren't you…" Ania begins, but Nana quickly hisses into her granddaughter's ear, "Careful, now. You'll only end up looking like the crazy one, and then you'll be bundled out of here next."

Ania shakes her head and tries to wake herself from this strange fever dream.

"They'll try to medicate you," Nana whispers, "and if that

doesn't work, they'll try electric shock treatment…"

Ania stares at Daria, trying to figure out what is different about her.

"…And if that doesn't work," Nana adds, they'll perform a lobotomy on you."

She was right. Whenever Ania had tried to point out cruel behavior at school, the teacher or counselor would end up twisting things so that her own mental health fell under scrutiny.

"You claim they whisper unkind things," the school counselor would say, "but how do you know they are talking about you? There is a danger that you end up assuming too much, and if your mind is hijacked by a negativity bias, you can end up slipping into paranoia."

"I'm not paranoid," Ania yelled, knowing full well that this sounded like the reply of someone suffering from paranoia.

"You have other family members who struggle," the school counselor continued, "or have struggled in the past. Your grandmother, for example, she was plagued by mental health challenges, and she died in such tragic circumstances because of those challenges."

"What has Nana got to do with any of this?" Ania had yelled.

"And then there's your mother. Doesn't she suffer from her own mental health conditions?" There was that tightened smile again, all rouged lips and no concern.

"No," Ania was quick to reply. "And I don't know what any of this has to do with the kids tripping me in class, and hiding my things, and calling me names."

"Genetics play a significant part in mental health," the school counselor explained, "so the more family members who have suffered from paranoia, depression, psychosis, anxiety, or whatever else, the more likely that you are to have it."

Of course, Ania went home that day and did her own online research. She hated to read the statistics, and she hated even more that the lipsticked woman was right.

"But that never made it inevitable," Nana added. "Besides, everyone is crazy."

"Are you okay?" Daria asks. "You look like you're unwell."

From the corner of the cabin, Cynthia emerges, a smile stretching her face into what seems like faux concern.

"Oh, Aaliyah," she says, "I hope you aren't coming down with something."

"What did you call me?" Ania asks.

"My goodness," the woman gasps, "you're sweating. If this keeps up, we'll need to take you to isolation. That seemed to help Daria."

"Maybe they've drugged you," Nana mutters, but Ania hasn't eaten or drunk anything. "Check your arms for pinpricks. They might've done it while you were asleep, and if you say anything, they'll only claim it was a spider bite."

Ania can't see the skin of her arms, and to lift off the cloak would draw too much attention to herself. Instead, she stares at Daria again. She doesn't seem to be hurt or scared by someone, in fact, she seems revitalized.

"Now come on, girls," Cynthia snaps as she claps her hands together. "Once you are in your nightwear, fold up your day clothes and place them in the drawer next to your bed. After you are washed, we will have lights out and no noise. Is that clear?"

All the girls nod in compliance. All except Ania, who stares at Daria some more. And then she realizes what is different about the girl; she isn't wearing her nose-ring.

Chapter Twenty

Not really here

Like automatons, the teenagers follow Cynthia's instructions with silent diligence. All except Ania, who sits on her bed and nurses a twisted stomach.

"You're jealous," Nana mutters as her granddaughter watches Cynthia snaking an arm around Daria's shoulders.

"Thought she was a troublemaker," Ania sneers to herself.

"Come now," Nana says with a sigh. "You've seen how jealousy can make a person ugly. Don't let it twist you."

"I'm not jealous," Ania insists.

"This is probably part of the plan," Nana continues, "to divide you. You've already been weakened by a swirl of chaos, and now you can't even turn to the people who might have supported you. Soon they'll present you a solution that you'll feel compelled to accept, just to end this chaos."

"Lights out," Cynthia demands, and Sophie plunges the cabin into darkness. Ania hasn't had time to get changed, but this doesn't seem to matter to the counselors who march out of the cabin and slam the door behind them.

Still in her hooded cloak, Ania slips beneath a thin sheet that is barely large enough to cover her.

She listens to the jangle of keys as someone locks the cabin door from the outside. With a dull thud, a bolt is slid across a chamber.

"All these latches and bolts and locks," Nana mutters, "and still the dangers can get in."

"Daria?" Ania whispers.

No response.

"Daria?" Ania repeats, only this time a little louder.

"What?" Daria snarls.

"Are you okay?" Ania asks.

"Yeah. Why?"

"You were…I heard you earlier on. When I was in a tunnel, I heard you making strange sounds, and… You sounded like…" She didn't know how to describe it, and she wasn't even sure it was the same person. "I don't know," Ania finally mutters. "Never mind."

"Go to sleep," Daria says.

"I will, but…I'm scared. I've seen some strange stuff. I mean, in Cynthia's office, she showed me some security monitors, and she wanted me to believe that it was only footage of the mall. She was trying to reassure me that we were safe here, only…When she left the room, one monitor, well, it showed a girl. I think it was a girl. I mean, she wasn't moving, so it could have been a mannequin. But the girl was in a bedroom and…"

Her words disappear in the darkness of the cabin. She thought by now there would be more light to creep in between the gaps in the shades. But it is a thick darkness that holds them in place in their beds.

"You need to stop," someone says. Ania thought it was Daria, but the voice was deeper. Bestial.

"Stop," it repeats.

"But the girl…"

"I said stop," someone yells, the cabin shuddering with the boom of the voice.

"You're gonna get us all into trouble," another voice adds. This one is quieter, sounding more like a teenage girl. "You need to just stop all of this and do what they say."

"Who is that?"

"It's Ellie. Listen, Ania, please, just stop all this. You shouldn't provoke them, shouldn't disobey them. You know there have been girls who have gone missing, so why risk it?"

Cold dread spreads through Ania's veins.

"I don't know why you're saying this," Ania lies, still unwilling to accept that any of this might be true. It is one thing for a bitter delivery man to talk about disappearances, but Ellie's words make it seem impossible to ignore.

"Yes, you do," Ellie replies. "I mean, they might go easier on you because you look like Cynthia's daughter, that might keep you safe. But that just means that we are more at risk. I don't want to suffer because you are making them angry."

"Oh, come on, they're running a camp. They're not dangerous."

"You've seen how they can get, how they can hurt you," Ellie continues.

Ania's cheek throbs, as if Sophie punched Ania a matter of minutes ago.

"Yes," Ania admits, "that hurt. And it hurt that you and Jill did nothing about it." She doesn't know why she suddenly feels so angry at this girl, but it makes her sit up in her bed so she can blink into the darkness and try to look the girl in the eye. All she sees is a dark shadow that she assumes to be Ellie laying on her bed. "You just looked the other way," Ania whispers. "You left me on the floor to get hurt like that. It was humiliating."

Silence.

"Why don't you have anything to say about that? You had plenty of opinions a moment ago."

Ania can hear something coming from Ellie's bed. Is she sniggering?

"Are you laughing at me?"

Muffled sounds of something scraping, distant conversation, and her chest tightens.

"The wolf pack," Nana snarls, and Ania's chest tightens some more. She tries to take in bigger mouthfuls of air, but this only makes her head lighter, and she starts to see stars.

If she tries to escape, will they block her route? Will she trip on their feet as they try to make her fall in the darkness?

"Then you'll be caught up in their web forever," Nana declares.

Another ripple of laughter.

"Oh, Aaaania," the voice croaks. "Silly little girl."

"Ellie? Is that you?"

"Little Annie, so helpless on the floor," the voice groans. "I've seen you, face down in the dirt. Did it hurt, little Annie?"

"Stop it. Why are you saying this?" Ania cries.

"Stupid. You're so stupid," someone whispers in the darkness. Then more sniggering. "We're watching you, waiting for you to fall." Another ripple of laughter.

"I want to go home," Ania whimpers, so softly that she barely makes a sound.

"Don't stress yourself," someone groans, the words stretching and distorting in the air. "So helpless, little Annie. Such a helpless little vessel."

"Caught in a trap," Nana whispers.

"And then what, Aaaniaaa?" the voice continues.

"This isn't sustainable," Nana adds, "to swim in this toxic brew. Don't forget that snow globe. It might be the only way to smash your way free."

Ania reaches into her pocket and her fingers grace the hard, glassy surface. The cold shocks her as she clings to it, a strange lifebuoy of sorts, but it's enough to fend off these fears.

"Slam it into their skull," someone mutters. "Break them open so you can see the yolky spillage." It isn't her grandmother's voice, but someone else, *something* else.

Ania imagines what it would be like to make slicing motions in the air with the glass object. How easy it might be to inflict so much damage.

"They're all asleep," someone whispers. "Like little sheep, all willing to follow the herd if it will keep them safe. All content to turn a blind eye to the violence as much as their reality. They're shadows, content to live in the in-between, just so none of the predators spot them. Which one are you, Ania, one of the sheep or a predator?"

"I don't know," Ania mutters. "I don't understand any of this."

"They're weakening you with mind games," Nana explains. "It's just a trick. Try not to listen."

Ania covers her ears with her hands, the coarse fabric of the cloak scratching her skin.

"I just want to go home," Ania mutters, each word an effort to articulate as they become ladened with exhaustion.

Something scampers from the direction of Ellie's bed.

"I don't know…" Ania slurs, her eyelids closing as she falls back onto her bed. She can hear the jingling of jewelry or keys.

"Or the footsteps of fairies," Nana whispers, and Ania is asleep.

Chapter Twenty-One

Arachnid

Awake. A splinter of moonlight breaks through a gap in the curtains, so Ania can see the outline of the bodies of three teenagers beneath their sheets. They are still, frozen in sleep, Ania presumes, so she tries not to make a sound as she slips from her bed.

Her movements feel different, more agile, and she makes quick progress across the cabin. She realizes she is lighter than usual, so there are no creaks of the splintered floorboards, no dull thud of a footstep. Is she even there?

She scampers some more, actually scampers, and then she realizes that she is small, so small, in fact, that she can slip between the gaps in the floorboards. No latch, bolt, or lock can confine her, no longer limited by the actions of others, she is free.

She races through the darkness, far from the cabin and across the courtyard. Finally, she plucks up the courage to glance down at her body, fully expecting to see the eight hairy legs of an arachnid. But she is intact, with two human legs and arms.

"You come from a long line of shape-shifters," Nana mutters. "You transformed so quickly from girl to woman, only for you to become something else. Now you can be whatever you like."

"I don't know what you are saying," Ania snaps. "I wish you wouldn't talk in such riddles."

"You know what my words mean, you really do. You just don't want to understand."

The cold is invigorating, and it energizes Ania so she can race faster, but she sees the forest ahead of her, and she staggers to a stop.

"I don't want this. Not this place," she pants in the cold night air. "Especially not alone."

"You can't go forward unless you go back," Nana murmurs.

Ania knows that just ahead the forest is the mall, where there are still more tunnels to explore. She still has hope that these will lead to her freedom, taking her to a nearby town, or even a highway, where someone will offer her help.

Still, the forest looms large in front of her. Again, she remembers the warnings from her parents, telling her about the dangers of oil cans and trash bags.

Behind her, she hears something. Sniggering? She thinks of Sophie and Carrie stalking her, playing hide-and-go-seek just so they can witness her torment. Revenge for telling Cynthia about their cruel words. She imagines how they might torment her some more the longer that she stays here. Will they wake her each night with the BS excuse of folding her clothes or cleaning up the bathroom? Will they make her stand alone in the middle of the cold yard, vulnerable to any prowling bear, fox, or wolf? Power tripping on trapped kids, like shooting fish in a barrel, it makes her want to scream, so she turns around. But no one is there.

"Ania," she hears. It could be the wind that has been freezing her ears, so they become numb.

"Ania," she hears again, and then footsteps, so this time she breaks into a run.

"Go on," Nana urges, and so she slips into the darkness of the forest. She is careful to duck beneath low-hanging branches, and her lungs start to heave. She can taste blood, and she knows that she will find the pungent scent of leather and something else, something metallic and spicy. But it doesn't slow her pace.

"Can't be hurt by memories," she says in unison with her grandmother.

Some trees are stooped, and their branches look like the outstretched arms of angry men in pursuit. She imagines their smaller branches, like fingers, curling round her wrists and pinning her to the ground. She imagines their force, grown over decades in this forest, and how it could squeeze her until she breaks. She imagines how fetid the dirt would smell as she is pushed into the ground again and again.

She can hear the mournful caw of a solitary raven, and she remembers screaming, “I don’t want this.” But no one was listening.

Chapter Twenty-Two

Schizosis

Subreddit: Psychosis

u/deadwolf#03:
Ever heard or seen anything?
u/rizlasykes#09:
You're gonna have to be more specific with your questions. Dumbass.
u/deadwolf#03:
Okay, wiseass, ever heard or seen anything that isn't there? You know, seeing and hearing things that don't really exist. I kinda made that clear by calling the sub psychosis, didn't I?
Who's the dumbass now?
u/rizlasykes#09:
Seeing things that don't exist? I can imagine you do. You probably see a girl who says she's interested in you, who calls to you, like some siren, and wants to do the dirty with you.
I can understand why you think she doesn't exist. Who would be interested in you? You can't get girlfriends, you dominate them.
u/deadwolf#03:
You know nothing about me. Stick to the topic or go troll someone else.

u/rizlasykes#09:
Some people can't take a joke.
u/deadwolf#03:
Jokes are supposed to be funny. That wasn't funny.
u/rizlasykes#09:
So, come on, what have you been seeing or hearing that isn't really there?
u/deadwolf#03:
I don't want to say.
u/rizlasykes#09:
So why start a sub on it?
u/deadwolf#03:
I can ask a question, can't I? I don't have to give details.
u/rizlasykes#09:
Come on, spill it. What you been seeing?
u/deadwolf#03:
I don't wanna say it online.
u/rizlasykes#09:
Pussy.
u/deadwolf#03:
Says you.
u/rizlasykes#09:
No, you.
u/deadwolf#03:
I don't wanna say it because someone might find out.
u/rizlasykes#09:
Trust me, no one cares about your subs.
u/deadwolf#03:
Yes, they do. There are people reading this right now, live, as I type it.
u/rizlasykes#09:
BS.
u/deadwolf#03:
It's true.
u/rizlasykes#09:
Now you can add paranoia to your hallucinations.
You realize what this is, what you're admitting to?
u/deadwolf#03:
?
u/rizlasykes#09:
Schizophrenia. Hallucinations, paranoia, it all points to

schizophrenia.
It's official, dude, you're a nut job. Should be locked up somewhere and medicated. Maybe chop some of your brain out if the electro-shock stuff doesn't work.
u/deadwolf#03:
You'd know about nut jobs. Besides, you can't say things like that. Aren't you supposed to be woke? Careful, now, you'll get cancelled.
u/rizlasykes#09:
Wacko.
u/deadwolf#03:
Whatever.
u/rizlasykes#09:
Always one bad apple in every crop.
Hey, relax, I'm just winding you up. Besides, who's to say what is real?
u/deadwolf#03:
?
u/rizlasykes#09:
You know, who's to say you are hallucinating or really seeing things that other people can't see? You know there's so much yet to explore, in time and space. Who's to say what you are seeing doesn't really exist?
u/deadwolf#03:
I don't know what you mean.
u/rizlasykes#09:
Yeah, I figured you wouldn't. So sad. All those teenagers diagnosed with schizophrenia when maybe, just maybe, they opened their eyes to what others couldn't see. Should we really persecute them, lock them up, manacle them, or forcibly medicate them just because we don't see or hear what they do? A blind man doesn't call you psychotic when they don't see what you do. None of us are in their skin, none of us can feel what they feel.
So, come on, tell me what you've seen and heard.
u/deadwolf#03:
No.
u/rizlasykes#09:
Is it a spider crawling down the back of your neck? Is it a wolf panting in your face when you try to sleep? Or hooded creatures that smell so bad?
u/deadwolf#03:
Stop.

u/rizlasykes#09:
Why? Come on, tell me what you've seen. Tell me what you've heard.
u/deadwolf#03:
I've told you, I can't. They're watching.
And they're watching you, too.
u/rizlasykes#09:
Whatevs.
I'm out.
u/deadwolf#03:
They're gonna find you.
They're coming.

Source: https//www.[redacted].com
Accessed November 4, 2020, at 7:30 PM

Chapter Twenty-Three

Awake

With a gasp, the forest recedes, and Ania returns to the cabin, somehow slipping through the gaps in the floorboards again.

Panting, she climbs onto her bed and slips beneath the sheets.

A muffled moan.

"Ellie?" Ania asks.

Silence clings to the darkness.

"Jill? Daria?"

Another muffled moan, only this time it is louder.

"Who is that?" Ania asks.

Silence again. Then a cough.

"Oh, shut up," the voice croaks. "You don't stop whining."

The light flicks on without warning, sending a burning glare through Ania's eyes.

Carrie. She's sitting on the edge of Ania's bed, sneering as she picks something from beneath her fingernails.

"*Lesbi-honest*, I don't want to be here any more than you want me here. But Cynthia told me to check on you, so that's what I'm doing. She heard screaming from the cabin, she was worried you might be upset or unwell or something. You haven't been crying for mommy, have you?"

"No."

"Good, cos she's not coming," Carrie sneers. "You're stuck here with us. And, *lesbi-honest*, I don't think you're gonna be leaving here anytime soon."

Something catches Ania's eye, something twinkling in the overhead light. A bracelet rattling on Carrie's big wrist. Ania reaches for her own arm, expecting to find a cluster of silver pendants beneath her palm, but all she feels is her bare skin.

"That's mine," Ania snarls. "Give it back."

"What? This? Cynthia gave it to me. I swear, you're losing it, Annie."

"Don't call me that," she snarls.

"Why? That's your name. *Lesbi-honest*, I could call you much worse." Carrie splutters a clumsy laugh and a droplet of her spittle lands on Ania's lip.

"Stop." She has no more fight in her, so she just turns in the bed so she doesn't have to face the counselor's oily sneer.

"Oh, come on," Carrie continues, "don't be like that. What's the matter, can't take a joke? *Lesbi-honest*. It's funny. You lost your sense of humor? You're such a snowflake."

"Say what you like," Ania says with a sigh, wishing the exhaustion would send her back to sleep.

"Okay, okay, I'll stop. Wouldn't want to upset you or anything. Wouldn't want you to go running to mommy Cynthia again, now, would I?"

Ania braces herself, expecting some kind of slap, at least.

"That wasn't smart of you, Annie. Thanks to you, Cynthia is pissed at me. Why did you have to open your big mouth?"

Ania pulls the hood around her ears and face, hoping that if she can't see her, then the counselor might cease to exist.

"I thought we were friends," Carrie adds.

This jars, and Ania wants to snap back at her, but she doesn't want to get hit.

"Girls need to stick together," Carrie declares. Her voice has gone up an octave, making her sound several years younger.

"Come on, Annie, aren't we bessies? Bessies need to stick together."

"What?"

The lights go out just as Ania turns back to look at Carrie. The counselor has jumped to her feet, transforming into a shadow that towers over her bed.

"Annie, I miss you," the voice hisses. "Annie, why don't you come back and play with us?"

"Why are you saying that?"

Ania tries to see in the darkness, but all she can see is the shadow moving about the cabin.

"Girls stick together," the voice repeats. "Stuck and sticky, so we'll tear if we try to go our separate ways. Isn't that right, Annie? No one liked you, not even your own mother. If she did, why would she send you here? Far away from her, cast out, like you're a foul stench."

"What is this?" Ania tries to yell, but she makes no sound. She shakes her head as she can hear the voice screeching at her.

"Let's go down to the woods today, Annie."

"No," Ania shouts, still silent, no matter the volcanic rage that erupts from within her. An implosion, silent and deadly.

Her head won't stop shaking back and forth, and the cabin blurs, and then she has shaken herself free of the flimsy wooden structure.

Once again, she finds herself in the cold night air. Her head feels so heavy that her neck aches under the pressure. Her mouth is dry and burns with some kind of bitter chemical. Voices are calling her, and they seem close enough for the heat of their breath on her neck, but they are nowhere to be seen. All she can see is a sunrise spilling out across the horizon just past the courtyard. It doesn't look right; the colors are too vivid and garish for it to be real. It reminds her of a badly illustrated commercial, or a strange fever dream.

Beyond the courtyard, she sees the forest, and she knows she must run again. But she doesn't have the strength. She wants to curl up beneath the sunrise and wait for rescue. She's seen this in films and soap operas, where her favorite characters just wait to be scooped up by someone big and strong. They never have to fight, never have to show so much strength.

"Bad things happen to bad people," she hears someone whisper, and a rage ignites in her. It makes her break into a run, plunging deep into the forest.

She keeps going, squeezing out every last breath to push her limbs onwards. Yet still the forest stretches out for as far as she could see when she started to run.

"Infinite. Perpetual torment," she hears someone say.

She stumbles. Her foot must have caught on something, a rock, maybe, and she staggers until she crumples into a pile on the ground. Her hands take the brunt of the fall, and in the amber light of dawn she can see the moist sheen of a bloody wound. She feels no pain.

A sudden snarl at her ear makes her run again, only this time she pushes herself beyond anything that feels healthy. So hard that she can feel the damp between her legs. She wants to believe it is sweat, but she knows it isn't, but it doesn't matter, so long as she can break free of this forest.

She keeps running faster, pushing further, only to find that darkness is descending. Instead of dawn, it is still the night, and it thickens all around her. She tries to run but her feet get heavy, and she staggers, and then comes to a stop. Still, the darkness thickens, and it pulls on her, dragging her down into the ground.

During one of her voyages across the dark web, she found what was claimed to be a person drowning in quicksand. She watched in horror and intrigue, knowing it was wrong, but she could not stop herself with no one there to shame her away from it.

She watched the entire video. The kid, a girl of around her age, drowned (suffocated?) before her eyes, and she tried to feel guilty for watching it.

"Bad things happen to bad people."

She refuses to succumb. She thrashes about, and even though the darkness fills her mouth as she tries to wail, she keeps fighting, harder and harder. Her mouth is filled, and so is her throat, in fact, it is swollen by the weight of it all, and she fears it might burst apart.

She shuts her eyes and she takes a deep breath.

And then it stops.

There is no crushing weight on her. She opens her eyes to a rush of light and air as she gasps and figures out her surroundings. She is back in her bed in the cabin, staring again at the wooden ceiling, and the silence is stirred by the soft sighs of the sleeping girls.

"You can't outpace your mind," Nana mutters. "You're looping. The only way to go is through the darkness, to stay in the forest until it is over. You need to make it through the trees to the other side."

Her whole body locks up at the thought of this.

"You aren't making progress," Nana continues, "because you're too afraid to truly look at the past."

"I'm not afraid," Ania insists. "Not anymore."

"Then admit it," Nana whispers to her. She knows she has to go gently. "Abigail was never your friend. She tricked you. She left you alone in those woods that night, where Smithson and his friends found you."

"Stop," Ania snaps. "I don't want to remember."

“Too late,” Nana whispers, “you already do.”

Chapter Twenty-Four

When you go down to the woods

The night of Halloween. When kids and parents dress up and pretend that they are not really ghouls and witches and tormentors. The one night of the year when they acknowledge all that is bloody and painful, all that is cruel. And they laugh at it, as if it is a parade of something far beyond the life they live.

She was told to meet Abigail here, and she knew she shouldn't go. Her parents told her never to go into the forest at the end of Mount Pelion Way. They warned her about the oil cans and trash bags and unwanted refrigerators that had been dumped there. Death traps for the unwary. But Abigail told her that she had to. "I need you," Abigail insisted, "and that's what friends do."

Her friend never showed, so Ania was left alone in the forest when Smithson appeared with Cory and Aedean.

"How you doing, Ania?" Smithson said with a snigger. "Yeah, how you doing?" Aedean and Cory echoed.

"Run," Nana bellowed. But Ania didn't run, she didn't want them to laugh at her showing signs of panic, so she took a few steps backwards. She stumbled, uncertain, so she turned away from them and started to walk away.

She plunged deeper into the forest, forcing the boys to follow.

She could hear their footsteps snapping twigs and crunching leaves. Her heart quickened with every pace, and a raven cawed from up above.

Hope of escape became obscured by the fading light, and she thought about what would happen next. Would it hurt? Would it be quick?

She sank into the darkness, as if she had slipped beneath the surface of a lake, and she felt a sense of calm. Birdsong was muted, the leaves were still, and even the syncopated shuffle of the train was shut out from her world.

When she heard their footsteps gaining on her, she cried out for them to "Stop." She wished her voice had sounded deeper, the growl of a predator rather than the fragile plea of their prey.

Too quickly they were so close that Ania could smell their vapor trail, the pungent male scent of leather and something else, something metallic and spicy.

"I don't know what games you girls are playing with us," she heard Smithson sneer. "But you or Abigail wanted to meet us. So here we are."

She stopped walking, but still she would not turn to face them. She could hear her breath, but she couldn't feel the movement of her body.

"You know, you're such a loser to do all this running around for her," he continued. "You're always trailing her around, always acting like her fucking slave. Why do you let her boss you around like that? Get a mind of your own, for fuck's sake."

She didn't know what to say to this, so she just stood there, waiting for his next move.

"I hope you aren't going to waste my time," Smithson added. "You need to make sure that you've made it worth my while."

He grabbed Ania's wrists. In one foolish moment, she imagined the trees sprouting arms and hands to seize her. At that time, she still had hope that Mother Earth would not turn against her like that, not when Ania had spent her life defending all her creatures. But then again, Mother Earth created these three boys, and entire armies of them, in nations throughout the world. Too late, she realized that Mother Earth had never been her friend.

Smithson squeezed her wrists so tightly that she feared she would snap. He used a force strong enough to topple her to the ground, face smushing in damp soil that stank of something rotten.

He ran his fingers over her cheeks and said, "Your skin is

surprisingly soft, silly girl," and then his hands slipped around her throat. She braced herself, half-expecting that to be the end. She wanted it to be, she didn't want any pain. But she didn't die.

He pushed his weight onto her, and Ania's face sank deeper in the dirt. She turned her head so she could breathe, and she could see in the distance a raven. It didn't try to save her, didn't even seem that bothered. Indifferent, it preened its feathers as it watched from a nearby tree.

At one point, she wondered if they were going to smash her skull with a rock. Would they form a pact to hide the body, in the thicker part of the forest, or up in the hills where there were no houses and prying eyes? She could have been buried with the items her mom left for her grandmother, more offerings for the dead to enjoy.

"Stop," she croaked through a hand-tightened throat. He squeezed a little tighter, feeling out the idea of killing her, but then he relented, allowing the air to reach her brain.

"Aw," he sneered, "poor little Annie. Do you need your mommy? Do you want your witch bitch of a mommy?"

"Please," Ania gasped. "Why are you doing this?"

She imagined how dirty his fingernails were as they started to claw at her. He explored her terrain, making good headway, and for a while he made no sound. She imagined him blank-faced and relentless, a zombie making its way from the underworld.

Then the spell was broken, and he spoke again.

"Oh come, now, little Annie, I thought you liked to play in here, far from the watchful eye."

"Why are you doing this?" she gasped.

"Am I doing this? Who's to tell."

He was possessed, his voice so deep it reverberated around the woodland.

"I want to go home," Ania tried to scream, but all she managed was a muffled wail. So she continued to silently wail in her head, "Let me go, let me go, let me go."

Afterwards, she managed to struggle to her feet. Her head swam with something fluid; ice water, a chemical imbalance. Thoughts trapped in a hardened snow globe.

Dizzy, she staggered through the dark forest. She felt branches whip at her head, but she didn't flinch. In the distance, she could hear trick or treaters whooping and yelling.

She heard the boys behind her, smelled their scent as they approached, and just when she thought they were upon her again, the light exploded, and she was free of the forest.

Chapter Twenty-Five

Monstermare

Screaming, someone is screaming.

Ania is frantic as the screaming gets worse. She is certain this child she can hear, a girl, perhaps, is slipping from her. Slipping into what? Jaws of metal, some kind of machine she has seen online that people use to crush all manner of objects. Squish mallows, inflatable balls, cans of tomato to splatter red paste all over the place. A doll? Surely it must have been a doll.

She scrabbles about her bed, trying to find this child, this girl, who needs help. Her fingers claw at the sheet, and then the mattress. Bestial, she keeps clawing and digging her way through bed springs to the wooden floor. She tears at the floorboards, revealing the dirt of outside, and then she is free again, crawling out into the cold night air in search of the forest.

She ignores the voices that once again call for her, and she ignores the sunrise or sunset or whatever might be spilling that yolky stain across the sky. Already, she is across the courtyard and plunging into the forest. Second thoughts are obscured by the fading light of the woods, and the trees and bushes whip by, but she is relentless.

She sees the rock that would have tripped her, and she jumps over it, bracing herself for the snarl in her ear. It doesn't come.

Through the trees, Ania thinks she sees the hill her mother used to climb, the place Eris would bury notes for Nana. Ania allows herself to become snared on an image of burying herself there, where her mother can find her and Nana. A portal to another dimension where all three generations unite. Ania can feel the weight of the dirt as she allows herself to be buried, but the tree roots reject her. They push and tear at her, telling her that she is not welcome. But then they relent. The roots recede, and she sinks deeper into the dirt, and she believes that she is safe. Until she is not. Until she feels the roots looping round her neck and pulling tight. They hold her fast.

"Leave me alone," Ania thinks she might gasp. But the pressure of the roots around her throat would make her words come out in a tangled mess of phlegm and desperation. "Aw," she might hear someone sneer. But that doesn't make sense, because trees don't sneer. She wonders if the gathering roots are making sounds as they rub against each other, and loop round her wrists and ankles.

She imagines they are going to taunt her.

"Aw," they might say, "poor little Annie. Do you need your mommy? Do you want your witch bitch of a mommy?"

And would she try to plead in response? Would she try to ask why they were doing this? If she did, dirt would fill her mouth and silence her. It would be too late to say or do anything, too late to escape and tell the truth. All she would do was scream silently in her head.

"I want to go home."

She doesn't climb any hill, and she doesn't bury herself. Instead, she keeps running faster, pushing further, and then the darkness gives way to the lights surrounding the mall. The endless concrete building looms on her horizon, making her quicken her pace.

What now? She feels foolish to admit that she had hopes of waking in her bed, having been sleeping as soundly as that girl in the security footage. Of course, that would be too simple, as unrealistic as the plots of her favorite soap operas.

She has no choice but to go into the mall; she can search Cynthia's office again and try to find car keys or a working cell phone. Failing that, she will have to push deeper into those tunnels.

Walking up to the entrance, she notices that the lettering above her head looks different. What was once the dark shadows of *Polemis Park Mall* now looked like something else. In the dim light, she can't make it out. The letters look more like symbols, and for a moment, Ania wonders if Cynthia has decided to use emojis instead of letters. Her pitiful attempt to connect with the young? Out of all the tasks to complete in this derelict building, and that woman decides to play around with the nameplate?

"Just another mind game?" Nana suggests.

Ania heaves open the heavy glass door and steps into the damp-filled gloom. The crunch of each footstep echoes in the vast empty space. A mannequin stands in a nearby window, head aloof and arms outstretched with pride for her sequin dress. Although she knows this is foolish, Ania can't help feeling watched and judged by the mannequin as she walks by.

Ahead of her, a wall has collapsed. Probably under the weight of a leaking pipe that froze and burst. Rubble has cascaded into the corridor that she is walking down, so she is going to have to climb over it. Her mind frays on the thought of a severed artery, torn on some piece of jagged metal or glass.

"There might be another way," Nana suggests.

Movement from behind her, so Ania turns, and she finds a dangling wire. It dances with life, and she knows she should be scared of it, but she is hypnotized by the sparks and buzz.

More movement, this time from the rubble ahead of her. Something is scampering. An arachnid? But it looks too large for that. It is round, with legs carrying it. She realizes what it is, but still won't believe it. A human head? It is moved by four legs that have sprouted from either side, like the roots of an overly ripe potato. She can see bloody wounds where the legs have broken through the skin, and the face moans with a groan of agony or hunger.

Ania takes a step back and the arachnid scuttles towards her. And then she recognizes the face on the head, its mouth distorting in a combination of pleasure and pain.

"*Jesus wept*," Smithson groans and squeals as his long tongue flickers again at the blood. "Ania, what have you done? What have you done to me?"

His voice is deep one moment and then distorted into a high-pitched squeal, like that of a child or a pig at the slaughter.

When she takes another step away, Smithson, this thing with eight legs, scuttles closer, and too quickly he is upon her, the smell of putrefying flesh so close that it makes her gag. She feels its legs crawling up her body to her face, its long tongue flickering near Ania's mouth.

Smithson's legs, the *arachnid's* legs, split at the tips to create pincers that make clicking sounds, and two of the pincer-tipped legs pinch hold of Ania's eyelids, peeling them back so she can watch as he inserts his other six legs into every orifice of every person she can imagine. People she cares about, like her mother and father and brother, but also people she barely knows, who she has met fleetingly, but he can gain access to through Ania's eyes and mind. No one is spared as the images flicker like an old-fashioned movie reel, the picture grainy and seemingly stained with something. They start to flash faster, horror sped up to intensify the pain of it all, and Ania longs for it to stop.

But Smithson isn't finished. He licks his lips with a greed that can never be satiated, and as their eyes meet, he reminds Ania of that Halloween night. He stares at her, urging her to let it happen again.

Ania knows there is no choice. She has to end this, for herself and this baby that will always be half Smithson. If she does not act now, she will play a part in haunting this world with a malevolence that might never end. Whatever she produces might produce more violence, and so it will continue.

Chapter Twenty-Six

Horror story

"But where's the baby," they holler and howl. "What have you done with it, you filthy creature? Where is the baby?" they holler and howl again, only this time a little louder, so loud and beset with rage that they sound like a girl. They're not a girl, of course, because girls do not have the power to demand things about babies. In fact, they take offence that you would suggest such a thing, to imply that they are debased and subjugated to the ranks of the weak, the fairer sex, the ones who must lie back and take it.

The ones who scream for the baby are men, of course, because they wear suits, and suits show that they have power, power to decide what girls should do and not do, how they should behave, and what they should do about a life that grows inside them. They create the rules even though they would never suffer a similar fate; they would never have to watch something growing each day as they wait for it to tear its way from their body. They would not have to look it in the eye and remember each day how it was created with such violence and rage, a rage that only men can possess and inflict on others through dark deeds in an equally dark forest, away from view and safe in the knowledge that their parents will never discover the shame of it. But those parents wouldn't judge them, not really, because they believe that nothing will break the bond between parent and child, not if their boy can get away with it and keep things hushed up in the darkness of that forest.

And if things escape? If the ripples of trauma distort their reality and darken their skies? Then these parents will paint the *tattle-tellers*, these snitches, as misfits or witches who deserve to be hanged or burned at the stake. Just see how these *tattle-tellers*, these scapegoats, can be hounded with the modern-day pitchforks of cell phones to record evidence of preconceptions that have been planted and propagated by the parents, and then confirmed by friends, therapists and psychologists alike. All will claim to see the same evidence of insanity in these scapegoats. A kind of social contagion will spread so that everyone sees through the same eyes. And if you cannot see it the same way? Then just cover your eyes because you don't want to be left out in the cold, a lone wolf vulnerable to the pack.

Once you see through the eyes of everyone else, it becomes easier to view these scapegoats as insane because you just tell yourself that their eyes cannot be trusted. Their eyes, after all, suffer from some kind of psychosis, and this makes sense because you've read about hallucinations and the upsurge in schizophrenia, especially amongst teens. This has all been proven, beyond a shadow of a doubt, by friends, therapists and psychologists alike who point to research that has been verified by other friends, therapists and psychologists, who have verified it with other friends, therapists and psychologists, and don't think too hard about how stuck you feel on a Möbius loop of verification, an echo chamber of reassurance, because if you blink and see things too clearly, they might just say that the insanity rests with you.

Doesn't it feel better to just pretend to believe what they tell you? Don't you feel safe again, now that you know that the wrongdoer is wrong, which makes you all right? And the parents of the boy feel right, too, so their child is not wrong, and they are not wrong, because D1 athletes are heroes not villains, after all, and they deserve to make more heroes who can also become D1 athletes, and so the story goes on and on, round the loop again, and all the boys can roam scot-free from their darkened forests, still swinging those sticks like a dick.

This is how a horror story grows.

Chapter Twenty-Seven

God-fearful

Subreddit: Abor-hating

u/deadwolf#03:
What's the deal with someone who's having a baby? Do they have to keep the baby if you want them to? Asking for a friend and I'd appreciate if everyone would keep the comments respectful. You know, no preaching.
u/rizlasykes#09:
Sure, dude, there you go again about your 'friend.'
u/deadwolf#03:
I don't know why you waste your time following me around these forums. Get a life.
u/rizlasykes#09:
Like you did? You went and got a life, made a life with some poor unsuspecting girl, and now what do you wanna do? Make the poor girl keep it or get rid of it? Either way, you're sick.
u/deadwolf#03:
How can this loser keep adding comments when I've blocked him?
u/deadwolf#03:
Asking again, in case it was missed the first time. How can someone make someone keep their baby? There must be laws and stuff.
u/VR_666:

I can certainly help you with that. There have been plenty of anti-abortion measures introduced. In particular, there are measures to require parental consent for certain procedures, there are restrictions on access (under certain conditions), and in some cases, there is an outright ban. It really depends on which procedure you are asking about.

u/deadwolf#03:

Are there any places that she can go to? My mom told me that in the old days, girls would be sent away to have the baby. They wanted to keep the shame away from the family, or something like that. I dunno, I got bored and stopped listening after a while.

u/rizlasykes#09:

And I bet your mom is so proud of you. Knocking some girl up. Ever heard of birth control? And what's that about shame? It isn't the girl who should be carrying the shame. That's on you.

u/deadwolf#03:

I'm gonna ignore the troll.

What about school kids?

u/VR_666:

I apologize, but you will need to clarify your question.

u/deadwolf#03:

What if the girl carrying the kid is a school kid?

u/rizlasykes#09:

You're sick.

u/VR_666:

Many measures apply regardless of the age of the mother carrying the baby.

u/deadwolf#03:

What about if she didn't want to do any of it.

u/rizlasykes#09:

Ugh. Someone have this person arrested.

u/deadwolf#03:

Asking again, so we can ignore the trolls: What about if she didn't want to do any of it.

u/VR_666:

I am sorry but I again ask that you clarify your question.

u/rizlasykes#09:

He's asking if you can force someone to carry the baby that you forcibly impregnated her with.

u/deadwolf#03:

Who said anything about force? You know nothing about this.

u/rizlasykes#09:
Oh, we know everything about this.
u/deadwolf#03:
What? About what? You know nothing.
u/rizlasykes#09:
Call yourself a Christian and God-fearing? You dress up smartly to go to church each Sunday, sure, but then you force a child to endure the pain of labor when you have forced her into this position? Doesn't sound very Christian to me.
u/deadwolf#03:
You don't know anything about me.
u/rizlasykes#09:
We know everything. We are everywhere, and we've been watching you.

Source: https//www.[redacted].com
Accessed November 4, 2020, at 7:30 PM

Chapter Twenty-Eight

A glitch in the matrix

Something scares Smithson, the arachnid, and it scuttles into the darkness.

Ania can hear a man's voice, and she thinks that she recognizes it.

"Dad?" she calls.

No one replies.

A shadow traces its way across the wall at the end of the corridor, near the dried-up fountain. As she approaches it, she notices that the coins have disappeared.

"They ran out of hope," Nana mutters, but Ania doesn't stop to listen. Already she has passed the silent escalators and the elevator, and she is at the door to Cynthia's office. From behind the opaque glass, light dances like an open flame.

"Burning evidence?" Nana suggests.

Opening the door, Ania realizes that the light is coming from the dancing static of the security monitors. The closet doors are wide open to reveal all the screens. The shots rotate through different corners of the mall, then to the cabin, and also the courtyard where she can see the edge of the forest.

The monitors change their shots again, footage from different cameras, and one screen shows the girl, or the mannequin, again.

She is still in a bed, only this time the image is clearer, with less jumping static. She can see the face, and the mono brow, and the hair that shines with grease. Abigail? She feels like someone is taunting her with this, trying to remind her of the days that followed Halloween.

After she missed her period, after she took the test, she told Abigail, because she thought that's what girls do.

She waited until after school, when they were in the privacy of Abigail's bedroom, before she told her friend about the child she was carrying.

Instead of hugging Ania, Abigail recoiled.

"That's disgusting," she sneered. "What the fuck is wrong with you? Ever heard of protection?"

"I didn't…"

"But who?" Abigail asked. "Who's the dad?"

Ania thought her friend had already guessed it, I mean, who else could it be?

"Smithson. The woods…"

"Are you kidding? That was a prank, a Halloween scare. You…You're disgusting. You knew I liked him.":

"I didn't…"

Already Abigail had a hold of Ania's elbow as she steered her out.

"Get out of my bedroom and get out of my house," she spat. "Get out and keep away from me, you bitch."

She returned home to the smell of something browning on a griddle. Eris was conjuring up new dishes to impress her family, and Ania could hear her humming contentedly as she moved about the kitchen.

Lost to herself, Ania floated past the stairs and toyed with the idea of climbing to the top and then letting herself freefall. She imagined the crimson stain that would emerge from between her legs, and she felt horrible for even thinking of it.

Too quickly, she pulled herself away from the stairs and forced herself to stay in the kitchen. She needed to get lost in their chaos, so she let her brother's words sink in, even though they held little meaning.

"…infantilizing her," Dylan muttered to their mother. "She never grew up," he added.

"I don't know what you are talking about," their mother replied.

"All that fussing after her. Admit it, you didn't want her to grow up because then she would've escaped your clutches. Then what would you have done? Kept a replica of her in the attic?"

Eris ignored him and started to slice some peppers.

"I'm not really here," Ania muttered.

"What was that?" Eris didn't look up from the chopping board.

"Where's my family?"

The sound of Ania's father, so sudden and so close to her ear, made her jump.

She watched as he planted a kiss on his wife's forehead, and the softness of this gesture made her want to cry.

"I'm glad to see you wearing that at last." Paris gestured to Eris' wrist where Ania could see that a bracelet was hanging. A bracelet with panda pendants.

"The jingling makes you sound like a fairground ride," Dylan sneered.

"Bad things happen to bad people," she heard someone say. The words repeated so relentlessly that she felt it burning into her skin.

"I'm not a bad person," she wanted to shriek.

"The jingling makes you sound like a fairground ride," Dylan repeated.

"I'm glad to see you wearing that at last," Paris repeated, and then adding, "Where's my family?" as his smile fell and, ashen faced, he retreated from the room. Even her mother stopped chopping, and the peppers shriveled to an ash-like grey.

A glitch in the matrix, a glitch in the algorithm, everyone stuck on repeat. Or maybe in retreat.

"I'm not really here," Ania muttered again, and then she wasn't.

Chapter Twenty-Nine

Buried treasure

"You know that Abigail told Smithson," Nana adds. "She told him about your pregnancy, and he went into damage control."

Ania knows and can see all of it. In fact, she sees so much that the guilt hurts her eyes. It was Ania who told Abigail about the clearing by the brook, explaining that this was how she would communicate with her mother if there was ever something difficult to say.

Abigail and Smithson would know that Ania buried a letter for her mother up there, telling her what Smithson had done. And she knows that one of them, maybe even both of them, crept up there to switch the letters and blame the pregnancy on someone else.

If they hadn't switched the letters, then this is what Eris would have found from her daughter:

Mom,

I wish I could tell you this to your face, but I cannot form the words in my mouth. So my hope is that you read this before it is too late. I am guessing that you know I have been following you here, where you've buried notes to your mom. It should only be a matter of time before you catch me here and then I can show you these letters.

Something horrible happened, and I never wanted it. He made me do it. I am sorry, I truly am. It disgusts me to even write this.

It was Smithson. Abigail told me to go to the woods that Halloween night. She made me think that she was meeting him there and that I should go to look after her. She made me believe that this is what friends do, that we look after each other. But I think she tricked me, I think she set me up so I would be alone there with Smithson and his friends.

He hurt me. I didn't want to do it, but he made me. I know you already hate him, and his parents, and all the others on Mount Pelion Way, and now I know why. They will probably cover this up, probably try to blame someone else, so that's why I need you to know the truth.

My period stopped a while back and I have been feeling funny. I am so scared that he has made me pregnant.
If I told Smithson, he would tell me that we should keep this a secret. But how is this going to stay a secret when my belly grows big? I am trapped and I don't know what to do.

I love you, and I want you to believe me.

Please believe me, Mom, and help me. I love you. Please don't hate me. Xxx

Abigail or Smithson, maybe both, replaced this letter with their own version of the truth about that Halloween night. In their version, Smithson could not be blamed. In their version, things were twisted so much that they blamed Ania's pregnancy on her own father, Paris.

Abigail knew how to forge Ania's handwriting. She had a habit of missing class, so she had a pile of Ania's notes that she could copy. She took her time to ensure that each g, each j, each q, each y was curved at just the right angle. Abigail or Smithson, maybe both, crept up the hill to the clearing by the brook, and this is what they buried for Eris to find:

Mom,

I wish I could tell you this to your face, but I cannot form the words in my mouth. So my hope is that you read this before it is too late. I am guessing that you know I have been following you here, where you've buried notes to your Mom. It should only be a matter of time before you catch me here and then I can show you these letters.

Something horrible happened, and I never wanted it. He made me do it. I am sorry, I truly am. It disgusts me to even write this.

I know you love him, and you have loved him for longer than Dylan or I have even lived, but he forced me.

My period stopped a while back and I have been feeling funny. I am so scared that he has made me pregnant. He used to tell me that we should keep this a secret.
But how is it going to stay that way when my belly grows big? I am trapped and I don't know what to do.

It wasn't Smithson or Cory or Aedean. I had a crush on them, and we fooled around in the woods that Halloween night, but they never hurt me. We never did anything that I didn't want to do, and never anything serious, nothing that would make me stop my period.

Only he did that, and he made me. He's been making me do it for a while. I never wanted to, I promise you. I love you, and I want you to believe me.

Please believe me, Mom. I love you. Please don't hate me. Xxx

"It's lies," Ania cries as her throat aches, "all lies. What kind of person could even dream up a lie like that? It's sick, twisted. My father was innocent, and yet Abigail was willing to lie about him to protect Smithson. She lied for the worst possible reason, and that was to protect a man."

The rage burns so intensely beneath Ania's skin that she has images of it vaporizing her, a blinding light sending heatwaves throughout her body. In this image, she can see herself, arms falling to her side, outstretched as she takes whatever is coming at her, an invisible force that makes her body jolt with every wave of it. And then she feels it, the surface of her skin breaking open as something red emerges from the cracks in her skin. She thinks it might be blood, but it is powdery, and as soon as it escapes from her, it gets caught up in the surrounding air. Ania can almost taste it, this metallic tinge peppering her face as she struggles not to lick her lips. She sees her own body crumbling from within, and just as she falls forward, she snaps out of it. Her body is still intact and cool. It was just a daydream.

"You are almost ready," Nana whispers.

"What? What did you say?"

"You went back," Nana continues. "Now you can go forward."

Chapter Thirty

Security footage

The monitor fizzles with more interference than the others, and Ania can see that the dried-up fountain is in the shot. There is movement, someone lying next to the fountain, so she steps up to the screen to take a closer look. There is a man curled up in the brace position. His shoulders shake. Is he crying?

It's Hank, the delivery man. Something makes her want to call out his name, but she stops herself. Instead, she watches as a long and dark object appears before him. It looks like a shadowy snake, long and straight as it heads straight into his mouth. He looks surprised and forms an "Oh!" with his lips, and then the footage changes again.

From this new camera angle, there is another man who is similar in height and build as Hank. This man's shoulders are also shaking, suggesting that he is crying. The image is grainy, but Ania can see that this man is sitting in a kitchen that seems familiar. She takes a step closer, the fizz of static prickling on the skin of her face. It can't be, surely it isn't.

The camera position changes again. This time it is a living room, and the image is clearer. It is her living room, at home in Rotherwell. There are the terracotta warriors, standing in silent sentinel, there are her mother's favorite books, all lined up in size order on the bookshelf. And there are her mother and brother, locked in a silent war as they sit on opposite sides of the room.

Another shot and this time it is a bedroom. Someone is in a bed, and she almost expects it now. The girl, only this time she can see that it is a teenage girl.

"Cynthia's daughter?" Nana suggests, but Ania knows this is impossible because she knows, for sure, that this is her own bedroom.

The camera position changes again, and now she can see her parents' bedroom. She sees them holding each other, curled up beneath the sheets in the same brace position Hank had been in. They are still, lifeless.

"Mom?" Ania calls through muffled tears. "Dad?"

She can hear the clock ticking again. She can't see it anywhere, even though it gets louder and louder.

"No use crying now," Nana mutters. "You must watch, though. Keep watching."

Ania wants to cover her eyes, but she also wants to see if they are okay, if she can see them breathing.

The camera position changes again, and she can see the fountain in the mall. There is Hank again, and there is the long dark object in front of him. Ania realizes it isn't a snake, it is something else. She only just forms the thought as he peers down the object, as if he is searching for something, and then she hears an explosion.

It was a gun.

She never looked away when it was footage on the dark web, but something made her cover her eyes.

"You must look," Nana urges, and Ania can feel something prising her fingers apart.

Through the gap between her fingers, Ania can see Hank's body, one leg twitching in the throes of death. She also realizes that the camera is pivoting like a wandering eye that is searching for its next target. And then it zooms in to an open doorway. The open door to Cynthia's office.

She can see a figure moving inside the office, and as she lets her hand drop from her face, the hand on the figure does the same. Of course, she realizes too late that the footage is live, and it is zooming in to her own back.

She runs from the office, stumbling past the dried-up fountain, but Hank is not there. There isn't any blood, not a trace of his existence.

A ringing from her pocket. Hank's cell phone.

She takes it out, presses a button to answer, and all she can hear is a crackling and a wail. It sounds like someone is trying to break through, making her think of the walkie talkies, and then she remembers Cynthia and her lifeless eyes.

Chapter Thirty-One

Blinding light

Ania continues to run, and she finds herself back in the part of the mall where the corridors are narrow. Ahead, she can see the broken wall panel, and from the cavernous space behind, she can hear a voice.

"Oh god," someone cries.

A few steps more and she manages to peer into the darkness. With the flashlight on Hank's phone, she scans the tunnel, and then the light bounces off something shiny.

"Oh god," the voice says again. It is coming from the direction of the shiny object, and as Ania's eyes get used to the gloom, she realizes that the shiny object is a nose-ring.

"Daria?" she calls. "What are you doing in there?"

"Ania," she croaks, "you shouldn't be here."

"Are you hurt?" Ania asks.

"You shouldn't be here," Daria repeats. "Now go. Please."

Daria has been staggering about the tunnel but now her knees buckle, and she falls to the ground.

Ania tries to climb in through the gap, ready to help her, but Daria yells.

"Don't! Don't touch me."

"Why? Is it contagious?" She thinks of the pandemic and the

stories that haunted her; tales of patients with glass-like substances blocking their lungs.

"Just stay away," Daria pleads.

In the grip of some kind of seizure, her body contorts. It is a sudden attack and as her eyes roll back in her head, it looks like rigor mortis has set in.

"Daria. For fuck's sake," Ania shouts as she starts to sob. "Let me get you help."

"No," Daria manages to groan. Something wet congeals at the back of her throat. "No one," she gargles as her head falls back. Another wave of something and then a blinding light. Ania can feel the heat of it on her skin, and she realizes, in horror, that the heat is coming from this girl. Something is happening to her body, some type of internal combustion.

At first, it makes Daria struggle; she thrashes about for a while, but then she calms. Her movements slow down and she shuts her eyes, embracing, finally, whatever this is. Her arms fall to her side, outstretched as she takes whatever is coming at her. It comes with an invisible force, making her body jolt with every wave of it. And then Ania can see the surface of her skin break open.

Ania tries to call out, but her words are swallowed by the solidity in the air. For the same reason, she can't take any steps forward to help this girl. All she can do is watch as something red emerges from the cracks in her skin. She thought it might be blood, but it is powdery, and as soon as it escapes from her, it gets caught up in the surrounding air. Ania can almost taste it, this metallic tinge peppering her face as she struggles not to lick her lips.

It isn't just her skin that is breaking apart. The whole shape of Daria shifts as if something is crumbling from within. Her face collapses inwards as her shoulders buckle. She falters and then collapses as more of her deteriorates. She is evaporating before Ania's eyes.

It takes a while, but eventually Ania is left with particles of her friend on her skin and in her hair.

She stumbles backwards and starts to run far from the narrow corridor. She keeps running until she can see the dried-up fountain, and beyond, the heavy glass doors to let her out of this mall. She tells herself that she is going to find someone who can do something for Daria, even though she knows that the girl is past any form of help. But the weight of that knowledge hangs on her, dragging down at her arms and legs to slow her pace. The possibility that Daria has slipped from her grasp makes her stumble a little, her eyelids closing, and then she falls into the darkness of a deep sleep.

Chapter Thirty-Two

Missing

Excerpts from the archives of WABC News:

Teen missing from mall.
A search is underway for a teen who went missing after visiting her local mall. [Name redacted] was reported missing by her family after the girl failed to return home from a day out with her friend. The 16-year-old friend of the missing girl has been questioned, and she explains that she saw a middle-aged woman talking to the teen before the disappearance.
Owners of the mall, [name redacted], [name redacted] and [name redacted] are under fire for failing to maintain the security cameras that covered the part of the complex where the teenager went missing.
The local Police Department confirmed a search is being conducted of the surrounding area, and they urge any potential witnesses to come forward.
For reasons unknown, the police have chosen not to issue an Amber Alert, although one witness claims that the police do not believe that the girl has been abducted.
The Police Department did not respond for additional comment at the time of publication.

This is a developing story. Visit [redacted].com for updates.

* * *

Search continues for missing Whitecliff County teen.

WHITECLIFF COUNTY, NJ. - The search continues for a Whitecliff County teenager a week after her disappearance.

The National Center for Missing & Exploited Children is asking the public for help to find 16-year-old [name redacted].

What we know:

According to the organization, the teen was last seen in her front yard, kicking a soccer ball against the wall of her home. When police arrived, her ball was still in the driveway.

Law enforcement agencies believe the teen may still be in the area - potentially in the woodland near a local mall.

The missing teen is described as being 5-feet-3-inches tall with a weight of 95 pounds. She has blue eyes and black hair.

What you can do:

If you have any information about where [name redacted] could be, call the Whitecliff County Police Department or the National Center for Missing & Exploited Children.

* * *

Search for missing girl, 16, continues following fatal crash

Budely, New York - A one-vehicle crash off US-64 into a forest has claimed the life of one person while the search for a missing 16-year-old girl continues.

News 27 cameras captured the flipped SUV that local residents discovered this morning as first responders rushed to locate the occupants of the vehicle.

The body of one of the two was recovered just before 1 p.m. yesterday. A City of Budely spokesperson said today that crews searched throughout most of the night to try to locate the missing girl, but to no avail.

Police cannot confirm the identity or age of the victim recovered at this time, but said the family of the victims has been notified. Police confirmed that the occupants of the vehicle had been travelling home after visiting a local mall at the time of the crash.

This is not the first fatality crash off US-64 in Budely. A Whitecliff woman was killed just last month.

This is a developing story. Stay with News 27 for updates.

* * *

16-year-old Baron County girl missing for 2 weeks
A 16-year-old Baron County girl has gone missing after visiting relatives in Whitecliff. The teen was last seen after she left a local mall with her two cousins, ages 18 and 19. Police were alerted by her parents when the teen failed to return home.
The police chose not to issue an Amber Alert, although the reasons remain unclear.
If you have any information, call the Baron County Police Department or the National Center for Missing & Exploited Children.

Comments:

u/deadwolf#03:
They were probably hoes. Should've been sent to a camp and incinerated.
u/rizlasykes#09:
Is this a joke?
u/deadwolf#03:
Dunno. Do you find it funny?
u/rizlasykes#09:
No, it's disgusting. You should be ashamed.
u/deadwolf#03:
What's it got to do with you, anyway?
u/rizlasykes#09:
Just so you know, I've reported your comment.
u/deadwolf#03:
I'm sure you feel proud of yourself, clicking that little report button. What are you, some keyboard warrior? Feel like the big man now, do you?
u/rizlasykes#09:
Why do you assume that I am a man?
Hang on, don't I know you? I recognize your username.
u/rizlasykes#09:
Oh, so now you're gonna try the strong and silent type, but a moment ago you had plenty to say.
u/rizlasykes#09:

Whatever. I'm not wasting any more time on you. I have better things to do.

u/deadwolf#03:

You're still here, though.

u/rizlasykes#09:

Just to make sure you don't leave any more vile comments.

u/deadwolf#03:

Why do you care? Get a job or something.

u/rizlasykes#09:

Think of the families of those missing girls. Imagine how they feel reading comments like the one you just added.

u/deadwolf#03:

They aren't likely to be sat online, reading this stuff. They're probably out looking for their kid, trying to work off some of that guilt that will gnaw at them for the rest of their lives. No one mentions that in the news headlines, that maybe, just maybe, if they'd paid more attention in the first place, they wouldn't have lost their kid to some maniac.

u/rizlasykes#09:

You are so disrespectful.

u/deadwolf#03:

What's disrespect got to do with this? They weren't looking after their kid, and so someone else did. They took them off their hands and looked after them real well.

u/rizlasykes#09:

How do you know that they've been taken?

u/rizlasykes#09:

Why won't you answer me?

u/rizlasykes#09:

Do you know something about these girls, and where they could be?

u/rizlasykes#09:

Are you there?

u/deadwolf#03:

I know a lot of things.

u/rizlasykes#09:

What?

u/deadwolf#03:

I can tell you the truth about the girls. That's if you want the truth.

u/rizlasykes#09:

I don't know what you mean. If you have information, you should go to the police.

u/deadwolf#03:
The police don't do shit. Many of them are in on it. Everyone wants a bit of the action. Do you know how much someone would pay for a sixteen-year-old?
u/rizlasykes#09:
What are you talking about? I'm going to report you again.
u/deadwolf#03:
Go ahead. Won't get those kids back.
u/rizlasykes#09:
Are you saying that those kids have been abducted?
u/deadwolf#03:
Maybe. Who knows?
u/rizlasykes#09:
Now you're just being stupid. If you have information about kidnapping or human trafficking or whatever you want to call it, you should tell the police. Do so, or I will.
u/deadwolf#03:
Go ahead.
u/deadwolf#03:
So do you want to know about those girls or not? I don't want you to waste my time.
u/deadwolf#03:
Now who's trying to be the strong and silent type?
u/deadwolf#03:
Hey, are you still there?
u/deadwolf#03:
You realize they used Route 80, they always do. You can grab a kid or two and drive all the way across the US, and chances are, you'll never see those kids again. And they aren't restrained by international borders. There are plenty of small airports where private planes take off with precious cargo. You have an endless supply of people who are willing to pay any price for a kid. And if she's pregnant, they'll pay an even higher price.
u/rizlasykes#09:
I don't know whether I believe any of this. I mean, I'm sure horrible stuff goes on, but I'm not so sure that you have any involvement. How do I know you aren't just a fantasist incel stuck in a tiny bedroom of your parents' house?
u/deadwolf#03:
Believe what you want. I really don't care. But just be careful where you go. Otherwise, you might just find the kind of person who is in

this line of work.
u/rizlasykes#09:
I know how to keep myself safe, thank you very much. I don't mix with these dark, shadowy people.
u/deadwolf#03:
How do you know? They could be living on your street, or sleeping in the other room of your house. They are everywhere; in abandoned warehouses and abandoned malls, in forests and campsites, and they are all over the dark web.
u/rizlasykes#09:
I'm calling the police.
u/deadwolf#03:
I told you already, the police won't do shit. And quit whining. You're living in a capitalist economy. Money talks. The ones who moan about it, with or without the guise of equality or human rights or basic fucking morality, are the ones who can't play the system. The losers. So, what do you want to be? A winner or a loser?

Source: https//www.[redacted].com
Accessed November 4, 2020, at 7:30 PM

Chapter Thirty-Three

Smother mother

Darkness. Something wet on her face. She imagines a beast licking her. Does she hear panting?

Ania claws at whatever is upon her, but instead of fur and claws, there is the cold skin of what feels like a hand.

"You were dreaming," the voice says. "You have to wake up."

She shakes her head, too afraid to open her eyes.

"Come on, Ania. You are safe. I've got you."

The teenager recognizes the voice. And there is the scent of a favorite perfume.

"Mom?" she asks. "Is that you Mom?"

"Don't worry. You are safe."

Cynthia.

Her eyes open, and she can see the slats of wood that form the cabin's walls. Ania is on her bed again, and Cynthia is perched next to her.

"I want to go home," Ania cries. "Just let me go home."

"I can't let that happen," Cynthia says as she dabs Ania's brow with a warm, damp cloth. It is soothing, and the teenager wishes she could lie back and let someone take care of her. But she fears this is a trap.

"Hank," Ania cries, "and Daria. What happened to them?" She chooses to remain silent about the arachnid version of Smithson, uncertain how this would sound.

"Best not to give her reason to lock you up or manacle you," Nana mutters.

Cynthia shakes her head. "Please don't worry."

"I mean it," Ania growls. "Something is horribly wrong with them. You should check the footage. Even if there are no cameras in the tunnels, you'll see what happened to Hank. He was by the fountain, and I think…I think he harmed himself. It looked serious."

Cynthia still refuses to listen. She gets up and paces, her fingers flexing into a clenched fist and then releasing. She keeps doing this, trying it out to decide upon her next move, and then she comes to stand over Ania's bed again.

Ania sits up and climbs out of the bed, reluctant to let this woman tower over her.

"I don't want you to worry," Cynthia explains. "Just relax and then everything will be okay."

"What about my family?" Ania demands. "Why are you watching them on your cameras?"

None of it makes sense, and Ania fears that even with an explanation from Cynthia, she still won't be reassured. She thinks of the snuff movies she has peeped at, certain that this is some kind of punishment for that.

Cynthia shakes her head. "You must have been mistaken. I know you are longing to see them, and I really do support that. In time, things will get easier…"

"No," Ania barks. "I'm not mistaken. I saw them with my own eyes. They were on your monitors, so you must know why. Who put cameras in their home?"

"Please," Cynthia whispers, "you'll wake the others."

Ania hadn't realized that anyone else was in the cabin, but now she can see the outline of three bodies in the surrounding beds.

Cynthia walks towards the door. She is finished with the conversation, and Ania can hear the jangle of keys as Cynthia gets ready to lock her in.

"You are going to sleep," Cynthia insists. "I don't know why you can't cooperate like the other three girls."

Ania glances at the other beds again. She still can't understand why the girls have not woken up with all the noise. Either they are too scared to move, or they've been drugged.

Ania returns her gaze to Cynthia. The woman's eyes are no longer lifeless but burning coals of fury.

"Sleep," the woman hisses. "It's always darkest before the dawn."

"No," Ania howls as she flies at this woman. She thinks of the arachnid, and how she could easily turn into it. She thinks of blood and broken bones piercing through the skin. She could inflict this on Cynthia, if it means that she could stop it happening to her family or herself.

She is upon the woman, trying to flail her with her fingernails, but Cynthia won't let her. Already she has Ania's wrists, gripping them so tight that it is painful, and the teenager starts to remember how she was hurt before.

"No," she wails again, "stop," she adds, "I don't want this."

"It won't take long," Cynthia mutters, "it will soon be sunrise, and you'll see everything clearly."

"I don't know what you're talking about," Ania hisses at her, "you're deranged."

"If it helps you to believe that, then go ahead," Cynthia retorts. The woman's face is softening, and in the dim light she transforms into someone else. Someone that Ania would never fight, never hurt.

"Mom?" she asks, surprising herself that she is even saying this. "Mom?" she asks again, but the woman shakes her head.

"You're not my mom," Ania acknowledges, the fight draining from every inch of her.

"I want to go home," she mutters. She knows it is pointless, but to say it feels soothing, in the way that rocking or pacing doesn't get you anywhere.

"You shouldn't stress yourself," Cynthia says. "It's harmful to the baby."

"What? Wait, what do you know about that?" Ania mutters. Instinctively, she folds her arms over her abdomen.

"I know everything," Cynthia adds. "I've told you; I have eyes everywhere."

Ania refuses to let her unborn baby become a reason for her weakness. She doesn't even want to think about it as more than cluster of cells that is multiplying like a cancerous growth.

"That's not a nice way to think," Nana snaps. "I never had any choice about my pregnancy either, but once I knew that I was expecting your mother, I shut my eyes to any other dimension, any version of my life that did not include her. Selfless devotion."

"Like a passive vessel," Ania jeers to herself, "a fucking automaton baby making machine."

"During sleep, babies grow," Cynthia explains. "So you should get some rest."

"Is that what this is," Ania cries, "you want me as some kind of handmaiden to bear children for you?"

They glance at the hooded cloak that is still wrapped around Ania's shoulders, and Cynthia shakes her head.

"I just wanted to keep you warm, that's all," the woman explains. "Can't you accept that someone is just trying to show you some kindness?"

Ania longs to relent, but as her muscles loosen just a tiny bit, the images of Daria and Hank come flooding back. It was all so sudden, so violent and inexplicable.

"Why are you keeping me prisoner here?" Ania cries. "What's going to happen to me?" She thinks of all the horrifying images and videos on the dark web, all the different forms of depravity. Her parents barely dipped beneath the surface when they warned her about dangers beyond the latches and bolts and locks of her home. They should have spoken about abductions, human trafficking, and all the ways that the human body can be debased, deformed and used for whatever purpose the paying party desires.

"Force-fed and medicated," someone whispers, "kept bound to a bed until you are swollen with that thing inside of you." This doesn't sound like Nana. She tries to place the voice, old and resonant, like the vibrations of ancient trees.

"And then what, Aaaniaaa?" the voice continues. She realizes that it has scared Nana into the shadows. Ania wants to cry out to her, pleading with her only companion not to leave, but the voice is like a force-field, and it tightens something over her mouth, threatening to crush her teeth if she speaks.

"After you have swollen to the point of popping," the voice adds, "what will happen then, Aaaniaaa? Will it tear its way out of you with dirty fingernails? Will it leave you as a rotting corpse in that forest out there, so it is free to wreak havoc on a world that you could never figure out? You must face this now, Ania, that some people are born to hide away behind latches and bolts and locks, and others are born to devour so they can thrive and conquer and multiply."

Ania glances around the cabin, certain that she will see something scampering, casting shadows up the walls and onto the ceiling. But all she can find is a scent of bourbon.

The voice is whispering some more, telling her of horrors to come. It speaks of softer parts of her that will be fed to others, and her spinal column fashioned as a whip, and all the while, Cynthia's words continue to speak of warmth and sleep. Ania knows her eyelids are shutting, but she is losing the ability to fight it.

She searches her pockets for a weapon, and her fingers grace the hard surface of the snow globe. The cold glass shocks her awake and she clings to it, a strange lifebuoy of sorts, but it's enough to keep her from slipping into the underworld.

Chapter Thirty-Four

Snow globe

"My family. Where are they?"

Ania has the snow globe out of her pocket, and her arm is stretched long. She looks like a pitcher ready to strike Cynthia out.

"Slam it into her skull," the resonant voice booms inside Ania's mind. "Break her open so you can see the yolky spillage. I bet you've thought about it, wondered what it would sound like; that crack of skull and squelch of the matter inside."

"You don't want to do this," Cynthia mutters. She seems less scared than Ania expected her to be, but this might be an act. All those plastic smiles, all those platitudes, this woman is a professional liar.

"My family," Ania repeats. "Why are you filming them? What is going on?"

"You don't have to worry about them," Cynthia responds softly. "They are safe."

"That's not what I asked you. What is going on?"

Cynthia shakes her head.

"If you really don't believe me, I can show you."

"What do you mean?" Ania asks.

"Come with me to my office and we can see your family. Trust me, they are at peace."

"What? What are you talking about? Ania spits.

"If you really want, we can try to say goodbye to them," Cynthia says gently.

"*What*?" Ania screeches.

"You can try to say goodnight to them," Cynthia continues.

"You said *goodbye*," Ania screeches again. "Why would I say goodbye to them if they are okay and I am going to see them again?" Ania starts to cry as she adds, "You're going to hurt them, aren't you? If I don't do what you tell me to do."

"Oh, come on, Ania, there's really nothing to worry about."

It's the kind of tone her mother would use when Ania would see a spider, and the longing for her family re-ignites a rage that burns inside the teenager.

Ania makes a sudden motion, pretending to slam the snow globe onto Cynthia's head, and the woman flinches. Satisfied, Ania nods. "Okay, so you understand me. Now talk. Explain what is going on."

Instead of talking, Cynthia's lips just stretch in a sickening smile.

"Talk!" Ania snarls.

"Are you sure you know what you've seen?" the woman asks. "Sometimes we only see what we long for. I used to do that all the time, seeing my daughter in every show, in every girl who would walk down the street. I still see her, even now," she mutters as she stares at Ania.

"I don't want to keep hearing about your daughter," Ania snaps. "You're stuck in a loop, going over and over stories about her. You're trapped in the past when there are more important things happening right here, right now."

"I know. I see her," Cynthia murmurs.

"What?'

"I see you," Cynthia adds. "I hear you and see you."

"You're crazy. Do you even have a daughter? Or was she just another girl you kidnapped and held here against her will? Did you find someone to pay a high price to her? And is that going to happen to me?"

"Stop it," Cynthia snarls, "I'm warning you."

"Or what? I'm the one with the weapon."

"That's not yours," Cynthia shrieks.

"It is for now. Tell me what happened, then, to this daughter of yours. Did you lose your patience with her and snap? I've heard of parents doing that, especially when their kids get to the teenage years. What happened? Did she steal money from you, or your prescription pills? Did she trash the house or call you names in front of your friends, and then one night, when you'd finally had enough, you crept in her room and strangled her?

Silence except the sound of Cynthia panting.

"I bet you did," Ania continues. "I bet you loved doing it until you saw her tongue hang slack from her mouth and you saw that she had wet herself. Then you regretted it. Then you were sorry and begged her to wake up, and you've been regretting so much that you dedicated your life to other *troubled souls*. Perpetual torment. Did you stuff the body in one of the tunnels or behind some wall panel? Is that what I can smell everywhere?"

"Stop it," Cynthia screams.

Ania expects the woman to fly at her, slicing her face with her nails, but she just looks away, her words falling like chalky flakes of ash.

"Please," she whispers, "you have to stop."

"Why? Why stop now?"

"Because you're not ready," Cynthia gasps. "Clearly, you're not. Not in the right frame of mind, not at the moment. Maybe in the morning things will feel differently if you just allowed yourself to sleep."

Ania doubts that she will last until the morning if she allows her heavy eyes to close.

"Tell me," Ania insists, as she musters all the energy she can find. "Where is she? Where is your daughter? And what happened to Daria and Hank? What's going on, and why am I being trapped here?"

Silence again.

"Please. What is happening," Ania repeats, her fingers tightening on the snow globe. She knows she can't swing it at her head because if she kills this woman, she will never find out any of it.

"You asked about my daughter. Well, you're right. She has gone. Just like Hank and Daria. No way of changing that now. If I could change anything, then…But there's no point going down that road. No point in regrets."

"What happened to Aaliyah?"

"Ania?" Cynthia blinks at the sixteen-year-old.

"What happened?' Ania insists. "Tell me."

"You know, they say all you need is one source of support, just one friend. And yet even that one friend turned against her. In the end, Annabelle found other friends, and she turned all the girls in their grade against my daughter. *Pack mentality*. Those wolves were vicious, and they had no problem tearing my kid apart. And all for the sake of a stupid, clumsy boy."

Cynthia squeezes her hands together, so the bones show beneath her paper-thin skin.

"She dreaded every morning of school. I had to bargain with her, plead with her, and sometimes she wouldn't go at all. I'd find out from a neighbor that she was hiding out somewhere, even when it was snowing. What sort of childhood is that? And do you know what I did? I kept forcing her to go. I didn't help her solve anything, I just screamed and shouted until she started to look numb. She just nodded, and said '*Sure, Mom.*' "

Ania doesn't want to know any more. Those words, they sound familiar.

"But you asked," Cynthia continues. "She saw a social influencer do it. Tyra Jackson was her name. I think she was live streaming somewhere. Probably one of the backroom channels or on the dark web. I really don't know. This crazy girl, this influencer, had a million followers, so she was like a god in the eyes of many teenagers. So, when she decided to do it, others followed suit. Spread like a contagion, and it killed my daughter."

Ania wants to cover her ears and eyes. She wants to fold herself up, so she is no longer here, so she can slip between the gaps of this cabin and let the wind carry her all the way home. But Cynthia keeps telling her story.

"It's your story, now," Cynthia explains. "No escaping that."

"In the end…as if there is any *end* to this perpetual torment… my daughter, defiant to the core, took matters into her own hands."

Cynthia raises her hands in defeat.

"I tried to protect her," Cynthia repeats. She watches Ania as the teenager stares at the woman's scarred wrists. "I'm not ashamed to admit that I did that to myself," she adds.

Through the crack in the curtains, Ania can see that ice-white shards of glass are falling on the nearby forest. Silent, gentle, they start to accumulate what might become a great weight to bear.

"I don't care what you did to your wrists, any more than I care what happened to your daughter," Ania snaps. "This has nothing to do with me."

"It has *everything* to do with you," Cynthia insists, her tone more tender than Ania expected. "You can't hurt me," she explains.

"I can try," Ania snarls, as she swings the snow globe at Cynthia's face.

Ducking, Cynthia only just saves herself from injury.

"You don't want this," the woman adds. "Not really."

"I do," Ania spits back at her. "It's you or me."

"What do you mean?"

"Either I kill you or I'm gonna kill myself. I can't take this anymore," Ania shrieks.

"Say it again," Cynthia whispers calmly.

"What?"

"You're saying that you want to die, right?" Cynthia adds.

Is Cynthia really smiling at this?

"You're sick," Ania spits.

"Listen to her," Nana urges.

"You don't have to be afraid," Cynthia explains. "You just have to accept the truth."

"It's true," Nana adds. "Listen to what she says."

Cynthia starts to laugh.

"You're laughing? You find this funny?" Ania cries. "Tell me what's going on. Where is my family?"

"You must trust me," Cynthia insists, "it's your only option."

"Fuck you. Just keep away."

"Come on, Ania. We are all tired. You need to calm down."

Ania heard the words, but she couldn't make sense of it. There was too much to process; too many different people in different dimensions: Cynthia's daughter, Aaliyah, but Daria and Hank, too. And what about Jill and Ellie, are they even alive as they lie in the bed beside her? Who is this strange Cynthia woman, and her tormenters, Sophie and Carrie? They all seem familiar, as if they are living in parallel to another life, where there are more tormentors who mean Ania harm. But there are also people who love her, her parents and brother, so why can't she reach them?

"I want to help you," Cynthia says. "But I can only help if you listen to the whole of my story. She hanged herself."

Finally, Cynthia says it.

A dull thud, a hangman's drop, and Ania realizes she has dropped the snow globe. It rolls to Cynthia's foot, and she just stares at it, transfixed by her reflection.

"I found her, and I wish I hadn't. I wish she could forever remain beautiful in my mind's eye, but instead, all I see is her disfigured neck."

Ania claws at her own neck, her throat closing in.

"She used some jute rope from my garage to break her neck, and if I'm honest, I can understand why. She had no choice; she was trapped in a dead-end that I had pushed her into. I wish I could have joined her the minute she did it. Just so she wasn't left alone."

Ania stares again at Cynthia's wrists.

"Such a thing of nightmares, this kinesthetic connection that still tethers me to my child," Cynthia mutters. "It's been so hard to watch you go through this," she explains, "when you two look so alike."

"I'm not your daughter," Ania says. Again, she can feel her throat tightening and she is finding it hard to breathe. "I'm not her," the teenager declares.

Cynthia won't hear it. She shakes her head hard, so that her long auburn hair ignites.

"That kind of grief," Cynthia mutters, "can trap you in a prism where you live and die at the same time and in the same space. You become haunted and tangled like a knot, until you get a second chance that might cut you free. This camp has been my second chance, to alchemize my daughter's loss and make something good of it, and to finally set myself free of all this pain. My daughter, my troubled soul, never got that chance. She tried everything to stop the pain; alcohol, drugs, and then she found that influencer."

Cynthia stares into the distance, as if she can see her daughter standing behind Ania.

"That influencer. I can barely say her name. That silly little sixteen-year-old hanged herself while she was live streaming on her cell phone, and I don't even think she meant to go through with it. She probably wanted to play with the idea, just for more views and comments and whatever else. But so many watched as she did it, and, of course, so many more followed suit."

Something shifts in Cynthia, and it makes her body stiffen. It was sudden, like a bolt of energy pulsating through her, and she stares at Ania with cold emerald eyes.

"I bathed her for the first time," she says with a gasp, her mouth wet with tears, "and I bathed her for the last time. They told me I could, after she had died. I didn't know if I would be able to do it, my hands were shaking so much. But in the end, I had no choice. I was her mother, after all. She was so small, a life barely out of its infancy."

"That toxic grief," Cynthia or Nana whispers, "to distort all manner of natural things, so the once nourishing becomes spoiled, so it is pungent like the stench of rotten flesh."

Ania tries to focus on these words, but her head starts to slip sideways.

"That stench of rotten flesh," Cynthia or Nana continues, "can attract some who like that kind of thing, the kind who searches the dark web for images of the dead or dying, and the sounds of the death rattle."

"Stay with it," Ania tells herself, "don't let them confuse you." But all she can think of is sleep.

"They have to go dark because this content is flagged and removed from the traditional webpages," Cynthia or Nana adds, "because no one wants to open their eyes to the inevitable, the sudden death that will grip them soon enough. They pretend it does not exist, and there is no bridge to link the two. They pretend that they cannot see that life and death exist as one. *As above, down below.*"

Ania tries to walk across the cabin but she staggers, her feet ladened by something. She reaches for the door handle, it floats out of reach as the door shifts in and out of focus.

"I need to…" Ania mutters, her words slurring. "Do I… What is this…I want to go home."

"You remember it now," Cynthia whispers, "you remember it all." She says it so softly that she sounds like Nana. The two seem to float in the ether, smokey phantoms circling her head to intoxicate her.

"You remember?" Cynthia, or Nana, asks.

Ania shakes her head and lunges for the door, but it is out of reach, and she stumbles against it. The handle catches her cheek, feeling like a punch.

"Sophie?" she asks. But she is nowhere to be seen.

"No, Ania, no one is going to hurt you now," Cynthia mutters into the teenager's ear.

Chapter Thirty-Five

Liminality

Subreddit: Liminality

u/deadwolf#03:
Anyone know what liminality is? This girl gave me the slip, can't find her anywhere, and someone said something about liminality. Not sure if they were trying to wind me up and all. Any info?
u/rizlasykes#09:
The way you talk about girls, it's no wonder she gave you the slip.
u/deadwolf#03:
You again? Leave me alone.
u/deadwolf#03:
Asking again, if anyone knows about this liminality thing, would appreciate it. I have a game on Sunday so I don't want it on my mind.
u/VR_666:
I can certainly help you with that. Liminality is the in-between or a transitional state, and there are plenty of theories to explain it. Most theories of liminality tend to fall into three categories:
Firstly, there is a quantum theory that explains that a particle can be in multiple states at once. In quantum mechanics, the concept of superposition defines this. In other words, quantum theory claims that a person can exist in multiple potentialities at once. Therefore,

liminality is a quantum-like state where reality is fluid and unpredictable.

A second category claims that liminality defines a transitional phase, such as a rite of passage, where a person moves from one status to another. This is a psychological theory of liminality, and it is defined by its ambiguity and disorientation. You might view the transition from adolescence to adulthood as a liminal state, or the transition from innocence to innocence lost.

The third category suggests that liminality is the result of mind control by the CIA. Many claim that people have been manipulated by the government, and they point to methods such as sleep deprivation, starvation, medication, and other means. These forms of manipulation put people in a liminal space where their sense of self, even their sense of reality, is undermined.

u/deadwolf#03:

And if you believe the third option, you're the wokest pseudo-science consuming snowflake I've ever encountered.

u/rizlasykes#09:

How do you know what's real, and what's not? I've heard of governments doing all types of manipulation on their subjects. You must've heard of the Hegelian dialectic.

u/deadwolf#03:

Sure I have.

u/rizlasykes#09:

Okay…so…????? If you've heard of that, why do you dismiss governmental manipulation?

u/deadwolf#03:

Whatever, dude.

u/rizlasykes#09:

Hang on, I don't think you even heard of the Hegelian dialectic. You're so full of bull it's unbelievable. It's a basic method of manipulation. They want you to feel the chaos. They want you to question what is real and what isn't. They want your world to be turned upside down, so it feels like the underworld, so you're so disoriented that you are desperate for whatever solution they have to offer. Even if that means you're gonna deprive yourself of your rights, your freedom. You'll do it just to make the chaos stop. Throughout history, governments have used this tactic so their subjects accept surveillance, diminished rights, even forced labor.

u/deadwolf#03:

You're kind of boring me now.

<u>*u/rizlasykes#09:*</u>
Okay, whatever. If you're not into government manipulation, how do you explain where your girl has gone?
<u>*u/deadwolf#03:*</u>
The hoe is just avoiding me. Probably turned lesbian.
<u>*u/rizlasykes#09:*</u>
You really are problematic.
<u>*u/deadwolf#03:*</u>
Doesn't stop you coming back for some more.
<u>*u/rizlasykes#09:*</u>
Next, you're gonna say I should be locked up in some camp.
<u>*u/deadwolf#03:*</u>
Yeah, and incinerated. How did you know I was gonna say that? LOL.
<u>*u/rizlasykes#09:*</u>
I know everything about you.
<u>*u/deadwolf#03:*</u>
You wish.
<u>*u/rizlasykes#09:*</u>
We've been watching you.
<u>*u/deadwolf#03:*</u>
Watch away. I don't give a sh*t.
<u>*u/rizlasykes#09:*</u>
You've been on 4chan again. In the backrooms. We saw you.
<u>*u/deadwolf#03:*</u>
What the f*ck are the backrooms?
<u>*u/rizlasykes#09:*</u>
You know.
<u>*u/deadwolf#03:*</u>
I don't, actually, but they sound interesting. After the Sunday game, I'll search for them. Where should I look?
<u>*u/rizlasykes#09:*</u>
They're anywhere and everywhere. They're endless.
<u>*u/deadwolf#03:*</u>
I don't think you know what you're going on about. You're just chatting sh*t because you have nothing better to do.
<u>*u/rizlasykes#09:*</u>
You'll find them when you play the new game.
Loop through the backdoor and put in the code.
<u>*u/deadwolf#03:*</u>
What code? What backdoor?

u/rizlasykes#09:
You're gonna have to figure that out
u/deadwolf#03:
Okay. Stay mysterious. Doesn't make you any more interesting.
u/rizlasykes#09:
You either.
u/deadwolf#03:
Whatevs.
u/rizlasykes#09:
It's called Soteira.
u/deadwolf#03:
What?
u/rizlasykes#09:
The game. Hekate Soteria.
u/deadwolf#03:
Okay, sweet.
u/rizlasykes#09:
The goddess of liminal time and space.
u/deadwolf#03:
Nice.
u/rizlasykes#09:
She guides us out of these in-between moments.
u/deadwolf#03:
Sounds creepy. I'm Christian, so I'm not into that witchcraft stuff.
u/rizlasykes#09:
Witch, goddess, all depends which side of misogyny you happen to be on.
u/deadwolf#03:
Whatevs.
u/rizlasykes#09:
It could help you. She could help you.
u/rizlasykes#09:
You're slipping between the cracks, aren't you? You're sorry for what you did, but you're still getting away with it. Kinda weird, huh? Weird state to be in. You keep having that nightmare about balancing on the edge of a cliff. Or walking a tightrope. Constantly balancing on the edge. Not living, but not dead.
u/deadwolf#03:
Not really.
u/rizlasykes#09:
Liar. You're at the threshold of something.

u/deadwolf#03:
Yeah, cool, gottit.
u/rizlasykes#09:
Look, the sun's rising. Can you see the dawn?
u/deadwolf#03:
Really? Well, that means I gotta go to school.
u/rizlasykes#09:
Liminum porta ad inferos.
u/deadwolf#03:
What?
u/deadwolf#03:
What was that? I'm trying Google translate and it isn't coming up. You f*cking with me? Cos you're creeping me out.
u/rizlasykes#09:
I lied. There's no game. It doesn't exist.
u/deadwolf#03:
What?
u/rizlasykes#09:
None of this is a game. It's real, only not the reality you know about. Endless liminality.
You'll see. A digital chronotope. You're gonna die a painful death, I'll see to that. And I'm gonna live stream it on the dark web and make my billons from it because money talks. Isn't that right? If you're not a billionaire, you're just bio-feed or bio-waste for their consumption.
u/deadwolf#03:
F*ck you.

Source: https//www.[redacted].com
Accessed November 4, 2020, at 7:30 PM

Chapter Thirty-Six

The orchard

Ania is in her backyard now. She knew she'd find her way there. She can see the gnarled old boughs of the apple trees.

"Now you see," she hears someone whisper.

There is the length of rope hanging from one of the boughs.

"You see it all now," the voice adds. "See how the rope is starting to stir?"

"No," Ania yells.

"See how the noose snakes round your throat?"

"No. Please stop. Please."

Ania tries to look away, but something grips her chin and holds her face in line with her own lifeless body. She sees her brown, polished shoes, like chestnuts that have only just ripened.

"You have to look back to go forward," someone mutters.

There is so much snow.

"Leave me alone," Ania pleads.

"No," the voice insists. "You have to see. You were only too willing to watch before, to watch others do it. Isn't that right? You watched Tyra Jackson do it and so now it's your turn."

Someone or something yanks at the rope, and Ania twitches into life, her limbs flickering like she is making snow angels. And still,

Ania knows there is worse yet to come.

"Come on, Ania. Take a look."

"Why are you so intent on torturing me?" Ania shouts.

"That's not what we intend," comes the reply.

Ania realizes there is more than one voice, only they are speaking in unison. A ghostly chorus to sing her goodbye.

"We're trying to set you free. Isn't that what you meant by doing this?"

Something yanks at the rope again, and then it finally happens. Ania's eyes open. And she remembers it all.

"Mom," she cries. "I want to go home." But she knows this is impossible, and it is no one's doing but her own.

With the noose around her throat constraining her vocal cords, Ania can barely make a sound. But there is a sound, and it is deadly; the loss of life in the form of air rushing from a hidden hole.

"Mom," she cries again. "It hurts."

And then the rope is yanked again, and her arms and legs thrash about for a final time, and then she is still.

"You see?" she hears. "Do you see now?"

Finally, the clock stops ticking.

Hours later, Ania's parents will run into the backyard. But it will be too late. Paris screamed as he tried to get her down. Eris helped too. They used their fingers and nails, and eventually Eris ran to the garage to get a knife.

Eris held her daughter as they cut her down, and when the rope finally went slack, Ania's cheek fell against her mother's. Eris stroked the softness of her daughter's skin, and Nana felt the softness of her own daughter, too. They were united at last, all three generations, and they heard the mournful caw of a solitary raven. But this time, it told them something they had known all along; that the bond between parent and child can never be broken.

Chapter Thirty-Seven

Regret

Each day that followed that Halloween night, Ania saw the apple tree and the length of rope. To know that the violence created something that would stay with her forever seemed like perpetual torment. Yet a bond cannot be broken between parent and child, she knew that much, and she was now carrying a child. So what was she to do?

She tried to think of any other way. For days, she ran through the forest and beyond, searching for a means to free herself but save her child. She dreamt of hidden doors that would lead to a secret attic which could serve as her perpetual hiding place. But when she awoke, and realized none of it was true, her daydreams grew dark and she imagined how she might find her freedom underground, through a network of tunnels that would plunge her into darkness. She could almost feel the roots growing around her as she waited there buried, hoping that her mother would finally discover the truth.

And then the arachnid appeared, in that Smithson form. He made her watch as he tunneled through nerve endings of countless people. He made them scream as he pushed in further and reached the vital organs that made them twitch. You would think this would kill them, and they would hope for death, but somehow, they remained alive, their eyes flickering as he rummaged about their innards, and his long tongue flickered at the bodily fluids that oozed and splattered about.

He wanted Ania to see more. He made excuses for his greed by trying to convince Ania that the world was filled with people who wished to inflict harm, who would seize whatever they want, just because they could. He wanted Ania to realize that even her own ancestors did this by invading the territory of others, creating empires just because they could.

"You see," he said, his voice thickened with a coating of blood. "There is always a reason, always a trauma hidden somewhere within the folds of your skin that you can pluck out and use as a *get out of jail* card, so you can keep hurting others as you loop round that trauma cycle like it is a merry-go-round."

He knew of the pregnancy, so he showed Ania what atrocities he could inflict through the future generations.

"You know of all the violence that can be unleashed," he sneered and slobbered. "You've already looked it up, haven't you? Don't think I didn't know what you were doing late at night, in your bedroom all alone. You were scrolling through the dark web that others see you scroll through, no matter how many times you erase your internet history or switch to *cognito* mode, they see all the pages of your filthy curiosity, because they are curious too."

Smithson promised that he would use Ania's eyes to prise open a portal from the underworld, and all manner of hell and violence would be unleashed.

Then she saw the apple tree and the length of rope again, and this time she made that split-second decision.

"Something I will always regret," she said in unison with her grandmother.

"Something that was inevitable?" she asked no one in particular. No one answered.

Chapter Thirty-Eight

Morgue

"You don't have to watch this," Nana whispered as Ania's body was wheeled through the funeral home. At first, she didn't look, but she knew there would be a steel-smooth table and harsh lights fizzing with brightness.

"I have to see," Ania cried, enthralled and repulsed at the same time as she peeped through a gap in her fingers.

She tried to distract herself from the horrific reality by criticizing the inconsequential. She found it disrespectful that the mortician chewed gum while he wheeled her in. She didn't like the choice of music as he set to work, soft rock instead of the strings of an orchestra, and the latex smell of the technician's gloves tickled her nose.

"I don't think this is a good idea," Nana added. "No one should have to watch something like this happen to their own body."

But Ania couldn't stop watching. She felt every incision, every tear of the skin, muscle, blood vessels, and capillaries. She didn't flinch, though, when she heard the crack of the rib cage, or the skull sliding about like the shell of a hard-boiled egg.

"Aren't you cold?" Nana asked. "Shouldn't you go somewhere to get warm?" She realized how foolish it was to say this, but she just could not bear to see her granddaughter watch as scalpel and bone saw clanked and clattered on metal trays.

"What's that smell?" Ania asked.

"Embalming fluids," Nana replied. "Can't we go now?"

"No," Ania snapped. She would rather stay here in this cold morgue, watching them drain her blood, than have to see the memorials that were popping up all over Rotherwell. Balloons and flowers left by the girls in her grade who had tormented her, who hated her and wished she'd been dead long before she was. They didn't regret those wishes, at least in their private thoughts, but publicly they sobbed on social media, live streaming the grief that others expected to see.

Ania tried to imagine each one of those girls lying on this mortician's slab. She wanted to take the scalpel, and the bone saw, and go to work on them. She knew each movement of the equipment because she'd watched plenty of autopsies on the dark web.

With every incision made into her own body, she wished for it tenfold for the girls in her grade. Especially Abigail. After all, Ania was the daughter of the wrathful goddess of discord and strife. In death, if not in life.

Chapter Thirty-Nine

Necromaniac

Subreddit: Grief

u/deadwolf#03:
What happens to a body straight after death? Asking for a friend.
u/rizlasykes#09:
You're sick.
u/deadwolf#03:
Leave me alone. A girl I know just died and I wanna know what happens. You're sick for judging the grieving.
u/rizlasykes#09:
You're not grieving. I know who you're talking about, and you never gave a f*ck about her.
u/deadwolf#03:
You don't know sh*t.
u/rizlasykes#09:
I know that she was pregnant.
u/deadwolf#03:
Who told you?
u/rizlasykes#09:
So I'm right. Lucky guess.
u/deadwolf#03:
Very good. Now go stalk someone else.

u/rizlasykes#09:
Admit it, you like the attention.
u/deadwolf#03:
I'd like it if you ended up in the morgue along with the girl.
u/rizlasykes#09:
I'd like to see you try.
So what's it like being the talk of the town? Only, I bet you didn't expect to be talked about in this way.
u/deadwolf#03:
Dunno what you mean.
u/rizlasykes#09:
Yes, you do. You know what they're saying. They know what happened. They know she did it because of you. So now you'll have blood on your hands. And you're gonna be hated, unless you can do something about it.
u/deadwolf#03:
You don't know what you're talking about.
u/rizlasykes#09:
Yes, I do. Pregnant. Can you imagine? A schoolgirl, pregnant. Bet you've been frantic, trying to figure out if it will be linked to you. We saw your search history. And then you got bored and started looking at the filth. You really are sick.
u/deadwolf#03:
I'm not the sick one. You know, they're saying that isn't even her body in the casket. It's a synthetic replica.
u/rizlasykes#09:
BS.
u/deadwolf#03:
It's true. The freak mother probably has her body in her attic, doing all sorts of weird things to her.
u/rizlasykes#09:
Projecting much?
u/deadwolf#03:
I'm serious. Her mother's a freak. Complete recluse.
u/rizlasykes#09:
Big word for you.
u/deadwolf#03:
If you wanna harass someone, go find her.
u/rizlasykes#09:
Oh, we know about her, and her husband and son. We also know what a nightmare you have created for them.

u/deadwolf#03:
You're welcome.
u/rizlasykes#09:
You really don't care about anything, do you?
u/deadwolf#03:
Not really. You can make all sorts of things out of rubber and latex. Maybe I'll make a synthetic version of myself, one that would care. Bet you'd like that, wouldn't you? A doll version of me to f*ck.
u/rizlasykes#09:
I'm sure you know all about that. I bet you can't even tell what's real anymore.
u/deadwolf#03:
Sure I can.
u/rizlasykes#09:
Am I real?
u/deadwolf#03:
Who cares?
u/rizlasykes#09:
Are you real?

Source: https//www.[redacted].com
Accessed November 4, 2020, at 7:30 PM

Chapter Forty

Surveillance

Gasping for breath, Ania wakes to find herself crumpled on the splintered floorboards of the cabin. She can hear Cynthia unlocking the door and opening it, and as she smiles, she says, “I’ve got you. It’s going to be alright.”

Through the open door, Ania can see the forest in the distance. A raven lands on the branch of a nearby tree, and it croaks its mournful caw. “Hello, you,” Ania calls to him.

The light still seems artificial, its brightness making the colors too garish, but it no longer unsettles the teenager. In fact, it comforts her, and she thinks that she can hear Mother Earth beckoning her by saying, “Come back to me.”

Cynthia takes Ania’s hand and helps her up, and then she leads her out of the cabin and across the gravel courtyard. The woman’s skin is warm and comforting.

“This won’t take long,” Cynthia explains. “This way,” she adds as she points to a dirt track.

Without hesitation, they plunge into the forest, and Ania can hear her footsteps snapping twigs and crunching leaves. Birdsong is muted and the leaves are still.

Before long, they can see a break in the trees, and then they are free of the forest, and the grey concrete and dirty glass of the mall looms on the horizon.

"Almost there," the woman adds with a squeeze of the girl's hand.

Cynthia pulls open the heavy glass door, and there is no smell of damp. Already, Ania can see that the hallway has been repaired. There are no dangling light fixtures, and the walls are freshly painted. Even the floor is clear of debris.

They walk on in silence until they reach the floodlit atrium. The two escalators are operational, making a gentle rushing sound, and the ornamental tree is flourishing.

Cynthia gestures towards her office, and they walk over to it. The door is already open, and it reveals a desk clear of any paperwork.

"Come in," the woman says as she walks across the threshold.

Ania can see that the door to the wooden closet is also open, and each monitor shows clear images of different sections of the mall.

Cynthia notices Ania's hesitation, and she smiles. "Come on, I know you want to see this." As she points to the monitors, Ania can see that the woman's wrists are clear of any scars, and there are no sounds of wheezing coming from the woman's chest.

"How's your throat?" she asks Ania.

"Better," the teenager replies as she walks into the office and up to the monitors.

"And you have your bracelet back," the woman remarks as she points down at Ania's wrist.

"Where did that come from?" Ania asks as she watches the panda pendants twinkling in the light from the monitors.

Cynthia shrugs her shoulders. "Does it matter? Does it matter, also, why or how Daria is better? In fact, she is better than she has ever been, which is all that matters. The how and why can wait for another time."

She points to one screen, and Ania can see Daria embracing a woman.

"Her mother," Cynthia explains. "And now she's free. Daria passed on from here, and the same happened to Hank. He's at peace with a daughter he lost some time ago. So sad, he just couldn't carry on teaching after she died. But now he is back with her. Look."

Another monitor shows Hank embracing a girl of a similar age to Ania.

"All of them have passed on from this camp," Cynthia explains, "and if you look carefully, there is a monitor for each of them. Jill, Ellie, Sophie and Carrie, they are all gone from here, beyond this liminal space. They just had to accept the truth that they had passed, and to let go of the people who are still alive. That's all we were waiting for."

Cynthia turns from the monitors to face Ania.

"It will be my time soon," she adds with a smile. "But not before you. Finally, you are ready to leave this camp, this liminal space, because you have accepted the truth of what happened. Now all you need to do is let go of the past and say goodbye."

"Just let go," Nana adds. "It's time."

"Why didn't you tell me the truth?" Ania asks. "You made me believe that Hank was..."

"You weren't ready for the truth. At that time, you were hanging on too tightly to the life you had just left, and it was confusing you. I had to say something to throw you off the scent. I'm sorry for lying to you. I hope you know, by now, that I was never a malevolent spirit who was holding you against your will or stalking you. I only wanted to help you but, for a while, you didn't want my help. Not until you accepted that you can't return home to Rotherwell. That's a big thing to come to terms with, a huge transition, so I had to give you time."

"The Einstellung effect," Nana mutters. "For a while, you could only find a solution by searching in the past, in your old life in Rotherwell, even though that is now out of reach."

"It's understandable that it took you a little time," Cynthia continues. "You looped a little because you were frozen by your trauma. The past still felt like the present for you. But once you saw what happened to Daria, the idea spread like a contagion, and you realized that you need to move on from here."

"What's going to happen?" Ania asks.

"It's already started."

The apple tree, the sagging bough. Ania's throat tightens with a jolt as her head snaps back. The length of rope. It was all so sudden.

"You see now," Cynthia says with a smile. "Until now, you were blind to the true nature of this place. But now you see."

Something sharp twists inside of Ania. It carves the shape of something she doesn't want, causing irreparable harm. Cynthia watches Ania flinch, and she nods.

"You're remembering some more. I don't want you to be in pain, but sometimes you have to go back to go forward."

"He hurt me," Ania groans, the rage hurting as much as anything else. "That Halloween night. Abigail tricked me and he ended up hurting me."

"I know," Cynthia growls. "Smithson will be dealt with, don't you worry about that. For now, you must focus on your own path to freedom. This isn't about him."

An alarm shrieks, an echo from the past. A smoke alarm.

"I could've told her. Mom was there, asking what was wrong as I burnt the evidence. And I said nothing."

When her mom touched her, Ania flinched as she saw in her mother's hands Smithson's meaty grip. In that moment, her mother's concern transformed into Smithson's sneer, and Ania ran from the house before her mother could ask any more.

"But the baby," Ania gasps. Pain surges through her as she is flooded with the truth.

"Such a thing of nightmares," Cynthia whispers, "this kinesthetic connection that still tethers you to your unborn child…"

"…as much as Eris is still tethered to the daughter who has slipped through her fingers.," Nana adds.

"I didn't mean to do it," Ania whimpers. "I would never want to harm my child."

"Bad things happen to bad people," someone murmurs through the suddenly bourbon-scented air.

"I'm not a bad person," Ania mutters.

"Say it again," Cynthia insists.

"I'm not a bad person."

"Absolutely right," Cynthia declares with a smile. "The violence, the shame, is all his. You can let go of that now."

"But the baby?" Ania asks again.

"She's coming with you," Cynthia declares with a smile. She then opens her arms, but the teenager falters. In that fortress, her mother taught her well about wrath and vengeance. And Eris, that goddess of discord and strife, was right all along: the greatest dangers were outside her home, lurking in the woods at the end of Mount Pelion Way. That vile boy with dirty fingernails, who was succored and strengthened by the suburban beast. Eris was right to detest him and all who surrounded him. But in her tales of danger, Eris forgot to teach her daughter one important lesson: that there are places of safety, too. If you know how to spot them, there will always be the ones who are trying to help.

"Oh, come on," Cynthia adds with a smile. "You can do this."

The woman pulls the teenager into her body and Ania can feel the heat radiating from within and without. She fears that she is going to melt into the woman's touch, so she breaks free and staggers away from her.

"I can't," Ania gasps. "I don't know why, but I can't."

"Maybe I was wrong, and you aren't ready."

The woman stares at the monitor for a moment, and then her face changes.

"I get it now," she says. "There. That one." She is pointing at one monitor that has just switched shots, and it shows Ania's parents. They are curled up beneath their sheets, seemingly sound asleep.

"First, you must say goodbye to the ones you will leave behind. Don't worry," Cynthia explains, "they are fine."

The footage is so clear that Ania can see the inwards and outwards breaths of each parent.

"I want to go home," Ania sobs, knowing this is the final time she will say it. This time, she says it as an act of letting go, and Cynthia nods in unison with the teenager.

"I love you, Mom," she calls to the monitor.

Her mother stirs, opening her eyes and sitting up. "Ania?" Eris calls.

"And I love you, Dad," Ania whispers.

Her father sits bolt upright, eyes still shut, and snorts. "What's that?"

"I love you both," Ania calls.

Her parents look at each other, their arms entwined, like roots of two trees that have grown old together. They start to cry as they hold each other, and Ania wants to stare at them forever, but the footage changes to Dylan in his own bedroom. He must have heard something too, because he is sitting bolt upright and gripping the sheets.

"I love you, Dyls," Ania sobs. "Don't ever change, or your *Midget* will haunt you!"

And then the monitors all go blank.

"Turn them back on!" Ania yells. "I wasn't finished."

"There's no more," Cynthia explains. "I'm so sorry. It's time."

"No. I don't want to. I miss them," Ania cries.

"I know, I know." Cynthia pulls Ania to her and squeeze her in an embrace. "It will get easier, believe me. Now that you have accepted it, now you are letting go, you are already on your way. I can feel it in you."

Ania doesn't have to ask what Cynthia means because she feels it too. The warmth of their touch has intensified to an inferno, but it doesn't hurt. It feels cleansing, just right, and Ania understands what happened to Daria and the others when they disintegrated.

A searing light is radiating all around them, and Ania realizes that it is coming from her, from her body. From within. She can feel every inch of herself start to break apart so that more light shines from her. Quickly, she smiles at Cynthia, and mouths the words *Thank you*, unsure how long she has left.

Cynthia is nodding, and smiling back at her, with eyes that are ignited with a bright life shining from her.

"Will I see them again?" Ania manages to ask.

"I can't say either way," Cynthia admits. "I'm sorry. My job was to help you see the truth about what had happened to you; what you did to yourself as much as where you are now, in this liminal space. Now your eyes are wide open, my job is done."

"I don't know if I'm ready," Ania mutters.

"It's time," Cynthia adds.

"It's time," Nana whispers.

"Let go," Cynthia continues. "You feel it beneath your skin, don't you? The burning. It shows that you are ready. Let go, and you'll be free."

"Will it hurt?" Ania asks.

Cynthia smiles and shakes her head. That smile. It seems to radiate throughout Cynthia's body and into Ania's. She feels it so much, that inner glow, that she knows what is going to happen next because she saw it happen to Daria. Looking down at her arms, she watches as the surface of her skin breaks open. Arms outstretched; it comes with the same invisible force she saw jolting Daria's body. But this time, as she is experiencing it, she feels the energy rise with such a force that she can smell it and taste it, and it has a color that she has never seen before.

Powdery red blood emerges from the cracks in her skin but she is not afraid because she is breaking free and getting ready to fly.

"I'll see you again," Cynthia says with a smile

"You aren't coming too?" Ania asks.

"Not yet. Just a few more troubled souls to help, and then I'll catch up with you."

"Okay. I'll miss you."

"I'll miss you too. But only for a short while, and then we'll see each other again."

Ania could feel the collapse from within. Every bone and every muscle disintegrated, and then she was dust and air and light.

Ania has gone.

Chapter Forty-One

Ring around a trafficking ring

Subreddit: Abduction?

u/deadwolf#03:
I don't want to be here. You have to send help or something.
u/rizlasykes#09:
You again? What now, you're gonna round up some girls and send them to a camp?
u/deadwolf#03:
You have to help me.
u/rizlasykes#09:
Quit playing. I still can't believe you said that stuff in another sub. "Camps and incineration"????????? I mean, who says things like that? You're gross.
u/deadwolf#03:
Please. Please send help. I don't know where I am. I'm being held in some camp. Please.
u/rizlasykes#09:
Oh, so now you've suddenly discovered manners? Now you can say please? This always happens with people like you, only ever contrite when you need something.
u/deadwolf#03:

I swear to god, you need to get help.
u/rizlasykes#09:
Don't.
u/deadwolf#03:
Don't what?
u/rizlasykes#09:
Say the G word.
u/deadwolf#03:
God?
u/rizlasykes#09:
Yeah, don't. They don't like it if you do that.
u/deadwolf#03:
Who are you talking about?
u/rizlasykes#09:
Them.
u/deadwolf#03:
I don't understand.
u/rizlasykes#09:
Clearly you don't know what you've stumbled upon. My suggestion is you get out now, while you still can.
u/deadwolf#03:
I told you, I can't. They've locked me in here. You have to send help.
u/rizlasykes#09:
I think I should go.
u/deadwolf#03:
No. Please help me.
u/deadwolf#03:
Why won't you help me?
u/rizlasykes#09:
Did you help that girl? I heard you hurt her.
u/deadwolf#03:
I didn't do anything.
u/rizlasykes#09:
Yes, you did. Stop lying.
u/deadwolf#03:
I never touched her.
u/rizlasykes#09:
Yes, you did. You know you did. And no matter how many people your parents threaten to sue, they know it too. Did you hear she went missing? What did you do with her? Where's she gone?

u/deadwolf#03:
I'm telling you that I don't know anything.
u/rizlasykes#09:
You and your buddies know plenty. They just followed you into those woods, that wolf pack of yours. They always follow your lead, so they've probably done something just as bad to some other girl. You're spreading your filth like a contagion.
u/deadwolf#03:
They can think for themselves.
u/rizlasykes#09:
Can they? You don't want them to. You want them right where you need them. In a group, you're the big man, but look at you now, all alone and shrunken and helpless. You're pathetic.
u/deadwolf#03:
Screw you.
u/rizlasykes#09:
Thought you needed my help? That isn't a very nice thing to say to someone whose help you need. You're not used to being in this position, are you? Always got what you wanted, without even having to ask. Being set up as this big D1 athlete who is entitled to the world. *A hero*, isn't that what your parents call you? You've always got your grubby hands into everything, your dirty fingernails burrowed in, just because you could, just because no one stopped you. You were relentless, vicious, and you'll do it again unless they lock you up.
u/deadwolf#03:
You know nothing.
u/rizlasykes#09:
Really? I've heard so many things, so I think I know quite a lot. I've heard she is at a camp, and I've heard they won't let her go. Not until she delivers.
u/deadwolf#03:
Delivers what?
u/rizlasykes#09:
Come on, don't play the dumbass. You know what I'm talking about.
u/deadwolf#03:
I'm calling BS on this.
u/rizlasykes#09:
Oh, so now you're calling the shots? I thought you needed my help.
u/deadwolf#03:
There is no girl in a camp. Not pregnant or otherwise. She's dead.

u/rizlasykes#09:
No, she isn't. They wanted everyone to think that.
u/deadwolf#03:
BS.
u/rizlasykes#09:
Believe what you like, but it's true.
u/deadwolf#03:
Her parents found the body. She did it in their backyard.
u/rizlasykes#09:
And you still think that was her lifeless body?
u/deadwolf#03:
I think her parents would know.
u/rizlasykes#09:
How? They've only held a living version of their daughter's body. How could they tell the difference between a dead daughter and a synthetic version? You know how lifelike those mannequins can be. Just a bit of latex rubber or silicone, human hair or synthetic hair, and you have something deathly real.
u/rizlasykes#09:
What's wrong? Said too much?
u/rizlasykes#09:
Are you there?
u/deadwolf#03:
Why would they do this?
u/rizlasykes#09:
Haven't I told you already?
u/deadwolf#03:
No.
u/rizlasykes#09:
She was pregnant.
u/deadwolf#03:
And?
u/rizlasykes#09:
She was searching the web for abortions. She didn't want anyone to know, but they found out.
u/deadwolf#03:
Who do you mean? Who is 'they'?
u/rizlasykes#09:
Them. The ones with power.
u/deadwolf#03:
The government?

u/rizlasykes#09:

That's funny. You think the government really has any power?

u/deadwolf#03:

Then who?

u/rizlasykes#09:

I'm not gonna say. I don't want to end up in one of those camps.

u/deadwolf#03:

I don't know what you are going on about. You're nuts.

u/rizlasykes#09:

They watch everyone's internet history. They've been watching her for years. They've seen all the depraved stuff she would search on the dark web, all the executions, suicides, all the snuff movies and torture, and none of that bothered them. It was only when she searched for a way to find an abortion that the alarms went off. She was switched for a synthetic doll, they left that at the base of the apple tree with a noose around its neck, and they took the real girl to a camp so she could have the baby.

u/deadwolf#03:

BS.

u/rizlasykes#09:

Believe what you like, but they've done it for years. Girls, women, they've always been taken to camps to have their babies. They're not gonna let people kill babies because it's babies. You know, everyone wants to protect the babies. Especially the Christians. They get really upset when you flush things down the drain and they claim that it was a baby.

u/deadwolf#03:

You're talking about abduction or kidnapping or whatever. The police would be all over this.

u/rizlasykes#09:

That's if anyone made a report. If they didn't think their kid was missing, if they thought she was dead, especially if they had what they thought to be her body, then what is there to report?

u/deadwolf#03:

The people who took her. If they were Christian, why would they want the girl to be taken from her parents? Wouldn't they want her to stay in a family with a mother and father?

u/rizlasykes#09:

Not if they thought the family wasn't raising her according to good traditional values. The girl wasn't happy. For years, she was bullied. Strike one. Then it turns out she was a sexual deviant. Strike two.

And then she got pregnant at sixteen, strike three, and she's out.
u/deadwolf#03:
Come on, I really think this is sounding like some wacko conspiracy.
u/rizlasykes#09:
If you want to believe that, go ahead. But others would say that it makes perfect sense, and this is part of the grand plan, to weaken you with chaos. And once you feel destabilized enough, they will come to you with a solution that you will be desperate to accept, just so this chaos can end. You will accept their solution no matter the cost.
u/deadwolf#03:
I don't understand.
u/rizlasykes#09:
And no one will challenge this. No one will object to a sixteen-year-old being locked away and forced to have a baby that she doesn't want. Because the alternative is too fearful.
u/deadwolf#03:
Which is?
u/rizlasykes#09:
That you will never find your way to freedom. That everything you know is not really how you understand it. That you are bio-feed or bio-waste for the billionaires. Take your pick. Which story, which version of reality would you like to believe?
u/deadwolf#03:
??????
u/rizlasykes#09:
You didn't like that, did you? Look, quit playing the innocent. You know all of this already.
u/deadwolf#03:
What?
u/rizlasykes#09:
We've seen your internet history, monitored your cell phone activity. Do you really expect us to believe that you are learning about this for the first time? Don't play us for a fool, you're smarter than that.
u/deadwolf#03:
How would you know how smart I am? You don't know anything about me.
u/rizlasykes#09:
We know everything about you, Smithson.
u/deadwolf#03:

?????

u/rizlasykes#09:

Smithson West of Mount Pelion Way, Rotherwell, New Jersey.

u/deadwolf#03:

Stop. I closed out of this. Why do you keep coming back?

u/rizlasykes#09:

You should be ashamed of yourself.

u/deadwolf#03:

u/rizlasykes#09:

Smithson.

u/deadwolf#03:

u/rizlasykes#09:

Smithson.

u/deadwolf#03:

u/rizlasykes#09:

We're on our way, Smithson. You can probably hear us outside. There's no point hiding from us. You know we were going to catch up with you in the end. You have to know that, Smithson. And it's okay, don't worry, this won't take long.

u/deadwolf#03:

u/rizlasykes#09:

Smithson, can you feel us yet? Can you feel us breathing on the back of your neck? Look behind you.

u/deadwolf#03:

u/rizlasykes#09:

Smithson, you like to rewrite narratives, don't you? You like to tell a different story? Well, how about we rewrite your own story? We can tell from your internet history that you know a thing or two about liminal spaces. And you know that liminal spaces are repetitive, aren't they, Smithson? You're such a clever boy for finding that out. Well, let's go round the loop again. Only, this time, let's see whether we can come up with a different ending. Shall we do that, Smithson? Would you like that? I'm sure you would, because you're a big, strong, athletic boy, aren't you? That's how you like your mommy to talk to you, isn't it? You like her to call you a big strong boy who lifts heavy weights, and you are so strong that you can leave big bruises on the wrists of girls. Isn't that right, you big strong boy? Those were some dark purples and blues that you wrapped around that girl's wrists that Halloween night. Like bracelets, weren't they? You see, Smithson, trauma distorts things. Did you find that out in your internet search? What about the dark web? Did that show you the kind of distortions that we are referring to? No? Well, you're in for a great surprise, my big strong boy with his bulging muscles. Because trauma distorts things so much that a perpetrator can transform into a victim. Isn't that crazy? You'd think, with those big bulging muscles, that you'd never be the one to be thrust into the dirt and left broken and bleeding. But can you feel it now, Smithson? Can you understand how trauma can have no bounds, and the ripples of it are unconstrained by space and time? Can you hear the jingling of those pendants on that bracelet that you felt so cold against your skin? There are people who miss that sound, and there are people who would do anything to get it back. So they'll find you in the end, even if they have to bend time and space to reach you. Can you feel them approaching? They're ready for you, in their hooded cloaks, smelling of oil and hemp and apples and bark. Are you ready, Smithson? Keep your eyes wide open because it's almost time for bad things to happen to bad people.

Sit back, my love, while I tell you a story

Source: https//www.[redacted].com
Accessed November 4, 2020, at 7:30 PM

Chapter Forty-Two

Hard hitter

It feels like Halloween. In the moments afterwards, ghoulishly unfamiliar faces stare at Smithson as they wait for him to make a decision. Instead of *Trick or treat?,* the choice is *collapse or retaliate?* The slap, more like a punch, still stings his cheek, but that isn't as important as getting to his feet. Crumpled on the splintered floorboards leaves him vulnerable to more violence, so he struggles to his feet so he can back away from this broad-shouldered girl who is positioning herself to hit Smithson again.

He thinks he might have concussion because he can't remember any of the people who surround him, let alone where he is right now.

"Run," a voice bellows in Smithson's ear as a door opens. Daylight pours in, making the air hiss under the intensity of the glare, but he manages to stagger across the room and out into the light. Across a courtyard, he can see a dirt track that leads into a forest. A raven lands on the branch of a nearby tree, and it croaks its mournful caw.

"Trauma repeats," someone whispers. "Caught like a ripple in time."

He runs across the courtyard and plunges into the forest, his footsteps snapping twigs and crunching leaves. As if he has slipped beneath the surface of a lake, birdsong is muted. The leaves are still.

There is a stirring of the branches ahead of him. A lonesome deer stops to calculate his next move.

"Lucky I don't have my baseball bat," he sneers at the beast. On he runs.

Finally, there is a break in the trees, and Smithson can see a building made of grey concrete and dirty glass. He races up to a pair of doors and finds that they are unlocked. He can't see through the glass so he has to open the door. The darkness clears, and he can see broken ceiling tiles and hanging wires.

"Hello?" he calls. "Anyone there?" He imagines that in the gloom, the vagrants and the wildlife are just waiting to attack, so he grabs a heavy rock before he makes his way in.

With each step, his shoes crunch on broken glass and debris.

"Anyone in here?" he calls. "If you are, I need to use your phone."

The smell of damp catches on the back of his throat and he starts to cough.

"Dunno what kind of shithole this place is, but you really need to clear up in here. Ever heard of bleach?"

A mannequin stands in a nearby window, head aloof and arms outstretched with pride for her sequin dress. Although he knows this is foolish, he can't help feeling watched and judged by the mannequin as he walks by.

"Bitch," he snaps. He wants to punch her, show her who's boss, but then he realizes she isn't real.

"Mind games," he jeers. "Bitches always playing."

The further he walks through this strange place, the narrower the corridors become.

Deciding to turn back, his elbow catches on something, and he flinches, the pain bringing him back to the punch that had landed on his cheek. He notices that blood is trickling down his left arm, and after he sees a broken wall panel, he realizes he must have caught himself on it. It juts out like a broken bone, and behind it, there is a dark cavernous space behind the panel.

"It's a trap," someone warns, but he ignores them.

"I'm not afraid," he insists as he squeezes himself into the gap.

Inside, he finds a tunnel that is tall enough for him to stand. It stretches far into the distance until it curves a corner out of sight, and there are lights screwed onto the walls; the kind of emergency lights he has seen in movies.

Laughter from up ahead. It is soft and fleeting, so he wonders if he hears it at all. But then a voice says something. Calls his name?

"Hello?" he calls.

Silence now.

He starts to run, cautious, though, that someone or something might be just round the corner, waiting to jump out at him.

A whispering, from the same direction as the voice he heard. He isn't mistaken, he is sure of it.

"Who's there?" Smithson calls.

"Smithson," he hears. It echoes round the walls of the tunnel.

"Who is that?" Fear is fading to anger, something he is more comfortable with. He lets it build in his body, pulsating through his veins to make him want to smash something. Instead, it only makes him run faster.

"Such a big strong boy," he hears.

"Whoever that is, quit messing."

"Why are you even talking to me?" he hears someone sneer. "You're gross."

As his anger swells, the ground starts to shudder. He quickens his pace, and then loses his footing, his hands slamming hard into the ground. Was that a foot? Did someone deliberately trip him so he could fall?

He hears laughter.

Who would do such a thing?

The shuddering has stopped, but instead there is a trembling in his hands and arms. He landed sharply, threw something out of whack, because pain is throbbing from his wrist and his hand is twisted at an angle, distorted into something unnatural.

Screaming, someone is screaming.

Smithson is frantic as the screaming gets worse. He thinks it might be a young child, it definitely sounds young. He is frozen with horrific images flashing through his mind of a kid in the jaws of metal, some kind of machine he has seen online that people use to crush all manner of objects. Squish mallows, inflatable balls, cans of tomato to splatter red paste all over the place. A doll? Surely it must have been a doll.

He scrabbles about, trying to get up without causing his wrist more damage.

"I want to go home," someone groans.

"Too right," he snaps back. But how?

Ahead of him, part of the tunnel wall has collapsed. There is movement amongst the rubble. A scampering. Surely it isn't.

He takes another step.

An arachnid? It looks too large for any kind of spider that he has seen before, but that is the shape. It is round, with legs carrying it. He realizes what it is, but still he won't believe it. A human head? It is moved by four legs that have sprouted from either side, like the roots of an overly ripe potato. He can see bloody wounds where the legs have broken through the skin, and the face moans with a groan of agony or hunger.

Smithson takes a step back and the arachnid scuttles towards him. And then he recognizes the face on the head, its mouth distorting in a combination of pleasure and pain.

"Jesus wept," Ania groans and squeals as her long tongue flickers again at the blood. "Smithson, what have you done? What have you done to me?"

Her voice is deep one moment and then distorted into a high-pitched squeal, like that of a child or a pig at the slaughter.

When he takes another step away, Ania, this thing with eight legs, scuttles closer, and too quickly she is upon him, the smell of putrefying flesh so close that it makes him gag. He feels its legs crawling up his body to his face, its long tongue flickering near Smithson's mouth.

Ania's legs, the *arachnid's* legs, split at the tips to create pincers that make clicking sounds, and two of the pincer-tipped legs pinch hold of Smithson's eyelids, peeling them back so he can watch as she inserts her other six legs into every orifice of every person he can imagine. People he cares about, like his mother and father and sister, but also people he barely knows, who he has met fleetingly, but she can gain access to through Smithson's eyes and mind. No one is spared as the images flicker like an old-fashioned movie reel, the picture grainy and seemingly stained with something. They start to flash faster, horror sped up to intensify the pain of it all, and Smithson longs for it to stop.

But Ania isn't finished. She licks her lips with a greed that can never be satiated, and as their eyes meet, she reminds Smithson of that Halloween night.

"Stop," he begs her, but she wants him to see it. She wants him trapped in a Möbius loop of violence and pain.

"Watch," she hisses, and then he sees. He sees himself plunging deep into the forest, his heart quickening with every pace. He hears footsteps crunching leaves behind him. It could be his own, or it could be someone else's.

"Stop," he pleads as the footsteps gain on him. "I don't want any of this." But he sees the forest, hears it, smells it. He can even feel the forest beneath his feet.

"Trauma repeats," someone whispers. "Caught like a ripple in time."

In that forest, someone grabs his wrists from behind. In a foolish moment, he imagines the trees have sprouted arms and hands to seize him.

His wrists are squeezed so tightly that he fears they will snap. A force topples him to the ground and his face smushes in damp soil that stinks of something rotten.

Someone runs their fingers over his cheeks and says that his skin is surprisingly soft.

"Silly boy," he can hear them purr as they slip their hands around his throat. He braces himself, half-expecting that to be the end. He wants it to be, he doesn't want any pain. But he doesn't die.

They push their weight onto him and Smithson's face sinks deeper in the dirt. He turns his head so he can breathe, and he can see in the distance a raven. It doesn't try to save him, doesn't even seem that bothered. Indifferent, it preens its feathers as it watches from a nearby tree.

At one point, he wonders if they are going to smash his skull with a rock. Would they hide his body in the thicker part of the forest, so he would be gnawed by wildlife at night until the dermestid beetles set to work?

"Stop," he croaks through a hand-tightened throat. They squeeze a little tighter as they feel out the idea of killing him, but then they relent, allowing the air to reach his brain.

"Aw," they sneer, "poor little Smithson. Do you need your mommy?"

"Please," Smithson manages to croak. "Why are you doing this?"

He imagines how dirty their fingernails are as they start to claw at him. They explore his terrain, making good headway, and for a while they make no sound. He imagines them blank-faced and relentless, a zombie making its way from the underworld.

Then the spell is broken, and they speak again.

"Oh come, now, Smithson, I thought you liked to play in here, far from the watchful eye."

"Why are you doing this?" he gasps.

"Am I doing this? Who's to tell?"

They were possessed, their voice so deep it reverberated around the woodland.

"I want to go home," Smithson tries to scream, but all he manages is a muffled wail. So he continues to silently scream in his head, "Let me go, let me go, let me go."

Afterwards, he manages to struggle to his feet. His head swims with something fluid; ice water, a chemical imbalance. Thoughts trapped in a hardened snow globe.

Dizzy, he staggers through the dark forest. He feels branches whip at his head, but he doesn't flinch. He can hear them behind him, smell their scent getting closer, so he quickens his pace, and just when he thinks they are upon him again, the light explodes, and he is free of the forest.

"Not so fast," the voice snarls in his ear. His cheek scrapes against the bark of some trees as he is dragged back into the forest.

"Such a thing of nightmares, this kinesthetic connection that tethers us together. We're stuck here," they hiss, "whether you like it or not."

"Trauma repeats," someone mutters, "caught like a ripple in time," and someone squeezes his wrists so tightly that he fears they will snap. He knows that he will be toppled again, face smushed in damp soil that stinks of something rotten. He's stuck here, in a Möbius loop of perpetual torment, and already he can feel someone run their fingers over his cheeks. They will tell him again how soft his skin is, and call him "silly boy," unless…

He can see the gnarled old boughs of an apple tree.

"Now you see," he hears someone whisper.

Already there is the length of rope hanging from one of the boughs.

"You see it all now," the voice continues. "See how the rope is starting to stir. See how the noose snakes round your throat?"

There is snow now, so much snow.

Someone or something yanks at the rope, and he is hanging from it as he twitches into life. His limbs flicker like he is making snow angels. And still, he knows there is worse yet to come.

"Come on, Smithson. You can do it."

"Mom," he cries. "I want to go home." But he knows this is impossible, and it is no one's doing but his own.

With the noose around his throat constraining his vocal cords, Smithson can barely make a sound. But there is a sound, and it is deadly; the loss of life in the form of air rushing from a hidden hole.

"Mom," he cries again. "It hurts."

And then the rope is yanked again, and his arms and legs thrash about for a final time, and then he is still.

"You see?" he hears. "Do you see now?"

~~~

Acknowledgements

~~~

Special thanks to M, L, and W.

~~~

Learn more

To learn more about this book, and others written by BB Clifford, use the following link to receive updates: https://www.bbclifford.com/signup.html

~~~

Other books by BB Clifford

Tangled Knot
The tale of Eris of suburbia

Like the whisperings of a ghost, this is a hellish tale of grief, isolation, and revenge. See how this family tree has become tangled and haunted by trauma, and learn whether anything can grow from this beyond poisoned fruit.

Eris once believed that she could keep herself safe from the suburban beast that slithered around the swampland of a small town on the US East Coast. She hid herself away behind latches and bolts and locks, making a fortress of her family home. They called this recluse a witch, and if she had lived in another age, this suburban misfit would have been hanged or burned at the stake.

Despite her fortress, the dangers still found Eris. As if myths and legends were true all along, her family was torn apart one snowy night when her teenage daughter was found dead. Ever since, Eris and her husband, Paris, remain tangled in a marriage knot riddled with grief. Every move Paris makes to free himself of this grief only tightens the knot like a hangman's noose around Eris's neck. For either of them to cut themselves free means they will fall into the unknown, which could mean a landing on softened soil ripe for regrowth, or a plunge into an abyss of hopelessness and despair.

Two years on since her nightmares became a reality, Eris thinks she has discovered the truth about her daughter's death. She stirs concoctions of poison and vengeance, but will this kill off all hope, proving herself to be a witch who should be condemned to isolation in a fortress that is haunted by grief? She fears that such a fate might leave her exposed to horrors that still haunt her: What good are locks on a fortress if the greatest danger threatens her from within? Anything is possible since the unnatural occurred and the bond was broken between parent and child. All manner of natural things has become unnatural as her life has become an underworld.

Compelling, poignant, and deeply real, Tangled Knot is an account of grief, isolation, and revenge that grabs you by the throat from the outset and will not let you go until you resolve for yourself whether the greatest threat is from the haunted world outside or the dangers that lurk within your own family—or even within the tangled knots of your mind.

~~~
~~~

Rainbow Warrior
The Tale of Ares, The Battle-Lustful Son

A dark, harrowing tale of grief and greed that contaminates the literary Gothic with eco horror to haunt the modern-day queer experience.

More than a year has passed since the fire. The destruction of a home is bad enough, but the remaining members of Dylan's family perished in the fire, so grief has followed Dylan in relentless pursuit.

Never one to pass up an opportunity, Max, Dylan's first love, seized what he could from a grief-stricken Dylan. He would have taken everything, but the fire gave Dylan an inexplicable strength to escape, so they fled Rotherwell in search of a new life across the Atlantic. But Max doesn't let his possessions slip through his fingers so easily. He is gaining on Dylan, and he intends to drag them back to Rotherwell to resolve their unfinished business.

Before they left Rotherwell, Dylan saw something scuttling about the charred bricks and broken window frames of their family home. They recognized the creature, and it was as familiar as the burning sensation deep beneath their skin. The creature revealed to Dylan that greed was causing the burning sensation, and it was this same greed that had driven Dylan's father to commit so much violence. Terrified that Dylan's father might inflict more horrors from beyond the grave, Dylan vowed never to return to Rotherwell.

Lost in the dismal grey of London, Dylan hopes that the incessant rain will cool the burning greed beneath their skin and keep them safe from Max. But an international border cannot contain horrors, just as one generation cannot contain trauma, genetic quirks, and contaminants. As time runs out for Dylan, they realize that the fire was just the beginning.

Twisted, powerful, and darkly liberating, *Rainbow Warrior* is a challenging work of queer horror that considers supernatural and real-world horrors that result from our greed and our manipulation of each other and the natural world.

~~~
~~~

About the author

BB Clifford has written *Tangled Knot, Rainbow Warrior,* and *Malevolent Fairy*.

BB Clifford is a queer author based in northern New Jersey. BB Clifford is greatly influenced by Shirley Jackson, Alison Rumfitt, Marcus Kliewer, Qntm, and Eliza Clark.